THE HOSTS OF THE AIR
THE STORY OF A QUEST IN THE GREAT WAR

By
JOSEPH A. ALTSHELER

The Hosts Of The Air
The Story Of A Quest In The Great War

by **Joseph A. Altsheler**

Copyright © 2023

All Rights reserved.
No part of this publication may be reproduced, stored in a retrieval system, or transmitted in any form or by any means, electronic, mechanical, photocopying or Otherwise, without the written permission of the publisher.

The author/editor asserts the moral right to be identified as the author/editor of this work.

ISBN: 978-93-57485-82-1

Published by

DOUBLE 9 BOOKS

2/13-B, Ansari Road, Daryaganj
New Delhi – 110002
info@double9books.com
www.double9books.com
Tel. 011-40042856

This book is under public domain

ABOUT THE AUTHOR

Joseph A. Altsheler was born on April 29, 1862, in Three Springs, Hart County, Kentucky, to Joseph and Louise Altsheler. He was a newspaper reporter, editor, and author of popular juvenile historical fiction. He wrote fifty novels and at least fifty-three short stories. Seven of his novels were in sequence. He worked as an editor at the Louisville Courier-Journal in 1885. In 1892, he started to work for New York World and then as the editor of the World's tri-weekly magazine. He wrote children's stories due to a lack of suitable stories. On May 30, 1880, Altsheler married Sarah Boles and had a son named Sidney. In 1914, during World War I Altsheler and his family were in Germany and they were forced to remain there. Altsheler died at the age of 57, on June 5, 1919, in New York. His wife, Sarah Boles died after 30 years. Their bodies are buried at the Cave Hill Cemetery in Louisville, Kentucky. Although each of the thirty-two novels constitutes an independent story, Altsheler suggested reading in sequence for each series (that is, he numbered the volumes). You can read the remaining eighteen novels in any order.

CONTENTS

CHAPTER I
 THE TRENCH 7

CHAPTER II
 THE YOUNG AUSTRIAN 23

CHAPTER III
 JULIE'S COMING 37

CHAPTER IV
 THE HOTEL AT CHASTEL 53

CHAPTER V
 THE REGISTER 64

CHAPTER VI
 JOHN'S RESOLVE 78

CHAPTER VII
 THE PURSUIT 92

CHAPTER VIII
 INTO GERMANY 113

CHAPTER IX
 THE GREAT CASTLE 126

CHAPTER X
 THE FAIR CAPTIVE 140

CHAPTER XI
 THE EFFICIENT HOSTLER 157

CHAPTER XII
 THE HUNTING LODGE 173

CHAPTER XIII
 THE DANGEROUS FLIGHT 193

CHAPTER XIV
 THE HAPPY ESCAPE 207

CHAPTER I
THE TRENCH

A young man was shaving. His feet rested upon a broad plank embedded in mud, and the tiny glass in which he saw himself hung upon a wall of raw, reeking earth. A sky, somber and leaden, arched above him, and now and then flakes of snow fell in the sodden trench, but John Scott went on placidly with his task.

The face that looked back at him had been changed greatly in the last six months. The smoothness of early youth was gone—for the time—and serious lines showed about the mouth and eyes. His cheeks were thinner and there was a slight sinking at the temples, telling of great privations, and of dangers endured. But the features were much stronger. The six months had been in effect six years. The boy of Dresden had become the man of the trenches.

He finished, rubbed his hand over his face to satisfy himself that the last trace of young beard and mustache was gone, put away his shaving materials in a little niche that he had dug with his own hands in the wall of the trench, and turned to the Englishman.

"Am I all right, Carstairs?" he asked.

"You do very well. There's mud on your boots, but I suppose you can't help it. The melting snow in our trench makes soggy footing in spite of all we can do. But you're trim, Scott. That new gray uniform with the blue threads running through it becomes you. All the Strangers are thankful for the change. It's a great improvement over those long blue coats and baggy red trousers."

"But we don't have any chance to show 'em," said Wharton, who sat upon a small stool, reading a novel. "Did I ever think that war would come to this? Buried while yet alive! A few feet of cold and muddy trench in which to pass one's life! This is an English story I'm reading. The lovely *Lady Ermentrude* and the gallant *Sir Harold* are walking in the garden among the roses, and he's about to ask her the great question. There are roses, roses, and the deep green grass and greener oaks everywhere, with the soft English shadows coming and going over them. The birds are singing in the boughs. I suppose they're nightingales, but do nightingales sing in the daytime? And when I shut my book I see only walls of raw, red earth, and a floor, likewise of earth, but stickier and more hideous. Even the narrow strip of sky above our heads is the color of lead, and has nothing soft about it."

"If you'll stand up straight," said John, "maybe you'll see the rural landscape for which you're evidently longing."

"And catch a German bullet between the eyes! Not for me. While I was taking a trip down to the end of our line this morning I raised my head by chance above the edge of the trench, and quick as a wink a sharpshooter cut off one of my precious brown locks. I could have my hair trimmed that way if I were patient and careful enough. Ah, here comes a messenger!"

They heard a roar that turned to a shriek, and caught a fleeting glimpse of a black shadow passing over their heads. Then a huge shell burst behind them, and the air was filled with hissing fragments of steel. But in their five feet of earth they were untouched, although horrible fumes as of lyddite or some other hideous compound assailed them.

"This is the life," said Wharton, resuming his usual cheerfulness. "I take back what I said about our beautiful trench. Just now I appreciate it more than I would the greenest and loveliest landscape in England or all America. Oh, it's a glorious trench! A splendid fortress for weak human flesh, finer than any castle that was ever built!"

"Don't be dithyrambic, Wharton," said Carstairs. "Besides the change is too sudden. It hasn't been a minute since you were pouring abuse upon our safe and happy little trench."

"It's time for the Germans to begin," said John, looking at his watch. "We'd better lie close for the next hour."

They heard the shrieking of more shells and soon the whole earth rocked with the fire of the great guns. The hostile trenches were only a few hundred yards in front of them, but the German batteries all masked, or placed in pits, were much further away. The French cannon were stationed in like fashion behind their own trenches.

John and his comrades, for the allotted hour, hugged the side of the trench nearest to the Germans. The shells from the heavy guns came at regular intervals. Far in the rear men were killed and others were wounded, but no fragment of steel dropped in their trench. There was not much danger unless one of the shells should burst almost directly over their heads, and they were so used to these bombardments that they paid little attention to them, except to keep close as long as they lasted.

Wharton resumed his novel, Carstairs, sitting on one end of a rude wooden bench, began a game of solitaire, and John, at the other end, gave himself over to dreaming, which the regulated thunder of many cannon did not disturb at all.

It had been months now since he had parted with Philip and Julie Lannes. He had seen Philip twice since, but Julie not at all When the German army made a successful stand near the river Aisne, and both sides went into trenches, Lannes had come in the *Arrow* and, in reply to John's restrained but none the less eager questions, had said that Julie was safe in Paris again with her mother, Antoine Picard and the faithful Suzanne. She had wanted to return to the front as a Red Cross nurse, but Madame Lannes would not let her go.

A month later he saw Lannes again and Julie was still in the capital, but he inferred from Philip's words rather than his tone that she was impatient. Thousands of French girls were at the front, attending to the wounded, and sharing hardship and danger. John knew that Julie had a will like her brother's and he believed that, in time, she would surely come again to the battle lines.

The thought made him smile, and he felt a light glow pass over his face. He knew it was due to the belief that he would see Julie once more, and yet the trenches now extended about four hundred miles across Northern France and Belgium. The chances seemed a hundred to one against her arrival in the particular trench, honored by the presence of the Strangers, but John felt that in reality they were a hundred to one in favor of it. He wished it so earnestly that it must come true.

"You're smiling, Scott," said Carstairs. "A good honest English penny for your thoughts."

"What do I care for money? What could I do with it if I had it, held here between walls of mud only four feet apart?"

"At least," interrupted Wharton, "the high cost of living is not troubling us. Next month's rent may come from where it pleases. It doesn't bother me."

A messenger turned the angle of the trench and summoned John to the presence of his commander, Captain Colton, who was about three hundred yards away. Young Scott, stooping in order to keep his head covered well, started down the trench. The artillery fire was at its height. The waves of air followed one another with great violence, and the fumes of picric acid and of other acids that he did not know became very strong. But he scarcely noticed it. The bombardment was all in the day's work, and when the Germans ceased, the French, after a decent interval, would begin their own cannonade, carried on at equal length.

John thought little of the fire of the guns, now almost a regular affair like the striking of a clock, but force of habit kept his head down and no German sharpshooter watching in the trench opposite had a chance at him. He advanced through a vast burrow. Trenches ran parallel, and other trenches cut across them. One could wander through them for miles. Most of them were uncovered, but others had roofs, partial or complete, of thatch or boards or canvas. Many had little alcoves and shelves, dug out by the patient hands of the soldiers, and these niches contained their most precious belongings.

Back of the trenches often lay great heaps of refuse like the kitchen middens of primeval man. Attempts at coziness had achieved a little success in some places, but nearly everywhere the abode of burrowing soldiers was raw, rank and fetid. Heavy and hideous odors arose from the four hundred miles of unwashed armies. Men lived amid disease, dirt and death. Civilization built up slowly through painful centuries had come to a sudden stop, and once more they were savages in caves seeking to destroy one another.

This, at least, was the external aspect of it, but the flower of civilization was still sound at the stem. When the storm was over it would grow and bloom again amid the wreckage. French and

Germans, in the intervals of battle, were often friendly with each other. They listened to the songs of the foe, and sometimes at night they talked together. John recognized the feeling. He knew that man at the core had not really returned to a savage state, and a soldier, but not a believer in war, he looked forward to the time when the grass should grow again over the vast maze of trenches.

A shell bursting almost overhead put all such thoughts out of his mind for the present. A hot piece of metal shooting downward struck on the bottom of the trench and lay there hissing. John stepped over it and passed on.

The cannonade was at its height, and he noticed that it was heavier than usual. Perhaps the increase of volume was due to the presence of some great dignitary, the Kaiser himself maybe, or the Crown Prince, or the Chief of the General Staff. But it was only a flitting thought. The subject did not interest him much.

The sky was turning darker and the heavy flakes of snow fell faster. John looked up apprehensively. Snow now troubled him more than guns. It was no welcome visitor in the trenches where it flooded some of them so badly as it melted that the men were compelled to move.

As he walked along he was hailed by many friendly voices. He was well known in that part of the gigantic burrow, and the adaptable young American had become a great favorite, not only with the Strangers, but with his French comrades. Fleury, coming out of a transverse cut, greeted him. The Savoyard had escaped during the fighting on the Aisne, and had rejoined the command of General Vaugirard, wounded in the arm, but now recovered.

"Duty?" he said to John.

"Yes. Captain Colton has sent for me, but I don't know what he wants."

"Don't get yourself captured again. Twice is enough."

"I won't. There isn't much taking of prisoners while both sides keep to their holes."

Fleury disappeared in one of the earthy aisles, and John went on, turning a little later into an aisle also, and arriving at Captain Cotton's post.

Daniel Colton had for his own use a wooden bench three feet long, set in an alcove dug in the clay. Some boards and the arch of the earth formed an uncertain shelter. An extra uniform hung against the wall of earth, and he also had a tiny looking-glass and shaving materials. He was as thin and dry as ever, addicted to the use of words of one syllable, and sparing even with them.

John saluted. He had a great respect and liking for his captain.

"Sit down," said Captain Colton, making room on the bench.

John sat.

"Know well a man named Weber?"

"Yes," replied John in surprise. He had not thought of the Alsatian in days, and yet they had been together in some memorable moments.

"Thought you'd say so. Been here an hour. Asks for you. Must see you, he says."

"I'll be glad to meet him again, sir. I've a regard for him. We've shared some great dangers. You've heard that he was in the armored automobile with Carstairs, Wharton and myself that time we ran it into the river?"

Captain Colton nodded.

"Then we were captured and both escaped during the fighting along the Marne. Lannes took me away in his aeroplane, but we missed Weber. I thought, though, that he'd get back to us, and I'm glad, very glad that he's here."

"See him now," said Colton, "and find out what he wants."

He blew a whistle, and an orderly appeared, saluting.

"Bring Weber," said the captain.

The orderly returned with Weber, the two coming from one of the narrow aisles, and John rose impulsively to meet the Alsatian. But before offering his hand Weber saluted the captain.

"Go ahead. Tell all," said Colton briefly.

Weber first shook John's hand warmly. Evidently he had not been living the life of the trenches, as he looked fresh, and his cheeks were full of color. His gray uniform, with the blue threads through it, was neat and clean, and his black pointed beard was trimmed like that of a painter with money.

"We're old comrades in war, Mr. Scott," he said, "and I'm glad, very glad to find you again. You and Lannes left me rather abruptly that time near the Marne, but it was the only thing you could do. If by an effort of the mind I could have sent a wireless message to you I'd have urged you to instant flight. I hid in the bushes, in time reached one of our armies, and since then I've been a bearer of dispatches along the front. I heard some time back that you were still alive, but my duty hitherto has kept me from seeing you. Now, it sends me to you."

His tone, at first eager and joyous, as was fitting in an old friend meeting an old friend, now became very grave, and John looked at him with some apprehension. Captain Colton motioned to a small stool.

"Sit down," he said to Weber. Then he offered the Alsatian a match and a cigarette which were accepted gratefully. He made the same offer to John, who shook his head saying that he did not smoke. The captain took two or three deliberate puffs, and contemplated Weber who had made himself comfortable on the stool.

"Military duty?" he asked. "If so, Scott's concern is my concern too."

"That is quite true, Captain Colton," said Weber, respectfully. "As Mr. Scott is under your command you have a right to know what message I bring."

"Knew you'd see it," said Colton, taking another puff at his cigarette. "There! Germans have ceased firing!"

"And our men begin!" said John.

The moment the distant German thunder ceased the French reply, nearer at hand and more like a rolling crash, began. It would continue about an hour, that is until nightfall, unless the heavy clouds and falling snow brought darkness much earlier than usual. The flakes were coming faster, but the three were protected from them by the rude board shelter. John again glanced anxiously at Weber. He felt that his news was of serious import.

"I saw your friend Lieutenant Philip Lannes about three weeks ago at a village called Catreaux, lying sixty miles west of us," said Weber. "He had just made a long flight from the west, where he had observed much of the heavy fighting around Ypres, and also had been present when the Germans made their great effort to break through to Dunkirk and Calais. I hear that he had more than a messenger's share in these engagements, throwing some timely bombs."

"Was he well when you saw him?" asked John. "He had not been hurt? He had not been in any accident?"

"He was in the best of health, hard and fit. But his activities in the *Arrow* had diminished recently. Snow, rain, icy hail make difficulties and dangers for aviators. But we wander. He had not heard from his mother, Madame Lannes, or his sister, the beautiful Mademoiselle Julie, for a long time, and he seemed anxious about them."

"He himself took Mademoiselle Julie back to Paris in the *Arrow*," said John.

"So he told me. They arrived safely, as you know, but Lannes was compelled to leave immediately for the extreme western front. The operations there were continuous and so exacting that he has been unable to return to Paris. He has not heard from his mother and sister in more than two months, and his great anxiety about them is quite natural."

"But since the retreat of the Germans there is no danger in Paris save from an occasional bomb."

"No. But a few days after seeing Lannes my own duties as a messenger carried me back to Paris, and I took it upon myself to visit Lannes' house. I had two objects, both I hope justifiable. I wanted to take to them good news of Lannes and I wanted to take to Lannes good news of them."

"You found them there?" said John, his anxiety showing in his tone.

"I did. But a letter from Lannes, by good luck, had just come through the day before. It was a noble letter. It expressed the fine spirit of that brave young man, a spirit universal now throughout France. He said the fighting had been so severe and the wounded were so many that all Frenchwomen who had the skill and strength to help must come to the hospitals, where the hurt in scores of thousands were lying."

"Did he mention any point to which she was to come?"

"A village just behind the fortress of Verdun. To say that she was willing was not enough. A great spirit, a magnificent spirit, Mr. Scott. The soul of chivalry may dwell in the heart of a young girl. She was eager to go. Madame, her mother, would have gone too, but she was ill, so she remained in the house, while the beautiful Mademoiselle Julie departed with the great peasant, Antoine Picard, and his daughter Suzanne."

"Do you know how they went?"

"By rail, I think, as far as they could go, and thence they were to travel by motor to the tiny village of Chastel, their destination. Knowing your interest in Mademoiselle Julie, I thought it would not displease you to hear this. Chastel is no vast distance from this point."

A blush would have been visible on John's face had he not been tanned so deeply, but he felt no resentment. Captain Colton took his cigarette from his lips and said tersely:

"Every man likes a pretty face. Man who doesn't—no man at all."

"I agree with you, Captain Colton," said Weber heartily. "When I no longer notice a beautiful woman I think it will be time for me to die. But I take no liberty, sir, when I say that in all the garden of flowers Mademoiselle Julie Lannes is the rarest and loveliest. She is the delicate and opening rose touched at dawn with pearly dew."

"A poet, Weber! A poet!" interjected Captain Colton.

"No, sir, I but speak the truth," said Weber seriously. "Mademoiselle Julie Lannes, though a young girl but yet, promises to become the most beautiful woman in Europe, and beauty carries with it many privileges. Men may have political equality, but women can never have an equality of looks."

"Right, Weber," said Captain Colton.

John's pulses had begun to leap. Julie was coming back to the front, and she would not be so far away. Some day he might see her again. But he felt anxiety.

"Is the journey to Chastel safe, after she leaves the railway?" he asked of Weber.

"Is anything safe now?"

"Nothing in Europe," interjected Captain Colton.

"But I don't think Mademoiselle Lannes will incur much danger," said Weber. "It's true, roving bands of Uhlans or hussars sometimes pass in our rear, but it's likely that she and other French girls going to the front march under strong escort."

His tone was reassuring, but his words left John still troubled.

"My object in telling you of Mademoiselle Lannes' movements, Mr. Scott," continued Weber, "was to enable you to notify Lieutenant Lannes of her exact location in case you should see him. Knowing your great friendship I thought it inevitable that you two should soon meet once more. If so, tell him that his sister is at Chastel. He will be glad to know of her arrival and, work permitting, will hurry to her there."

"Gladly I'll do it," said John. "I wish I could see Philip now."

But when he said "Philip" he was thinking of Julie, although the bond of friendship between him and young Lannes had not diminished one whit.

"And now," said Weber, "with Captain Colton's permission I'll go. My duties take me southward, and night is coming fast."

"And it will be dark, cold and snowy," said John, shivering a little. "These trenches are not exactly palace halls, but I'd rather be in them now than out there on such a night."

The dusk had come and the French fire was dying. In a few more minutes it would cease entirely, and then the French hour with the guns having matched the German hour, the night would be without battle.

But the silence that succeeded the thunder of the guns was somber. In all that terrible winter John had not seen a more forbidding night. The snow increased and with it came a strong wind that reached them despite their shelter. The muddy trenches began to freeze lightly, but the men's feet broke through the film of ice and they walked in an awful slush. It seemed impossible that the earth could ever have been green and warm and sunny, and that Death was not always sitting at one's elbow.

The darkness was heavy, but nevertheless as they talked they did not dare to raise their heads above the trenches. The German searchlights might blaze upon them at any moment, showing the mark for the sharpshooters. But Captain Colton pressed his electric torch and the three in the earthy alcove saw one another well.

"Will you go to Chastel yourself?" asked John of Weber.

"Not at present. I bear a message which takes me in the Forest of Argonne, but I shall return along this line in a day or two, and it may be that I can reach the village. If so, I shall tell Mademoiselle Julie and the Picards that I have seen you here, and perhaps I can communicate also with Lannes."

"I thank you for your kindness in coming to tell me this."

"It was no more than I should have done. I knew you would be glad to hear, and now, with your permission, Captain Colton, I'll go."

"Take narrow, transverse trench, leading south. Good of you to see us," said the captain of the Strangers.

The Alsatian shook hands with John and disappeared in the cut which led a long distance from the front. Colton extinguished the torch and the two sat a little while in the darkness. Although vast armies faced one another along a front of four hundred miles, little could be heard where John and his captain sat, save the sighing of the wind and the faint sound made by the steady fall of the snow, which was heaping up at their feet.

Not a light shone in the trench. John knew that innumerable sentinels were on guard, striving to see and hear, but a million or two million men lay buried alive there, while the snow drifted down continually. The illusion that the days of primeval man had come back was strong upon him again. They had become, in effect, cave-dwellers once more, and their chief object was to kill. He listened to the light swish of the snow, and thought of the blue heights into which he had often soared with Lannes.

Captain Colton lighted another cigarette and it glowed in the dark.

"Uncanny," he said.

"I find it more so than usual tonight," said John. "Maybe it's the visit of Weber that makes me feel that way, recalling to me that I was once a man, a civilized human being who bathed regularly and who put on clean clothes at frequent intervals."

"Such days may come again—for some of us."

"So they may. But it's ghastly here, holed up like animals for the winter."

"Comparison not fair to animals. They choose snug dens. Warm leaves and brush all about 'em."

"While we lie or stand in mud or snow. After all, Captain, the animals have more sense in some ways than we. They kill one another only for food, while we kill because of hate or ignorance."

"Mostly ignorance."

"I suppose so. Hear that! It's a pleasant sound."

"So it is. Makes me think of home."

Some one further down the trench was playing a mouth organ. It was merely a thin stream of sound, but it had a soft seductive note. The tune was American, a popular air. It was glorified so far away and in such terrible places, and John suddenly grew sick for home and the pleasant people in the sane republic beyond the seas. But he crushed the emotion and listened in silence as the player played on.

"A hundred of those little mouth-organs reached our brigade this morning," said Colton. "Men in the trenches must have something to lift up their minds, and little things outside current of war will do it."

It was a long speech for him to make and John felt its truth, but he atoned for it by complete silence while they listened to many tunes, mostly American, played on the mouth-organ. John's mind continually went back to the great republic overseas, so safe and so sane. While he was listening to the thin tinkle in the dark and snowy trench his friends were going to the great opera house in New York to hear "Aida" or "Lohengrin" maybe. And yet he would not have been back there. The wish did not occur to him. Through the dark and the snow he saw the golden hair and the deep blue eyes of Julie Lannes float before him, and it pleased him too to think that he was a minute part in the huge event now shaking the world.

A sudden white light blazed through the snow, and then was gone, like a flash of lightning.

"German searchlight seeking us out," said Colton.

"I wonder what they want," said John. "They can't be thinking of a rush on such a night as this."

"Don't know, but must be on guard. Better return to your station and warn everybody as you go along. You can use your torch, but hold it low."

As John walked back he saw by the light of his little electric torch men sound asleep on the narrow shelves they had dug in the side of the trench, their feet and often a shoulder covered with the drifting snow. Strange homes were these fitted up with the warriors' arms and clothes, and now and then with some pathetic little gift from home.

He met other men on guard like himself walking up and down the trench and also carrying similar torches. He found Carstairs and Wharton still awake, and occupied as they were when he had left them.

"What was it, Scott?" asked Carstairs. "Has the British army taken Berlin?"

"No, nor has the German army taken London."

"Good old London! I'd like to drop down on it for a while just now."

"They say that at night it's as black as this trench. Zeppelins!"

"I could find my way around it in the dark. I'd go to the Ritz or the Carlton and order the finest dinner for three that the most experienced chef ever heard of. You don't know how good a dinner I can give—if I only have the money. I invite you both to become my guests in London as soon as this war is over and share my gustatory triumph."

"I accept," said John.

"And I too," said Wharton, "though we may have to send to Berlin for our captive host."

"Never fear," said Carstairs. "I wasn't born to be taken. What did Captain Colton want with you, Scott, if it's no great military or state secret?"

"To see Fernand Weber, the Alsatian, whom you must remember."

"Of course we recall him! Didn't we take that dive in the river together? But he's an elusive chap, regular will-o'-the-wisp, messenger and spy of ours, and other things too, I suppose."

"He's done me some good turns," said John. "Been pretty handy several times when I needed a handy man most. He brought news that Mademoiselle Julie Lannes and her servants, the Picards, father and daughter, are on their way to or are at Chastel, a little village not far from here, where the French have established a huge hospital for the wounded. She left Paris in obedience to a letter from her brother, and we are to tell Philip if we should happen to see him."

"Pretty girl! Deucedly pretty!" said Carstairs.

"I don't think the somewhat petty adjective 'pretty' is at all adequate," said John with dignity.

"Maybe not," said Carstairs, noticing the earnest tone in his comrade's voice. "She's bound to become a splendid woman. Is Weber still with the captain?"

"No, he's gone on his mission, whatever it is."

"A fine night for travel," said Wharton sardonically. "A raw wind, driving snow, pitchy darkness, slush and everything objectionable underfoot. Yet I'd like to be in Weber's place. A curse upon the man who invented life in the trenches! Of all the dirty, foul, squalid monotony it is this!"

"You'll have to curse war first," said John. "War made the trench."

"Here comes a man with an electric torch," said Carstairs. "Something is going to happen in our happy lives."

They saw the faint glimmer of the torch held low, and an orderly arrived with a message from Captain Colton, commanding them to wake everybody and to stand to their arms. Then the orderly passed quickly on with similar orders for others.

"Old Never Sleep," said Carstairs, referring to Colton, "thinks we get too much rest. Why couldn't he let us tuck ourselves away in our mud on a night like this?"

"I fancy it's not restlessness," said John. "The order doubtless comes from a further and higher source. Good old Papa Vaugirard is not more than a quarter of a mile away."

"I hear they had to enlarge the trench for him," grumbled Carstairs. "He's always bound to keep us stirring."

"But he watches over us like a father. They say his troops are in the best condition of all."

The three young men traveled about the vast burrow along the main trenches, the side trenches and those connecting. The order to be on guard was given everywhere, and the men dragged themselves from their sodden beds. Then they took their rifles and were ready. But it was dark save for the glimmer of the little pocket electrics.

The task finished, the three returned to their usual position. John did not know what to expect. It might be a device of Papa Vaugirard to drag them out of a dangerous lethargy, but he did not think so. A kind heart dwelled in the body of the huge general, and he would not try them needlessly on a wild and sullen night. But whatever the emergency might be the men were ready and on the right of the Strangers was that Paris regiment under Bougainville. What a wonderful man Bougainville had proved himself to be! Fiery and yet discreet, able to read the mind of the enemy, liked by his men whom nevertheless he led where the danger was greatest. John was glad that the Paris regiment lay so close.

"Nothing is going to happen," said Carstairs. "Why can't I lay me down on my little muddy shelf and go to sleep? Nobody would send a dog out on such a night!"

"Man will often go where a dog won't," said Wharton, sententiously.

"And the night is growing worse," continued Carstairs. "Hear that wind howl! Why, it's driving the snow before it in sheets! The trenches won't dry out in a week!"

"You might be worth hearing if you'd only quit talking and say something, Carstairs," said Wharton.

"If you obeyed that rule, Wharton, you'd be known as the dumb man."

John stood up straight and looked over the trench toward the German lines, where he saw nothing. The night filled with so much driving snow had become a kind of white gloom, less penetrable than the darkness.

Only that shifting white wall met his gaze, and listen as he would, he could hear nothing. The feeling of something sinister and uncanny, something vast and mighty returned. Man had made war for ages, but never before on so huge a scale.

"Well, Sister Anna, otherwise John Scott, make your report," said Carstairs lightly. "What do you see?"

"Only a veil of snow so thick that my eyes can't penetrate it."

"And that's all you will see. Papa Vaugirard is a good man and he cares for his many children, but he's making a mistake tonight."

"I think not," said John, dropping suddenly back into the trench. A blinding white glare, cutting through the gloom of the snow, had dazzled him for a moment.

"The searchlight again!" exclaimed Wharton.

"And it means something," said John.

The blaze, whiter and more intense than usual, played for a few minutes over the French trenches, sweeping to right and left and back again and then dying away at a far distant point. After it came the same white gloom and deep silence.

"Just a way of greeting," said Carstairs.

"I think not," said John. "Papa Vaugirard makes few mistakes. To my mind the intensity of the silence is sinister. Often we hear the Germans singing in their trenches, but now we hear nothing."

Another half-hour of the long and trying waiting followed. Then the white light flared again for a moment, and powerful lights behind the French lines flared back, but did not go out. The great beams, shooting through the white gloom, disclosed masses of men in gray uniforms and spiked helmets rushing forward.

CHAPTER II
THE YOUNG AUSTRIAN

It seemed to John that the heavy German masses were almost upon them, when they were revealed in the glare of the searchlights, sweeping forward in solid masses, and uttering a tremendous hurrah. But the French lights continued to throw an intense vivid white blaze over the advancing columns, broad German faces and stalwart German figures standing out vividly. Officers, reckless of death, waving their swords and shouting the word of command, led them on.

The French field guns behind their trenches opened, sending showers of missiles over their heads and into the charging ranks, and the trenches themselves blazed with the fire of the rifles.

"A surprise that isn't a surprise?" shouted Carstairs. "They thought to catch us napping in the night and the snow!"

The battle spread with astonishing rapidity over a front of more than a mile, and in the driving snow and white gloom it assumed a frightful character. The German guns fired for a little while over their troops at the French artillery beyond, but soon ceased lest they pour shells into their own men, and the heavy French batteries ceased also, lest they, too, mow down friend as well as foe. But the light machine guns posted in the trenches kept up a rapid and terrible crackle. The front lines of the Germans were cut down again and again, always to be replaced by fresh men, who unflinchingly exposed their bodies to the deadly hail.

"The massed attack!" exclaimed Wharton. "What courage! Nobody was ever more willing to die for victory than these Germans!"

Even in the moment of danger and utmost excitement he could not refuse tribute to the enemy. Nevertheless he snatched up a rifle and was firing as fast as he could into the gray ranks. John and

Carstairs were doing the same and the trench held by the Strangers was a continuous red blaze. There was so much fire and smoke and so much whirling snow that John could not see clearly. He was a prey to illusions. Now the Germans were apparently at the very edge of the trench, and then they were further away than he had first seen them. The white gloom was shot with a red haze, and the shouts of soldiers, the commands of officers and groans of wounded were mingled in a terrible turmoil of sound. But John knew that the Germans would be driven tack. Only surprise could have enabled them to win, and the vigilance of the French scouts had put their commanders on guard.

Captain Colton walked up and down the trench, his face ghastly white, although it was the flare of the searchlight and not any retreat of the blood that made it so. Now and then under the frightful crash of the rifles and machine guns he addressed brief words of warning and encouragement to his men:

"Don't raise your heads too high! Keep cool! Aim at something! Here they come again! Fire low!"

All of John's pulses were throbbing hard with excitement. He wished the Germans would go back, and his wish was prompted — less by the desire of victory than the sickening of his soul at so much slaughter. Why would their leaders continue to hurl these simple and honest peasants upon that invincible line of rifles and machine guns? The dead and wounded were piling up fast in the driving snow, but the willing servants of an emperor came on as steadily as ever to be killed. So much slaughter for so little purpose! The height of battle, excitement and danger, could not keep him from thinking of it.

Occasionally a man fell in the trench and lay in the mud and snow, but the others never ceased for a moment to send bullets into the gray masses which fell back only to come on again. Nothing but modern weapons, machine guns from which missiles fairly flowed in an unending stream, and rifles which a man fired as fast as he could pull the trigger could check them. "Why don't they stop! Why don't they stop!" John was shouting to himself through burned lips, and again he shuddered with sick horror, when he saw a whole line of men blown away, as if they had been grain swept by a tornado.

Once they came to the very edge of the trench to be slain there, and the body of a German fell in at John's very feet. He never knew how many times they charged, but human flesh and blood must yield, in the end, before unyielding steel, and at last through the crash and confusion the notes of trumpets sounded. Then the German masses melted away and the heavy white gloom once more enveloped the ground before the trenches from which came faint cries. The wounded lay thickly there with the dead, but neither side dared to go for them. An upright human figure would draw at once a hail of bullets.

Several machine guns still purred and crackled, but no reply came. Presently they, too, ceased, and the silence in front was complete, save for the faint groans and the swish of the drifting snow. John shivered, and it was not with cold. His feeling of horror was increasing. Many men had been killed and as many maimed, and he was sure that all of them had fallen for nothing.

"It's a victory," said Carstairs, "isolated and detached, but a victory nevertheless."

"So it is," said John, "but it's just a little segment on a vast curving line of four hundred miles. Maybe the Germans have taken a trench somewhere else."

"And maybe we have, at yet another point. This isn't much like the war we've read about, is it, Scott? A great battlefield, vast batteries blazing, long lines of infantry in brilliant uniforms advancing, twenty thousand cavalry charging at the gallop the earth reeling under the hoofs of their horses!"

"No, it's just murder in the dark."

"Once they came to the very edge of the trench to be slain there"

"But a black night would oppress me less than the ghastly whitish glare of the snow. I can't see a thing out there, Scott, but those low sounds I hear appall me."

The wind and the fall of snow alike were increasing in violence. The great flakes poured in a feathery storm into the trench, and, before them, all things were hidden. John knew, too, that it was covering the many dead in their front with a blanket of white and that the wounded who were unable to crawl back would probably lie frozen beneath it in the morning. Once more that shiver of horror and utter repulsion seized him. Despite himself, he could not control it, and he merely remained quiet until his nerves became steady again.

But a low moaning just beyond the trench held his attention. It did not seem to him that it was more than a dozen feet away, and he felt a great sympathy and pity. He did not doubt that some German boy hurt terribly lay almost within reach of his arm. He moved once in order that he might not hear the dreadful sound, but an irresistible attraction drew him back. Then he heard it more plainly, but the thick pouring snow covered all things.

"Carstairs," he said, "I'm going to get a wounded man out there. I just can't stand it any longer."

"Don't be foolish. They may send a volley at any time through the snow, and one of their bullets is likely to get you."

"I'll chance it."

"It's against orders."

"I'm going anyhow. Maybe I've suddenly grown squeamish, but I mean to save that wounded German from freezing to death."

"Stop, Scott! You mustn't risk your life this way. I'll report you to Captain Colton!"

But it was too late. John had climbed up the side of the trench, and, standing in the deep snow, was feeling about for the one who groaned. Guided by the sound his hands soon touched a human body.

The fallen man was lying on his side and he was already half buried in the snow. John ran his hand along his arm and shoulder, and felt cold thick blood, clotting his sleeve. But he was yet alive, because he groaned again, and John believed from the quality of his voice that he was very young. The hurt was in the shoulder and the loss of blood had been great.

He knelt beside the wounded lad and spoke to him in English and French, and in German that he had learned recently. A faint reply came; but it was too low for him to understand. Then he knelt in the snow beside him and was just barely able to see that he had a blond youth younger than himself. Shots came from the German line as he knelt there, but they were merely random bullets whistling through the snowy gloom. He was made of tenacious material, and the danger from the flying bullets merely confirmed him in his purpose. Moreover, he could not bear to return, and listen to those groans so near him. He grasped the young German under the shoulders and dragged him to the edge of the trench. Then he called softly:

"Carstairs, Wharton! I've got him! Help me down!"

Carstairs and Wharton appeared and Carstairs said:

"Well, you light-headed Yankee, you have come back!"

"Yes, and I've brought with me what I went after. Help me down with him. Easy there now! He's hit hard in the shoulder!"

The two lifted him into the trench and John slid after him, just as a half-dozen random shots whistled over his head. There they drew the rescued youth into one of the alcoves dug in the wall and Carstairs flashed his electric torch on his face, revealing features boyish, delicate, and white as death now. His gray uniform was of richer material than usual and an iron cross was pinned upon his breast.

"A brave lad as the cross shows," said Carstairs, "and I should judge too from his appearance that he's of high rank. Maybe he's a prince or the son of a prince. You've already had adventures with two of them."

"One of whom I liked."

"He looks like a good fellow," said Wharton. "I'm glad you saved him. Rub his hands while I give him a taste of this."

John and Carstairs rubbed his palms until he opened his eyes, when Wharton put a flask to his lips and made him drink. He groaned again and tried to sit up.

"Just you lie still, Herr Katzenellenbogen," said Wharton. "You're in the hands of your friends, the enemy, but we're saving your life or rather it's been done already by the man on your left; name, John Scott; nationality, American; service, French."

Captain Colton appeared and threw a white light with his own electric torch upon the little group.

"What have you there?" he asked.

"Young German who lay groaning too near the edge of our trench," replied Carstairs. "Scott couldn't stand it, so he went out and brought him in. Fancy his name is Katzenellenbogen, Kaiserslautern, Hohenfriedberg, or something else short and simple."

Captain Colton permitted himself a grim smile.

"Your act of mercy, Scott, does honor to you," he said, "though it's no part of your business to get yourself killed helping a wounded enemy. Bring him round, then send him to hospital in rear."

He walked on, continuing his inspection of the Strangers although sure that no other attack would be made that night, and the three young men applied themselves with renewed energy to the revival of their injured captive. Wharton cut the uniform away from his shoulder and, after announcing that the bullet had gone entirely through, bound up the two wounds with considerable skill. Then he gave him another but small drink out of the flask and, as they saw the color come back into his face, they felt all the pleasure of a surgeon when he sees his efforts succeed. The boy glanced at his shoulder, and then gave the three a grateful look.

"You're all right," said Carstairs cheerfully in English. "You're guest or prisoner, whichever you choose to call it and we three are your hosts or captors. My name is Carstairs and these two assistants of mine are Wharton and Scott, distant cousins, that is to say, Yankees. It was Scott who saved you."

The boy smiled faintly. He was in truth handsome with a delicate fairness one did not see often among the Germans, who were generally cast in a sterner mold.

"And I am Leopold Kratzek," he replied in good English.

"Kratzek," said John. "Ah, you're an Austrian. Now I remember there's an Austrian field-marshal of that name."

"He is my father but he is in the East. My regiment was sent with an Austrian corp to the western front. It seems that I am in great luck. My wound is not mortal, but I should certainly have frozen to death out there if one of you had not come for me."

"Scott went, of course," said Carstairs. "He's an American and naturally a tuft-hunter. He's been making a long list of princely acquaintances recently, and he was bound to bring in the son of a field-marshal and make a friend of him, too."

"Shut up, Carstairs," said John. "You talk this way to hide your own imperfections. You know that at heart every Englishman is a snob."

"Snobby is as snobby does," laughed Carstairs. "Now, Kratzek, lie back again and we'll spread these blankets over you."

The young Austrian smiled.

"I've fallen into very good company," he said.

John, whose character was serious, felt some sadness as he looked at him. He remembered those gay Viennese who had set the torch of the great war, and how merry they were over it with their visions of quick victory and glory. Poor, gay, likable, light-headed Austrians! Brave but short-sighted, they were likely to suffer more than any other nation! The fair, handsome youth, wrapped now in the blankets, seemed to him to typify all the Austrian qualities.

"You'd better go to sleep if you can," said John. "We can't move you yet, but in time you'll reach a good hospital of ours in the rear."

"I'll obey you," said Kratzek, in the most tractable manner, and closing his eyes he soon fell asleep despite his wound.

"Now, having caught your Austrian, what are you going to do with him?" said Carstairs to John.

"Nothing for the present, but later on I'll have him taken down one of the transverse trenches to a hospital. Maybe you think I'm foolish, Carstairs, but I've an idea that I've made a friend, though I didn't have that purpose in view when I went out for him. I never think that anybody hates me unless he proves it. People as a rule don't take the time and trouble to hate and plot."

"You're right, Scott. Hating is a terribly tiresome business, and I notice that you're by nature friendly."

"Which may be because I'm American."

"Oh, well, we English are friendly, too."

"But seldom polite, although I think you're unaware of the latter fact."

"If a man doesn't know he's impolite, then he isn't. It's the intention that counts."

"We'll let it go, but I've a strong premonition that this Austrian boy is going to do me a great favor some day."

"I have premonitions, too, often, but they're invariably wrong. Now, I see an orderly coming. I hope he hasn't a message from Captain Colton for us to prowl around in the snow somewhere."

Happily, the message released them from further duty that night and bade them seek rest. Young Kratzek was lying in John's bed and was sleeping. He looked so young and so pale that the heart of his captor and rescuer was moved to pity. Light-headed the Austrians might be, but no one could deny them valor.

Just beyond the niche was another and smaller one, seldom used, owing to its extreme narrowness, but John decided that he could sleep in it. At any rate, if he fell off he would land in six or eight inches of soft snow.

The flakes were still coming down heavily. It was the biggest snow that he had yet seen in Europe and he believed that it would fall all night. They had plenty of blankets and spreading two on the shelf which was no broader than himself he lay down and put two more over him.

He was in a pleasant mental glow, because he had saved young Kratzek, forgetting the rest who lay out there under the snow. All his instincts were for mercy and gentleness, but like others, he was being hardened by war, or at least he was made forgetful. Resting in the earthen side of a trench, the horrors of the battle passed out of his mind. The white gloom was so heavy there that he could not see the other wall four feet away, and the falling flakes almost grazed his face as they passed, but he had a marvelous sense of comfort and ease, even of luxury. The caveman had fared no better, often worse, because he had no blankets, and John drew a deep sigh of content.

A gun thundered somewhere far back in the German lines, and a gun also far back in the French lines thundered in reply. Then came a random and scattering fire of rifles through the falling snow from both sides, but John was not disturbed in the least by these reports. He felt as safe in his narrow trench as if he had been a hundred miles from the field of battle, and compared, with the driving storm outside, his six feet by one of an earthen bed was all he wished. The pleasant warmth from the blankets flowed through his veins, and his limbs and senses relaxed. There was firing again, faint and from a distant point, but it was soothing now like the tune played on the little mouth-organ earlier in the evening, and he fell into a deep and peaceful slumber.

When he awoke in the morning the sun was shining in the trench, the bottom of which was covered with eight inches of snow, now slushy on top from the red beams. John felt himself restored and strong, and he stepped down into the snow and slush, having first tucked his blue-gray trousers into his high boots. He was lucky in the possession of a fine pair of boots that would turn the last drop of water, and in such times as these they were worth more than gold.

A shell screaming high overhead was his morning salutation, and then came other shells, desultory but noisy. John paid no more attention to them than if they had been distant bees buzzing. He looked at his young prisoner, Kratzek, and found that he was still sleeping, with a healthy color in his face. John was impressed anew by his youth. "Why do they let such babies come to the war?" he asked himself, but he added, "They're brave babies, though."

"Well, he's pulling along all right," said Carstairs. "I was up before you and I learned that Captain Colton sent a surgeon in the night to examine him. Wharton had done a good job with his bandages, he admitted, but he cleaned and dressed the wound and said the patient was in such a healthy condition that he would be entirely well again in a short time. He's only a young boy, isn't he, Scott?"

"Yes, I suppose that's why I have such a fatherly feeling for him."

"That, or because you brought him in from sure death. We're always attached to anyone we save."

"I mean to have him exchanged and sent back to his mother in Austria. He's bound to have a mother there and she'll thank me though she may never see me. I wish these pleasant Austrians had more sense."

Kratzek opened his eyes and looked blankly at the two young men. He strove to rise, but fell back with a low sigh of pain. Then he closed his eyes, but John saw the muscles of his face working.

"He's trying to remember," whispered Carstairs.

Memory came back to Kratzek in a few moments, and he opened his eyes again.

"I was saved by somebody last night and I think it was you," he said, looking at John. "I want to say to you that I am very grateful. I do not wish to appear boastful, but I have relatives in both the Austrian and German armies who are very powerful—ours is both a North German and South German house, and East German, too."

"That is, it's *wohlgeboren* and *hochwohlgeboren*," said Wharton, who appeared at that moment.

"Yes," said the Austrian boy, smiling faintly. "I am highborn and very highborn, although it's not my fault. You, I take it, by your accent, are American and these things, of course, don't count with you."

"I don't know, they seem to count pretty heavily with some of our women, if you can judge by the newspapers."

"Who are these men of whom you speak?" asked John.

"The chief is Prince Karl of Auersperg, who is not far from your front. I betray no military secret when I say that. I shall send word to him that you have saved my life, and, if you should fall a prisoner into German hands, he will do as much for you as you have done for me."

The Austrian boy did not notice the quick glances exchanged by the three, and he went on:

"Prince Karl of Auersperg is a general of ability, and owing to that and his very high birth, he has great influence with both emperors. You have nothing to fear from our brave Germans if you should fall into their hands, but I beg you in any event, to get word to the prince and to give him my name."

"I'll do it," replied John, but he soothed his conscience by telling himself that it was a white lie. If he should be captured for the third time Prince Karl of Auersperg was the last one whom he wanted to know of it. Neither was he pleased to hear that this medieval baron was again so near, although he did not realize why until later.

"We've talked enough now," said John, "and I'll see that food is sent you. Then it's off with you to the hospital. It's a French hospital, but they'll treat a German shoulder just as they would one of their own."

The life in the vast honeycomb of trenches was awakening fast. Two million men perhaps, devoted to the task of killing one another, crept from their burrows and stood up. Along the whole line almost of twenty score miles snow had fallen, but the rifles and cannon were firing already, spasmodic sharpshooting at some points, and fierce little battles at others.

John peered over the edge of the trench. A man was allowed to put his head in the German range but not his hand. So long as he lived he must preserve a hand which could pull the trigger or wield the bayonet.

They were not firing in the immediate front, and he had a good view of fields and low hills, deep in snow. Just before him the ground was leveled, and he saw many raised places in the snow there. He knew that bodies lay beneath, and once more he shuddered violently. But the world was full of beauty that morning. The sun was a vast sheet of gold, giving a luminous tint to the snow, and two clusters of trees, covered to the last bough and twig with snow, were a delicate tracery of white, shot at times by the sun with a pale yellow glow like that of a rose. On the horizon a faint misty smoke, the color of silver, was rising, and he knew that it came from the cooking fires of the Germans.

It reminded him that he was very hungry. Cave life under fire, if it did not kill a man, gave him a ferocious appetite, and turning into one of the transverse trenches he followed a stream of the Strangers who were already on the way to their hotel.

The narrow cut led them nearly a mile, and then they came out in a valley the edges of which were fringed with beeches. But in the wide space within the valley most of the snow had been cleared away and enormous automobile kitchens stood giving forth the pleasant odors of food and drink. At one side officers were already satisfying their hunger and farther on men were doing the same. They were within easy range of the German guns, but it was not the habit of either side to send morning shells unless a direct attack was to be made.

John had no thought of danger. Youth was youth and one could get hardened to anything. He had been surprised more than once in this war to find how his spirits could go from the depths to the heights and now they were of the best. He was full of life and the world was very beautiful that morning. It was the fair land of France again, but it was under a thick robe of snow, the golden tint on the white, as the large yellow sun slowly sailed clear of the high hills on their right.

General Vaugirard stood near the first of the wagons, drinking cup after cup of hot steaming coffee, and devouring thick slices of bread and butter. He wore a long blue overcoat over his uniform, and high boots. But the dominant note was given to his appearance by the thick white beard which seemed to be touched with a light silver frost. Under the great thatch of eyebrow the keen little eyes twinkled. He made John think of a huge, white and inoffensive bear.

The general's roving eye caught sight of Scott and he exclaimed:

"Come here, you young Yankee! I hear that you distinguished yourself last night by saving the life of one of our enemies, thus enabling him perhaps to fight against us once more."

"I beg your pardon, General," said John, "but I'm no Yankee."

"What, denying your birthright! I never heard an American do that before! Everybody knows you're a Yankee."

"Pardon me. General, you and all other Europeans make a mistake about the Yankees. At home the people of the Southern States generally apply it to those living in the Northern states, but in the North it is carried still further and is properly applied to the residents of the six New England states. I don't come from one of those states, and so I'm not in a real sense a Yankee."

"What, sir, have I, a Frenchman, to do with your local distinctions? Yankees you all are and Yankee you shall remain. It's a fine name, and from what I've seen in this war you're great fighting men, worthy to stand with Frenchmen."

"Thank you for the compliment, General," said John, smiling. "Hereafter I shall always remain a Yankee."

"And now do you and your friends take your food there with de Rougemont. I've had my breakfast, and a big and good one it was. I'm going to the edge of the hill and use my glasses."

He waddled away, looking more than ever an enormous, good-natured bear. John's heart, as always, warmed to him. Truly he was the father of his children, ten thousand or more, who fought around him, and for whose welfare he had a most vigilant eye and mind.

The three joined a group of the Strangers, Captain Colton at their head, and they stood there together, eating and drinking, their appetites made wonderfully keen by the sharp morning and a hard life in the open air. Bougainville, the little colonel, came from the next valley and remained with them awhile. He was almost the color of an Indian now, but his uniform was remarkably trim and clean and he bore himself with dignity. He was distinctly a personality and John knew that no one would care to undertake liberties with him.

In the long months following the battle on the Marne Bougainville had done great deeds. Again and again he had thrown his regiment into some weak spot in the line just at the right moment. He seemed, like Napoleon and Stonewall Jackson, to have an extraordinary, intuitive power of divining the enemy's intentions, and General Vaugirard, to whose command his regiment belonged, never hesitated to consult him and often took his advice. "Ah, that child of Montmartre!" he would say. "He will go far, if he does not meet a shell too soon. He keeps a hand of steel on his regiment, there is no discipline sterner than his, and yet his men love him."

Bougainville showed pleasure at seeing John again, and gave him his hand American fashion.

"We both still live," he said briefly.

"And hope for complete victory."

"We do," said Bougainville, earnestly, "but it will take all the strength of the allied nations to achieve it. Much has happened, Monsieur Scott, since we stood that day in the lantern of Basilique du Sacré-Coeur on the Butte Montmartre and saw the Prussian cavalry riding toward Paris."

"But what has happened is much less than that which will happen before this war is over."

"You speak a great truth, Monsieur Scott. And now I must go. Hearing that the Strangers were in this valley I wished to come and see with my own eyes that you were alive and well. I have seen and I am glad."

He saluted, Captain Colton and the others saluted in return, and then he walked over the hill to his own "children."

"An antique! An old Roman! Spirit defying death," said Captain Colton looking after him.

"He has impressed me that way, too, sir," said John. But his mind quickly left Bougainville, and turned to the message that Weber had brought the night before. He was glad that Julie Lannes would be so near again, and yet he was sorry. He had not been sorry when he first heard it, but the apprehension had come later. He tried to trace the cause, and then he remembered the name of Auersperg, the prince whom his cousin, the Austrian captive, had said was near. He sought to laugh at himself for his fears. The mental connection was too vague, he said, but the relieving laughter would not come.

John hoped that a lucky chance might bring Lannes, and involuntarily he looked up at the heavens. But they were clear of aeroplanes. The heavy snow of the night before had driven in the hosts of the air, and they had not reappeared.

Then John resolved to go to Chastel himself. He did not know how he would go or what he would do when he got there, but the impulse was strong and it remained with him.

CHAPTER III
JULIE'S COMING

That day, the next night and the next day passed without any event save the usual desultory firing of cannon and rifles. Many men were killed and more were wounded by the sharpshooters. Little battles were fought at distant points along the lines, the Allies winning some while the Germans were victorious in others, but the result was nothing. The deadlock was unbroken.

Meanwhile the weather turned somewhat warmer and the melting snow poured fresh deluges of water into the trenches. Most of it was pumped out, but it would sink back into the ground and return. John again gave thanks for the splendid pair of high boots that he wore, and also he often searched the air for Lannes. But he saw no sign of the lithe and swift *Arrow* and his anxiety for Julie increased steadily. She must now be at Chastel, but he had not yet found any excuse that would release him from the trenches and let him go there.

He inquired for Weber, but no one had seen or heard of him again. No doubt he was far away on some perilous mission, serving France on the ground as Lannes served her in the air.

Young Kratzek in the hospital was improving fast and John secured leave of absence long enough to see him once. He was fervent in his gratitude and renewed his promises that somehow and somewhere he would surely repay young Scott. News that he was alive, but a prisoner, had reached the German lines and already an exchange for him had been arranged, the Germans, owing to his rank, being willing to return a French brigadier in his place. The prospect filled him with happiness and he talked much. John noticed once more how very young he was, not much more than seventeen, and with manners decidedly boyish. He had the utmost confidence in the success of Germany and Austria, despite the check at the Marne, and talked freely of another advance. John led him adroitly to his cousin of Auersperg, of whom he wished to hear more. He soon discovered that Auersperg was a very great prince to Kratzek.

"I stand in some awe of him. I need scarcely tell you that Herr Scott, my captor," he said, "because he represents so much. Ah, the history and the legends clustering about our house, that goes far back into the dim ages! The Auerspergs were counts and princes of the Holy Roman Empire, and they have been grand dukes. They have decided the choice of more than one emperor at Frankfort, and they have stood with the highest when they were crowned at Augsburg. Please don't think I am boasting for myself, Herr Scott, it is only for my cousin, the august Prince Karl, *hochwohlgeboren*!"

"I understand," said John, smiling. "But I want to tell you, Leopold Kratzek, that I'm *hochwohlgeboren* myself."

"Why, how is that? You are neither German nor Austrian."

"No, I'm American, but I'm very highborn nevertheless. There are a hundred millions of us and all of us are very highborn not excepting our colored people, many of whom are descended from African princes who have a power over their people not approached by either of the kaisers."

The boy smiled.

"Now, I know you jest," he said. "You have no classes, but I've heard that all of you claim to be kings."

John saw that he had made no impression upon him. Frank, honest and brave, an Auersperg was nevertheless in the boy's mind an Auersperg, something superior, a product of untold centuries, a small and sublimated group of the human race to which nothing else could aspire, not even talent, learning, courage and honesty. To all Auerspergs, Napoleon and Shakespeare were mere men of genius, to be patronized. John smiled, too. He did not feel hurt at all. In his turn he felt a superiority, a superiority of perception, and a superiority in the sense of proportion.

"Prince Karl of Auersperg is always resolved to maintain his pride of blood, is he not?" he asked.

"He considers it his duty. The head of a house that has been princely for fifteen centuries could not do less. He could never forget or forgive an insult to his person."

"If he were insulted he would hold that all the Auerspergs who were now living and all who had lived in the last fifteen hundred years were insulted also."

"Undoubtedly!" replied Kratzek, with great emphasis.

"I merely wished to know," said John, gravely, "in order that I may know how to bear myself in case I should meet Prince Karl of Auersperg"—he had not told that he had met him already—"and now I'm going to tell you good-by, Leopold. I think it likely that I shall be sent away on a mission and before I return it is probable that you will be exchanged."

"Good-by, Mr. Scott. Don't forget my promise. If you should ever fall into our hands please try to communicate with me."

John returned to his trench. He had been very thoughtful that day, and he had evolved a plan. A considerable body of wounded soldiers were to be sent to Chastel, and as they must have a guard he had asked Captain Colton to use his influence with General Vaugirard and have him appointed a member of the guard.

Now he found Captain Colton sitting in his little alcove smoking one of his eternal cigarettes and looking very contented. He took an especially long puff when he saw John and looked at him quizzically.

"Well, Scott!" he said.

"Well, sir!" said John.

"General Vaugirard thinks your desire to guard wounded, see to their welfare, great credit to you."

"I thank him, sir, through you."

"Approve of such zeal myself."

"I thank you in person."

"Did not tell him—French girl, Mademoiselle Julie Lannes, also going to Chastel to attend to wounded. Handsome girl, wonderfully handsome girl, don't you think so, Scott?"

"I do, sir," said John, reddening.

"You and she—going to Chastel about same time. Remarkable coincidence, but nothing in it, of course, just coincidence."

"It's not a coincidence, sir. You've always been a friend to me. Captain Colton, and I'm willing to tell you that I've sought this mission to Chastel because Mademoiselle Julie Lannes is there, or is going there, and for no other reason whatever. I'm afraid she's in danger, and anyway I long for a sight of her face as we long for the sun after a storm."

Captain Colton, with his cigarette poised between his thumb and forefinger, looked John up and down.

"Good!" he said. "Frank statement of truth—I knew already. Nothing for you to be ashamed of. If girl beautiful and noble as Mademoiselle Julie Lannes looked at me as she has looked at you I'd break down walls and run gantlets to reach her. Go, John, boy. Luck to you in all the things in which you wish luck."

He held out his hand and John wrung it. And so, the terse captain himself had a soft heart which he seldom showed!

The convoy started the next morning, John with five soldiers in an armored automobile bringing up the rear. There were other men on the flank and in front, and a captain commanded. The day was wintry and gloomy. Heavy clouds obscured the sky, and the slush was deep in the roads. A desolate wind moaned through the leafless trees, and afar the cannon grumbled and groaned.

But neither the somber day nor the melancholy convoy affected John's spirits. Chastel, a village of light—light for him—would be at the end of his journey.

Despite mud, slush and snow, traveling was pleasant. The automobile had made wonderful changes. One could go almost anywhere in it, and its daring drivers whisked it gaily over fields, through forests and up hills, which in reality could be called mountains. War had merely increased their enterprise, and they took all kinds of risks, usually with success.

John was very comfortable now, as he leaned back in the armored car, driven by a young Frenchman. He wore a heavy blue overcoat over his uniform, and his only weapon was a powerful automatic revolver in his belt, but it was enough. The ambulances, filled with wounded, stretched a half-mile in front of him, but he had grown so used to such sights that they did not move him long. Moreover in this war a man was not dead until he *was* dead. The small bullets of the high-powered rifle either killed or harmed but little. It was the shrapnel that tore.

The road led across low hills, and down slopes which he knew were kissed by a warm sun in summer. It was here that the vines flourished, but the snow could not hide the fact that it was torn and trampled now. Huge armies had surged back and forth over it, and yet John, who was of a thoughtful mind, knew that in a few more summers it would be as it had been before. In this warm and watered France Nature would clothe the earth in a green robe which winter itself could not wholly drive away.

A reader of history, he knew that Europe had been torn and ravaged by war, times past counting, and yet geologically it was among the youngest and freshest of lands. Everything would pass and new youth would take the place of the youth that the shells and bullets were now carrying away.

He shook himself. Reflections like these were for men of middle years. The tide of his own youth flowed back upon him and the world, even under snow and with stray guns thundering behind him, was full of splendor. Moreover, there was the village of Chastel before him! Chastel! Chastel! He had never heard of it until two or three days ago, and yet it now loomed in his mind as large as Paris or New York. Julie must have arrived already, and he would see her again after so many months of hideous war, but deep down in his mind persisted the belief that she should not have come. Lannes must have had some reason that he could not surmise, or he would not have written the letter asking her to meet him at Chastel.

The village, he learned from one of the men in the automobile, was only ten miles away and it was built upon a broad, low hill at the base of which a little river flowed. It was very ancient. A town of the Belgæ stood there in Cæsar's time, but it contained not more than two thousand inhabitants, and its chief feature was a very beautiful Gothic cathedral.

John's automobile could have reached Chastel in less than an hour, despite the snow and the slush, but the train of the wounded was compelled to move slowly, and he must keep with it. Meanwhile he scanned the sky with powerful glasses, which he had been careful to secure after his escape from Auersperg. Nearly all officers carried strong glasses in this war, and yet even to the keenest eyes the hosts of the air were visible only in part.

John now and then saw telephone wires running through the clumps of forest and across the fields. There was a perfect web of them, reaching all the way from Alsace and the Forest of Argonne to the sea. Generals talked to one another over them, and over these wires the signal officers sent messages to the men in the batteries telling them how to fire their guns.

The telegraph, too, was at work. The wires were clicking everywhere, and the air was filled also with messages which went on no wires at all, but which took invisible wings unto themselves. The wireless, despite its constant use, remained a mystery and wonder to John. One of his most vivid memories was that night on the roof of the château, when Wharton talked through space to the German generals, and learned their plans.

He looked up now and his eyes were shut, but he almost fancied that he could see the words passing in clouds over his head, written on nothing, but there, nevertheless, the most mysterious and, in some ways, the most powerful part of the hosts of the air, the hosts that within a generation had changed the ways of armies and battles. He opened his eyes and found himself searching for aeroplanes, the most tangible portion of those hosts of the air, with which man had to fight. He saw several behind him, where the French and German lines almost met, but there was no shape resembling the *Arrow*.

The aeroplanes and Zeppelins had been much less active since winter had come in full tide. They were essentially birds of sunshine and fair weather, liking but little clouds and storms. And as the skies still looked very threatening John judged that they would not be abroad much that day. The conditions were far from promising, as a heavy massing of the clouds in the southwest indicated more snow.

"There is Chastel, sir," said Mallet, his chauffeur. "You can see the steeple of the cathedral shining through the clouds."

John's eyes followed the pointing finger, and he caught a high gleam, although all beneath was a mass of floating gray mist. But he knew it was a few beams of the sun piercing through the clouds and striking upon some solid object. He put the glasses to his eyes and then he was able to discern an old, old town, standing on a cliff above a stream that he would have called a creek at home. Some of the houses were of stone, and others were of timber and concrete, but it was evident that war had passed already over Chastel. As he rode nearer he beheld buildings ruined by shells or fire. Many of them seemed to be razed almost level with the ground. The evidences of battle were everywhere. He surmised that it had been held for a while by the Germans on their retreat from the Marne, and that the lighting there had been desperate.

In the lower ground on the near side of the stream were many small board houses arranged in a square, and these he knew were the hospital. He would remain there until the last of the wounded were discharged, and then he would enter Chastel. Mallet informed him that his surmises were correct and he saw for himself that the head of the train had already turned into the square around which the little board houses were built.

The transferring of the hurt, took nearly all the morning, and John faithfully performed his part. There was Chastel only a few hundred yards away, now clearly visible despite the massive clouds that floated persistently across the sky. Yet he made no attempt to reach it until his work was done, nor did he speak of it, not even to the chauffeur, Mallet, of whom he had made a good friend.

Near noon, the task finished, he ate luncheon and started toward Chastel. His orders from Captain Colton allowed him much liberty, and he was not compelled to account to anyone, when he chose to enter the town. He crossed the stream, muddy from the melting snow, on a small stone bridge, which he believed from its steep arch must date almost back to the time of the Romans, and pausing on the other side looked up once more at Chastel. He had no doubt that, seen in the sunshine and as it was, it had been both picturesque and beautiful. But now it lay half in ruins, under a sullen sky, and he beheld no sign of life. Just above him within its grounds stood a large château, that had been riven through and through by shells. The walls looked as if they were ready to fall apart and John shivered a little. Farther on was a public building of some kind, destroyed by fire, all save the walls which stood, blackened and desolate, and now he saw that the cathedral too had been damaged.

A flake of snow, large and damp, settled on his hand. The clouds were massing, directly over his head, and he feared another fall. It was unfortunate, but nothing could drive him back, and finding a flight of stone steps he ascended them and entered the village.

Chastel had looked somber from the plain below, where some of the effect, John had thought, might be due to distance, but here it was a silent ruin, tragic and terrible. Over this village, once so neat and trim, as he could easily see, war had swept in its most hideous fashion. Houses were riddled and the gray light showed through them from wall to wall where the great shells had passed. A bronze statue standing in a fountain in the center of the little place or square had been struck, and it lay prone and shattered in the water.

The first flakes of the new snow began to fall, and the sinister sky, heavy with clouds, took on the darkness of twilight, although night was far away. Yet the huge rents and holes in the houses and the fallen masonry seemed to grow more distinct in the gloom. The village consisted chiefly of one long street, and as John looked up and down it, he did not see a single human being. Nothing was visible to him but the iron hoof of war crushing everything under it, and he shuddered violently.

The snow began to drive, whipped by a bitter wind, and he drew the heavy blue overcoat closely about him. The shuddering which was not of the snow and the cold, passed, but his heart was ice. The abandoned town over which Germans and French had fought oppressed him like a nightmare. What had become of Julie? Why had Philip asked her to meet him at such a place? There was the hospital, but it was in the plain below, where lights now shone faintly through the heavy gray air and the driving snow.

Surely Lannes could not have made any mistake! John had learned to trust his judgment thoroughly and Philip, too, knew the country so well. If he had sent for Julie to come to Chastel he must have had a good reason for it, although the snow was bound to delay the coming of the *Arrow* to meet her. If she had reached Chastel she would remain there, and not go to the hospital in the plain below. She trusted her brother as implicitly as John did.

John, taking thought with himself, concluded that she must be now in the village. It was not possible that Chastel, silent as it was and desolate as it seemed, could be entirely deserted. Although leaving ruin behind, the fury of battle had passed and some of the people would return to their homes. Chastel lay behind the French lines, a great hospital camp was not far away, and the fear of further German invasion could not be present now.

He put one hand in his overcoat pocket over the butt of the automatic, and then, remembering how General Vaugirard whistled, he too whistled, not for want of thought but to encourage himself, to make his heart beat a little less violently, and to hear a cheerful sound where there was nothing else but the soft swish of the snow and the desolate moaning of the wind among the ruins.

He walked down the main street, and unconsciously stopped whistling. Then the awful silence and desolation brooded over him again. The storm was thickening, and the lights in the plain below were entirely gone now. He was not yet able to find any proof of human life in Chastel, and, after all, the fighting in the town might have been so recent and so fierce that not one of the inhabitants yet dared to return. The thought made his heart throb painfully. What, then, had become of Julie?

He stopped before the cathedral, and looked up at the lofty Gothic spire which seemed to tower above the whirling snow. As well as he could see some damage had been done to the roof by shells, but the beautiful stained-glass windows were uninjured. He stood there gazing, and he knew in his heart that he was looking for a sign, like that which he and Lannes had seen on the Arc de Triomphe when the fortunes of France seemed lost forever.

A stalwart figure suddenly emerged from the white gloom and heavy hands were laid upon him. John's own fingers in his overcoat pocket tightened over the automatic, but the hands on his shoulders were those of friendship.

"Ah, it is thou, Monsieur Scott!" exclaimed a deep voice. "The master has not come but thou art thrice welcome in his place!"

It was Picard, no less than Antoine Picard himself, looming white and gigantic through the storm, and John could not doubt the genuine warmth in his voice. He was in truth welcome and he knew it. As Picard's hands dropped from his shoulders he seized them in his and wrung them hard.

"Mademoiselle Julie!" he exclaimed. "What of her? Did she come? Or have you only come in her place?"

"She is here, sir! In the church with Suzanne, my daughter. We arrived two hours ago. I wanted to go on to the camp that we could see in the plain below, but Mademoiselle Lannes would not hear of it.

It was here that Monsieur Philip wished her to meet him, and if she went on he would miss her. We expected to find food and rooms, but, my God, sir, the town is deserted! Most of the houses have been shot to pieces by the artillery and if people are here we cannot find them. Because of that we have taken shelter, for the present, in the church."

But John in his eagerness was already pushing open one of the huge bronze doors, and Picard, brushing some of the snow from his clothes, followed him. The door swung shut behind them both, and he stood beside one of the pews staring into the dusky interior.

But his eyes became used to the gloom, and soon it did not seem so somber as it was outside. Instead the light from the stained-glass windows made the mists and shadows luminous. A nave, the lofty pillars dividing it from the side aisles, the choir and the altar emerged slowly into view. From the walls pictures of the Madonna and the saints, unstained and untouched, looked down upon him. One of the candles near the altar had been lighted, and it burned with a steady, beckoning flame.

The cathedral, a great building for a small town, as happens so often in Europe, presented a warm and cheerful interior to John. It seemed to him soon after the huge bronze door sank into place behind him that war, cold, desolation and loneliness were shut out. The luminous glow streaming through the stained glass windows and the candle burning near the altar were beacons.

Then he saw Julie, sitting wrapped in a heavy cloak, in one of the pews before the choir, and the grim Suzanne, also shrouded in a heavy cloak, sat beside her. John's heart was in a glow. He knew now that he loved his comrade Philip's sister. Two or three of the golden curls escaping from her hood, fell down her back, and they were twined about his heart. He knew too that it was not the light from the stained windows, but Julie herself who had filled the church with splendor. She was to John a young goddess, perfect in her beauty, one who could do no wrong. His love had all the tenderness and purity of young love, the poetic love that comes only to youth.

But when he realized that Julie Lannes had become so much to him he felt a sudden shyness, and he let the gigantic Picard lead the way. They had made no noise in opening and closing the door, and their boots had been soundless on the stone floor.

"The American, Lieutenant Scott, Mademoiselle," said Picard respectfully.

John saw her little start of surprise, but when she stood up she was quite self-possessed. Her color was a little deeper than usual, but it might be the luminous glow from the stained-glass windows, or the cloak of dark red which wrapped her from chin to feet may have given that added touch.

She had been weary and anxious, and John thought he detected a gleam of welcome in her glance. At least it pleased him to think so. The stern Suzanne had given him a startled look, but the glance seemed to John less hostile than it used to be.

"I was told, Miss Lannes," said John in English, "that you had received a letter from your brother, Philip, to meet him here in Chastel. One Weber, an Alsatian, an able and trustworthy man whom I know, gave me the news."

It had often been his habit, when speaking his own language, to call her, American fashion, "Miss" instead of "Mademoiselle," and now she smiled at the little, remembered touch.

"It was Mr. Weber who brought the letter to me in Paris, Mr. Scott," she said. "You know it was my wish to serve our brave soldiers hurt in battle, and I was not surprised that the letter from Philip should come."

"In what manner did you arrive here?"

"In a small automobile. It is standing behind the cathedral now. Antoine is an excellent driver. But, Oh, Mr. Scott, it has been a strange and lonely ride! Once we thought we were going to be captured. As we passed through a forest Antoine was quite sure that he caught a gleam of German lances far away, but much too near for assurance, and he drove the motor forward at a great rate."

"And then you arrived in Chastel?"

"Yes, Mr. Scott, then we came to Chastel."

"But you did not see what you expected to see."

She shivered and the brilliant color left her face for a moment.

"No, Mr. Scott, I did not find what I thought would be here. Philip had not come, but that did not alarm me so much, and I knew that for awhile the snow had made the flight of aeroplanes impossible.

No, it was not the absence of Philip that filled me with terror. Surely when he sent for me he did not anticipate such fighting as must have occurred here so recently."

"He would never have drawn you into danger."

"I know it, and that is why I am so puzzled and so full of apprehension. The sight of Chastel appalls me and it has had its influence upon Antoine and Suzanne, strong as they are. We saw ruins, Mr. Scott, the terrible path of battle, and no human being until you came."

"I had the same feeling myself, nor did I see life either until I met Antoine, Miss Julie, if I may call you so instead of Miss Lannes?"

"Yes, of course, Mr. Scott. But what does it mean? Why haven't the people come back?"

They were still talking in English, and Suzanne's customary look had returned to her face in all its grimness, but they went on, unmindful of her.

"I confess, Miss Julie, I don't understand it," replied John. "The fighting here seems to have occurred within the last two or three days. It is behind our lines and I did not hear of it, but so much has happens of which we do not hear, and there has been so much shifting of the lines in recent days that a battle could easily have occurred at Chastel without my knowledge. And the shock of cannon fire with the enormous guns now used is so tremendous that the fleeing people may not have recovered from it yet. Doubtless they will return tomorrow or the next day."

"I hope so, Mr. Scott. A ruined town with nobody in it oppresses terribly."

A sudden thought stabbed at John's heart. It was possible that the people of Chastel did not return because they were fearing another attack. If Antoine had caught the gleam of German lances in the wood then a considerable German force might be behind the French lines. Snowstorms formed a good cover for secret operations.

Julie noticed the passing shadow in his face and she knew it to be the sign of alarm.

"What is it, Mr. Scott?" she asked. "Do you know of any danger?"

"No," he replied truthfully, because he had dismissed his thought as incredible, "but you will not remain here, Miss Julie. You and your servant will go to the hospital camp, will you not? It is not much more than a mile beyond the river."

But to his surprise she shook her head.

"I must stay in Chastel," she said. "It is here that Philip wished me to come, and if I am not here when he arrives he will not know where to find me. And there is no danger. You know that, Mr. Scott. If Antoine really saw German lances as he claims, it is no proof that German horsemen will come to Chastel, running into danger. What have they to gain by raiding a ruined town?"

"There is much reason in what you say. Certainly it would avail the Germans nothing to gallop through shattered Chastel in a snowstorm. But you can't spend the night in the church. I've no doubt that we can find bed and board for all of us in some abandoned house."

The driving snow had reconciled John somewhat to the idea of Julie passing the night in Chastel. The road leading down to the river was steep and the bridge over which he had crossed was narrow with a very high arch. A motor might easily miss the way in the darkening storm, and then meet disaster.

Julie looked at him inquiringly as if she wished his indorsement of her plan, although her lips were closed tightly.

"Of course you'll stay, Miss Julie," he said, "and I'll stay too, although I'm not invited."

"You're invited now."

"Thanks. Consider me a follower, or rather a dragoman, to use the eastern term."

Then he said to Antoine in French:

"Mademoiselle Lannes is resolved to remain tonight in Chastel. She thinks that if her brother were to come her absence would upset all his plans."

Picard nodded. His was the soul of loyalty.

"It is right," he said. "It is here that Monsieur Philip expects to find her and we can guard her."

John liked the inclusive "we."

"And now to work, Antoine and Suzanne," he said. "We've agreed that we can't spend the night in the cathedral. Perhaps there is no better refuge so far as the storm is concerned, but a pew is not a good bed, except for hardened old soldiers like you and me, Antoine."

"No, Mr. Scott, it is not."

"Then I suggest that we leave Mademoiselle Lannes and Suzanne here while we look for shelter."

But Julie would not agree. They must all go out together. What was a little snow? Should a Lannes mind it? She drew her great red cloak more closely around her and led the way from the choir to the bronze doors, the others following in silence.

John felt that Julie had shown much decision and firmness. When she had declared that she would not remain in the church her tone and manner were wonderfully like those of her brother Philip. She was altogether worthy of the name of Lannes, and the fact appealed strongly to young Scott, who liked strength and courage.

When they were outside they saw that the storm had increased. The snow was driving so thickly that they could not see fifty yards ahead, and their quest of a house for the night would be difficult. But the lofty steeple of the church with its protecting cross still towered above them and John felt, if their search was vain, that the cathedral would always be there to shelter them. Doubtless the provident Picard also had provisions in the motor.

"I believe you told me your machine was behind the cathedral, Antoine," he said. "We ought first to take a look at it, and see that it's all right."

"That's very true, sir," replied Picard. "Shall we not go there and see it, Mademoiselle Julie?"

She nodded and they passed to the rear of the cathedral, where the machine stood under a shed. It was a small limousine with a powerful body, and John, although knowing little of automobiles, liked its looks.

"How about the gasoline supply?" he asked Picard.

"Enough, sir, for a long journey."

"You've brought food?"

"Food and wine both, sir, under the seats."

"That's very good, but I knew you'd be far-seeing, Picard. If we don't find a good place we can take the supplies and return to the cathedral."

"But we will find lodgings, Sir Jean the Scott," said Julie, catching the trick of the name from her brother. "I command you to lead the way and discover them."

Her dark red cloak was now white with the driven snow, and her face, rosy with the cold, looked from a dark red hood, also turned white. John saw that her eyes laughed. He realized suddenly that she felt neither fear nor apprehension. He had discovered a new quality, the same heroic soul that her brother Philip had, the unquenchable courage of the great marshal. He realized that she found a certain enjoyment in the situation, that the spirit of adventure was upon her. His own pulses leaped and his soul responded.

"Come on," he said in a strong voice. "If there's a habitation in this place fit for you I'll find it." John had resumed command, but Julie walked at his elbow, a brave and strong lieutenant. The two Picards followed close behind. Suzanne, at this moment, when the resources of Scott were needed so much, had relaxed somewhat of her grimness. She and Antoine said nothing as they bent their heads to the snow. Unconsciously they had resigned decision and leadership to the young pair who walked before them.

John glanced toward the river and the plain beyond, but he merely looked into a wall, cold, white and impenetrable. No ray of light or life came from it. The hospital camp had been blotted out completely. But from the north came a faint sullen note, and he knew that it was the throb of a great gun. Julie heard it too.

"They're still firing," she said.

"Yes, but it may not be snowing so hard a few miles away from here. I discovered when I was up in the air with Philip that the air moves in eddies and gusts and currents like the ocean, and that it has bays and straits, and this may be a narrow strait of snow that envelops us here. Hear that! Guns to the south, too! One side is shelling the other's trenches. You remember how it was in all the long fighting that we call the Battle of the Marne. Day and night, night and day the guns thundered and crashed. I seemed when I slept to hear 'em in my dreams. They never stopped."

"It makes me, too, think of that time, Mr. Scott, except that this is winter and that was summer. The cloud of battle is just the same."

"But the results are much less. It's a deadlock, and has been a deadlock for months. I don't expect anything decisive until spring, and maybe not then. Here is a good house, Miss Julie. It looks as if the mayor, or Chastel's banker might have lived here. Suppose we try it."

But the house had been stripped. All the rooms were cold and bare, and in the rear a huge shell had exploded leaving yawning gaps in the walls, through which the snow was driving fast. Julie shivered.

"Let's go away from it," she said. "I couldn't sleep in this house. It's continually talking to us in a language I don't like to hear."

"I don't hear its talk," said John, "but I see its ghosts walking, and I'm as anxious to get away from it as you are."

Nor were Antoine and Suzanne reluctant, and they hurried out to enter another house which had suffered a similar fate. They passed through a half-dozen, all torn and shattered by monster shells, and at last they came to one which had before it a stretch of grass, a pebbled walk, a fountain, now dry, and benches painted green, under their covering of snow.

"An inn!" said John. "This is surely Chastel's hotel. Either the de l'Europe, the Grand or the Hollande, because more than half the hotels in Europe bear one or the other of those names. Is it not fitting, Miss Julie, that we should enter and take our rest in an inn?"

She looked at it with sparkling eyes. Again the spirit of adventure was high within her.

"It seems to be undamaged," she said. "Perhaps we'll find someone there."

John shook his head.

"No, Miss Julie," he said, "I'm convinced that it's silent and alone. You'll observe that no smoke is rising from any of its chimneys, and every window that we can see is dark."

"What do you say, Antoine, and you Suzanne?" asked Julie.

"It is evident, since the inn has no other guests, that we have been sent here by the Supreme Power, for what purpose I know not," replied Suzanne, devoutly.

"Then there is no need to delay longer," said John, and, leading the way up the pebbled walk, he pushed open the central door.

CHAPTER IV
THE HOTEL AT CHASTEL

John was fast finding that in a crowded country like Europe, suddenly ravaged by war, nothing was more common than abandoned houses. People were continually fleeing at a moment's warning. He had already made use of two or three, at a time when they were needed most, and here was another awaiting him. Before he pushed open the door he had already read above it, despite the incrustations of snow, the sign, "Hôtel de l'Europe," and he felt intuitively that they were coming into good quarters. He was so confident of it that his cheerful mood deepened, turned in fact into joyousness.

As he held open the door he took off his cap, bowed low and said:

"Enter my humble hôtel, Madame la Princesse. Our guests are all too few now, but I promise you, Your Highness, that you and your entourage shall have the best the house affords. Behold, the orchestra began the moment you entered!"

As he spoke the deep thunder of guns came from invisible points along the long battle-line. The firing of the cannon was far away but the jarring of the air was distinct in Chastel, and the windows of the hotel shook in their frames. John and Julie had become so used to it that it merely heightened their fantastic mood.

"Yours is, in truth, a most welcome hotel," she said, "and I see that we shall not be annoyed by other guests."

She shook the snow from her hood and cloak and entered, and Picard and Suzanne, also divesting themselves of snow coverings, followed her. Then John too went in, and once more closed a door between them and the storm. He noticed that the great Antoine gave him a glance of strong approval, and even the somber Suzanne seemed to be thawing.

John was sorry that the European hotels did not have a big lobby after the American fashion. It would have given them a welcome now, but all was as usual in the Hôtel de l'Europe, Chastel. There was the small office for the cashier, and the smaller one for the bookkeeper. Near them was the bureau and upon it lay an open register. Through an open door beyond, the smoking-room was visible, and from where he stood John could see French and English illustrated weeklies lying upon the tables. Nothing had been taken, nothing was in disorder, the hotel was complete, save that it was as bare as *Crusoe's* deserted island. But John did not feel any loneliness. Julie and the two Picards were with him, and the aspect of the Hôtel de l'Europe changed all at once.

"We'll register first," said John. "I know it's customary to send a waiter to the rooms for the names, but as our waiters have all gone out we'll use the book now."

Pen and ink stood beside the register and he wrote in a bold hand:

Mademoiselle Julie Lannes, Paris, France.

Mademoiselle Suzanne Picard, Paris, France.

Monsieur Antoine Picard, Paris, France.

Mr. John Scott, New York, U.S.A.

Julie looked over his shoulder.

"It is well," she said. "If Philip arrives perhaps he will come to the hotel and see our names registered here."

"And we'll reserve a good room for him," said John, "but although I don't want to appear a pessimist, Miss Julie, I don't think he'll come just now, at least not in the *Arrow*. All aeroplane, balloon and Zeppelin trains have stopped running during the blizzard. Blizzard is an American word of ours meaning a driving storm. It's expressive, and it can be used with advantage in Europe. What accommodations do you wish, Madame la Princesse?"

"A sitting-room, a bedroom and a bath for myself, and a room each for my maid, Suzanne, and my faithful retainer, her father, Antoine Picard."

"You shall have all that you wish and more," said John, and then dropping into his usual tone he said: "I think we'd better look over the rooms together. It's barely possible some looter may be prowling in the house. Of course, the electric power is cut off, but Suzanne will know where to find candles, and we can provide for all the light we need."

He thought of light, because the heavy storm outside kept the hotel in shadow, and he knew that when night came, depression and gloom would settle upon them, unless they found some way to dispel the darkness. Despite the silence of the hotel they had a sense of comfort. They had been oppressed in the cathedral by its majesty and religious gloom, but this was the haunt of men and women who used to come in cheerfully from the day's business and who laughed and talked in rooms and on the stairways.

John's imaginative mind was alive at once. He beheld pleasant specters all about him. Chastel was off the great highways, but many quiet tourists must have come here. The beautiful cathedral, the picturesque situation of the little town above the little river and the very ancient Gothic buildings must have been an attraction to the knowing. He could shut his eyes and see them now, many of them his own countrymen and countrywomen, walking in the halls after a day of sightseeing, comparing notes, or looking through the windows down at the little river that foamed below. Yes, Chastel had been a pleasant town and one could pass many days in right company in its Hôtel de l'Europe.

"What are you smiling at, Mr. John?" asked Julie.

It was the first time she had called him "Mr. John," the equivalent for his "Miss Julie," and he liked it. But he hid his pleasure and apparently took no notice of it.

"I was seeing our hotel in times of peace," he said. "It was a sort of mental transference, I suppose, but the place looked good to me. It was crowded with people, many of whom were from America, and some of whom I would like to know. I've never had a horror of tourists — in fact I think the horror of them that most people pretend to feel is a sort of affectation, a false attempt at superiority — and I always liked, when I was a sightseer myself, to come back to the hotel in the evening and meet the cheerful crowd full of chatter and gossip."

"That is what I should want to do if ever I should go to America. They say that your distances there are great and your hotels large and bright. I shouldn't want to miss seeing the people in the evenings under the blazing electric lights."

"You'll see them, Miss Julie, because I know that you're going to America some time or other."

They were speaking in English again and Suzanne, wrapped in a gray cloak and looking very large, assumed her old grim look. John glanced at her and for the moment he was just a little afraid of her. He saw her eyes saying very plainly: "You're an American and a foreigner and my mistress, Mademoiselle Julie Lannes, a very young girl, is French. You should not be talking together at all, and if you were not so necessary to us in our hour of danger I would see that she was quickly taken far away from you."

He led the way into the smoking-room, where there were many comfortable chairs, and writing-desks with pen, ink and paper at hand. Everything was ready for use, but guests and waiters were lacking.

"Let's go into the main dining-room," said John, who had opened another door. "It's a fine, big place and the windows look directly over the river. Doubtless we'd have a good view from here if it were not for the driving snow."

It was, in fact, a handsome long room, proving the truth of John's surmise that many guests came at times to Chastel, and, to their great surprise, they found several of the tables fully dressed, as if some of the people had just been sitting down to dinner, when the voice of the shells bade them go.

"You see it's waiting for us," said John. "Why, we'd have done its proprietor a wrong if we'd missed the Hôtel de l'Europe. The table is set and, hospitable Frenchman that he is, he'll be glad to know that somebody is enjoying his house in his absence. The pepper, the salt and the vinegar are there, and I actually see a small bottle of wine on one of the tables."

"Poor man!" said Julie. "It must have cost him much to go. You don't know, Mr. John, how we French love our homes and houses."

"Oh, yes, I do, and we in America, since there's no longer any Wild West in which we can seek romance and change, are settling down into the same habits."

"Would Mademoiselle and Mr. Scott wish us to serve their dinner here?" asked Antoine gravely, the duties of his position ever uppermost in his mind.

"Not now, Antoine," said Julie, "but we will later. I'm glad to see, though, that you are making the best of it. You show a spirit worthy of a Picard."

Picard bowed and smiled with gratification. John suggested that they look upstairs for rooms, and then, after putting them in order, they could return for dinner. But before ascending the grand stairway, they lighted several candles which Suzanne had found, and put them at convenient places. They were not sufficient to illuminate the interior of the hotel, but they threw a soft glow which John found warm and pleasing.

Above was the main drawing-room, and a great array of guest chambers, continued also on the third floor, which was the last. John selected the best suite, looking over the river, for Julie and also for Suzanne, who, under the circumstances, must remain with her. A running water system had not been installed in the houses of Chastel but the great pitchers were filled, and the stalwart Suzanne could easily bring more. They were good rooms, perhaps with an excess of gilt and glass after the continental fashion, but they were comfortable, and John said to Julie:

"Maybe you'd like to remain here a half-hour or so, while Antoine and I choose a place for ourselves. It's best that the members of our party remain close together in view of possible emergencies."

"Yes, Suzanne and I will stay," said Julie. "I felt no weariness a few moments ago, but I've grown suddenly tired. A short rest will restore me."

"Very well," said John. "I bid you a brief *au revoir*, and when you hear a knock on your sitting-room door don't be alarmed, because it will be Antoine and I returning. Come, Antoine, we'll let the ladies rest while you and I look for the state apartments for ourselves."

Picard permitted a grin to pass over his broad face. His heart belonged to his daughter Suzanne and the Lannes family, and it was not moved easily by outsiders. Yet, this young John Scott from across the sea was beginning to find a favorable place in his mind. He spoke good French, he fought well for the French, he was highly esteemed by Monsieur Philip, he had done great service for Mademoiselle Julie and in the present crisis he was a tower of strength for them all. His daughter, Suzanne, regarded young Scott with a certain fear, but he,

Antoine, could not share it. Henceforth John would have his distinct approval, and he felt a measure of pride in being now his comrade in danger.

When John had closed the door of the sitting-room and he knew that neither Julie nor Suzanne could hear him, he said:

"Picard, have you any weapon?"

Picard drew a heavy automatic revolver from the pocket of his jacket.

"Before I started I provided myself with this, knowing the dangers of the journey," he replied.

"Good, but don't use it, except in the last resort. Remember how near you came to execution as a *franc-tireur*."

"Does Monsieur apprehend an attack?"

"I scarcely know, Antoine. But things have come about too easily. We find here a furnished hotel waiting for us. I've no doubt that the kitchens of the Hôtel de l'Europe are well stocked, and we have all the comforts, even the luxuries sufficient for a hundred guests. So far as we know there is not a soul in all this town save our four selves. It doesn't look natural, my good Antoine. It's positively uncanny."

"But, sir, if what we want is here waiting for us, why shouldn't we take it?"

"That's true, wise Antoine. 'Take the goods the gods provide thee whilst the lovely Thaïs sits beside thee,' as Mr. Dryden said."

"Who is Mr. Dryden? Must I infer, sir, from his name, that he is one of our brave English allies?"

"Doubtless he would be if he were living, but he has been dead some time, Antoine."

"Alas, sir, the way of all flesh!"

"So it is, Antoine, but I refuse to grieve about it or get morbid over it. I like to live and living I mean to live. What do you think of this big room, Antoine? It has two beds in it, one for you and one for me, and it's near enough to hear any call from the suite, occupied by Mademoiselle Julie and your daughter."

"A wise precaution. Monsieur Scott thinks of everything."

"No, not of everything, Antoine, but the presence of Mademoiselle Lannes is bound to sharpen the wits of anyone who is trying to take care of her."

"Will you make your toilet here, sir? I will call Suzanne and we will prepare dinner. When it is ready we will serve Mademoiselle Lannes and you."

The stalwart Picard had become all at once the discreet and thoughtful servant, and John felt a sudden sense of restfulness. Intense democrat that he was, he realized in his moment of weariness that all could not be masters.

"Thank you, Picard," he said gratefully. "The afternoon is wearing on and I do need to shake myself up."

"You'll find plenty of water in the pitchers, sir, and there are clean towels on the rack. One would think, sir, that the manager of the Hôtel de l'Europe before taking his departure, made careful preparation for our coming."

"It looks like it, Picard, and it certainly will be true, if you and Suzanne find the well-filled kitchen that you predict."

"Never a doubt of it, sir. The perfect condition in which we find everything above-stairs indicates that we shall find the same below."

He went out, leaving the door open, according to John's wish, and the young American heard his firm step pass down the hall and to the stairway. He drew a deep sigh of content, and lying down on a red plush sofa rested for a little while. It was luck, most wonderful luck, that he had come into Chastel, and had found Julie and her servants, and it was luck, most marvelous luck, that this well-equipped hotel was here waiting for them.

He rose and looped back the heavy lace curtains from the windows which looked over the river. But the snow was falling so fast that he could not see far into the dense, white cataract. The stream was completely hidden, and so, of course, was the hospital camp beyond. Yet through all the driving storm came a faint moan, a light pulsing of the air, which he knew to be the far throb of the great guns.

He turned impatiently away. Why couldn't they stop at such a time? As for himself, he would think of Julie, and a very handsome, tanned young man looking into the glass over the dresser smiled, although it was not at his own reflection. Then he bathed his face and hands, straightened out his hair with the small pocket comb and brush that he, like most other young officers, carried, and felt as if he had been made over.

He hung up his hat and heavy overcoat, and, resuming his place on the sofa, waited until Julie should announce her readiness. But she took more than a half-hour. He had not expected anything else. Truly a girl in her position was entitled to at least an hour if she wanted it. So he continued to wait with great patience. Besides it was very comfortable there on the sofa, and the swish of the driving snow against the window-panes was soothing. Now and then the low mutter of the guns came, but it did not disturb him.

"I'm ready if you are, Mr. John," called a clear voice, and springing from the sofa he joined Julie in the hall. She had smoothed her hair and her Red Cross dress, and the rest had restored all her brilliant color. She was as calm, too, as if they were not alone under the cloud of war, and the hotel was full of real guests. It was her courage as much as her beauty that appealed to John. At no time in all the dangers through which they had gone had he seen her flinch. He had heard much of the courage shown by the women in the great Civil War in his own country, and this maid of France was proving anew that a girl could be as brave as a man.

"May I take you down to dinner, Mademoiselle Lannes?" he asked.

"You may, Mr. Scott," she replied, and they walked together down the hall and the stairway into the great dining-room. Antoine, a napkin on his arm, ceremoniously held open the door for them and Suzanne showed them to opposite seats at a small table by the window.

"We have found an abundance, Mademoiselle," she said, "and you shall be served as if you were real guests."

The memory of that dinner will always be vivid in the mind of John Scott, though he live to be a hundred. Julie and he were invincible youth that always blooms anew. War and its horrors and dangers fell from them. Their sportive fancy that they were guests in the hotel and nothing ailed the world just then held true. As Antoine and his daughter served the excellent dinner that Suzanne had prepared these two found amusement in everything. The barrier of race that had been becoming more slender all the time melted quite away, and they were boy and girl looking into each other's eyes across a narrow table.

Picard and Suzanne even felt a touch of their fantastic spirits. Suzanne from the north of France, powerful in her prejudices, a Frenchwoman to the core, had viewed John from the first with a distinct hostility, softening slowly, very slowly, as time passed. It was not that she disliked his voice, his figure, his manner, or anything about him. He was a brave and true young man and he had rendered great service to the contemporary house of Lannes, but he was not a Frenchman.

But it seemed to Suzanne, as she served the courses and watched with an eye which nothing escaped, that Monsieur Jean the Scott was becoming a Frenchman—almost at least. She had seen young Frenchmen act very much as the young American was acting. The Frenchman, too, would lean forward to speak when the girl to whom he was speaking was as lovely as her Mademoiselle Julie. No, that was impossible! None other was as lovely as her Mademoiselle Julie. The glow that illumined his face was just the same, quite of the best French manner, too. She had seen people who *were* people and she knew. She admitted, too, that he was very handsome, with the slenderness of youth, but strong and muscular, and above all, his face was good.

Antoine with the napkin over his arm did most of the serving, and being a man the conventional differences did not seem to him so great as they did to his daughter.

"A handsome pair," he said to her.

But while willing to admit much to herself, Suzanne would not admit it to her father.

"Aye, handsome," she replied in a fierce whisper, "but not well matched. He comes from an uncivilized continent on the other side of the world, and soon he'll be going back there. I would that her brother, Monsieur Philip, were here where he ought to be. Perhaps he'd be foolish, too, because he likes the strange American, but it would relieve us of care."

"But America is not a barbarous continent, Suzanne, at least some of it is not. I have heard that in the eastern part of their country many of them act very much as we do, and we have seen those in Paris who appear to be quite civilized. And Suzanne, often they are rich, very rich. Before I left Paris the second time I made it a point to inquire about this young man, and I discovered that he had an immensely wealthy uncle, whose sole heir he is."

"Ah!" said Suzanne, making a long intake of the breath. It was easier than she had thought for John to become French.

"And the fortunes of the house of Lannes are moderate now, as you and I know quite well, Suzanne," continued the wise Antoine. "Surely it must have occurred to Madame her mother, when our little Mademoiselle Julie was yet but a beautiful young child, that she might make a great marriage some day. In this world of ours, Suzanne, many millions of good francs should not be allowed to escape from France."

"It is so, my father," said Suzanne. "France will need numberless millions when this war is over. Here is the vinegar for the salad. Not too much. Mademoiselle Julie likes only a little of it. What fortune it was to find a hotel furnished with everything! The faint sighing sound that still comes on the wind, is it not that of the guns, my father?"

"Aye, Suzanne, it's that of the cannon thundering far away, but Mademoiselle Julie and Mr. Scott have forgotten all about it, and it would be a pity to recall them to it."

Suzanne nodded. For a little space she, too, was compelled to relax. The salad now being complete she served it herself, and as she did so she relaxed still further, murmuring that they were just boy and girl together, but that they were very handsome. She had lifted two of the candles and put them upon the table, their light touching Julie's hair of deep gold with a ruddy tint and heightening the brilliant color of her cheeks. The heavy curtains before the window near them had been looped back a little, and the glass revealed the snow pouring down like a cataract, but they did not see it.

"It's the best dinner I ever ate," said John.

"Now you are finding what capable people Antoine and Suzanne are," said Julie.

"I give them all the credit due them," said John, as he made mental reservations.

"They're wonderfully capable, but it will always be Antoine's bitter regret that he does not serve in this war. If he could, he would be glad to represent himself fifteen years younger than he really is."

"His chance will come. Again I say to myself, Miss Julie, what luck I had in arriving at Chastel!"

"And it was lucky for us, too. We need your courage and resource, Mr. John. I know that Philip cannot come today or tonight and perhaps not tomorrow."

"In that event, what plans have you, Miss Julie?"

"To remain in Chastel. We have an excellent hotel here at our service, and as we're behind the French army we're in perfect safety."

John opened his lips to speak, but changed his intention and did not say what was in his thought. He said instead:

"Antoine is looking unusually important. He is going to serve us wine. He has mineral water, too. Will you take a little of it with your wine? It's a white wine, and the water improves it for me."

"Yes, Mr. John, I'll take mine the same way."

Any dinner, although it may have a flavor which the food and drink themselves, no matter how good, cannot give, must draw to an end, and when the dessert had been served and eaten John looped back the heavy curtain still further and looked out at the white cataract.

"The snowfall will certainly continue the rest of the day," he said, "and perhaps all through the night. Suppose we go to the smoking-room. Antoine and Suzanne must eat also. It's their hour now."

"That is true, Mr. John. The smoking-room is a good place, but I'm afraid that you have no cigarette."

"I don't smoke, but we can talk there, of your brother Philip, of your mother, safe now, of Paris, delivered as if by a miracle from the German menace, and of other good events that have happened."

He held open the door of the dining-room and when she went out he followed her, leaving Picard and Suzanne to their hour.

CHAPTER V
THE REGISTER

John and Julie in the smoking-room were not lonely. They talked of many of the events he had suggested, and of more. Two of the windows looked out upon the town instead of the river, but they could see little there save the towering spire of the cathedral and the blank and ruined walls. The snow was already very deep, but the fall was not diminishing. The gray gloom of coming twilight, however, was beginning to show through it and once more John returned silent thanks that he had come into Chastel and found Julie. He was serving vicariously for Philip who undoubtedly had been held back by the snow.

"It will be night soon," he said. "It's likely that the snow will cease in the morning, and then I'm quite sure that Philip will come for you. It must have been his intention for you to help at the hospital camp below."

"I think so, too."

"Then why not go there in the morning?"

"And he would miss me. He would be searching all Chastel for me, and perhaps would then go away, believing that I had not come."

He was about to say that Philip, missing her in the town would be sure to look for her in the hospital camp, but he forebore. It was very pleasant for them there in the hotel, and why hurry?

"At any rate, it would be unwise to leave tonight," he said. "I think Suzanne herself will agree with me in that statement. I'll ask her, as she'll be in here very soon now."

"Why so soon?"

"Because I've noticed that Suzanne, besides being your maid is also your chaperon."

"She's been that as far back as I can remember, and I believe a most excellent one. Suzanne, I know, loves me."

"I'm sure of it. I don't blame her."

"Look how the snow is leaping up against the window, Mr. John! Ah, Suzanne is ahead of your prediction! She's coming now."

Suzanne stood in the doorway. John surmised from her look that her distrust, at least in a mild form, had sent her there.

"Now that your maid can be with you," he said, "I think I'll take another look at the front of the hotel. Possibly, a new guest has arrived and registered since we last saw the bureau. Will you excuse me for a few minutes, Miss Julie?"

John was merely impelled by a sense of duty to take a look about the hotel, not that he expected to find anything, but because a good soldier should never neglect his scouting operations. He went first into the little lobby at the entrance, where the offices were. Antoine had lighted a candle and left it on the desk of the bureau. Otherwise he could have seen little in the room as the twilight was advancing fast, and the white gloom, made by the falling snow, was shading into gray.

He opened the front door. There was nothing in the street. The tower of the cathedral was almost hidden by the storm and the twilight and the gaunt ruins of the houses, covered now with snow, looked inexpressibly dreary and lonely. The dismal spectacle without heightened the bright gladness within, where he and Julie had sat face to face, only a narrow table between, and Antoine and Suzanne had served.

He stood awhile in the open door, the snow whirling now and then against him, and the faint mutter of great guns coming at almost regular intervals to his ears. He was trying to decide what to do, free from any influence, however noble, which might unconsciously turn him from his duty. His was in the nature of a roving commission, and yet he must not rove too far. He decided that if Lannes did not come in the morning he would insist upon Julie going with him to the hospital camp. It would be hard for him to go against her wishes, but he was bound to do it, and easy in little things, young John Scott had a will in greater affairs that could not be overborne.

But his heart remained singularly light. This was a good hotel, the Hôtel de l'Europe. He had not found a finer or better in Europe. Others might be larger and more magnificent, but not one of them had offered him such light and hospitality at a time when they were needed most. He went back to the bureau, where the register still lay open. He had a vague impression that it was not lying just as they had left it, that it was turned much more to one side, and he glanced at the names, which a quaint fancy had made them write on the open page. His own name had been inscribed there last, and he started when he saw another written beneath it in a bold flowing hand. But the light was so dim that he could not at first make it out, and despite all his courage and power of will an uncanny feeling seized him. A chill ran along his spine, and his hair lifted a little.

With a cry of anger at himself, he seized the candle and held it over the page. Then he read the new name:

Fernand Weber, Paris and Alsace.

With another exclamation, but this time of relief, he put the candle back upon the desk. Two beads of perspiration that had formed upon his brow rolled from it, and fell upon the register. And Weber had come, too! He was not surprised at it. Since he was Lannes' messenger, and he was free to come and go as he pleased, it was altogether likely that he would appear in Chastel to see the reunion of brother and sister, and his work well done. Moreover, he was a man who knew. John had often noticed that Weber's characteristic was knowledge and now he would help them.

He lifted the candle high above his head and looked around the lobby, but there was no sign of the Alsatian. He must have gone outside again. Saying nothing to Julie or the Picards, John resolved to seek him. He needed his heavy overcoat and he was able to secure it unobserved, because Julie had gone up to her room, and Antoine and Suzanne had disappeared in the back regions of the hotel.

He had a faint hope that when he returned to the lobby he might find Weber there, but it was still lone and silent, and drawing the collar well about his ears and throat he thrust himself out into the snow. Turning his back to the driving flakes he walked eastward, searching everywhere through the advancing twilight. Weber, of course, knew of their presence in the hotel as he had seen their names on the register, and the lighted candle on the bureau. It must have been a sudden alarm that called him away so quickly, else he would have gone in at once, and have spoken to his friends.

Unfortunately the night was coming fast. Thick gray gloom clothed the whole east, and but little light showed in the west. Looking back he saw no light in the hotel, but that was to be expected, as Picard would certainly loop the curtains heavily over the windows. Out here in the ruined town much of his extraordinary buoyancy departed. The cold and the desolation of the world made him shiver a little. He thrust his hand into the pocket of his overcoat, and closed it upon the butt of the automatic.

He thought once of calling at the top of his voice for Weber, but instinctive caution kept him from doing so. Then he caught sight of a slender moving figure far ahead and feeling sure that it must be the Alsatian he hurried forward. The figure moved on as fast as he, but, eager in pursuit, he followed. It was shadowy and slim at the distance, but he knew that it was a human being, and either it was Weber or some man of Chastel returning to see what had happened to his town. In either event he wished to overtake him.

But the figure led him a long chase. The man seemed to be moving with some definite purpose, and kept a general course toward the east. Now John called out once or twice, though not loudly, but the stranger apparently did not hear him. Then he pushed the pursuit more vigorously, breaking into a run, and just beyond the eastern rim of Chastel, feeling sure now that it was the Alsatian, he called once more:

"Weber! Weber!"

The man paused and he seemed to John to look back, but the snow drifted heavily between them just then, and when the cataract had passed he was again moving on, more slender and dim than ever. Beyond him lay a little wood, torn and mangled by shells and shrapnel, as the town had been, and John, afraid that he would lose him in it, ran as fast as he could through the deep snow, calling once more, and loudly now:

"Weber! Weber! Weber!"

The figure stopped at the edge of the wood and turned. John, holding up his hands to show that he meant no harm, continued his panting rush through the snow. The man stood upright, magnified into gigantic size by the half light and the storm, and, as John came close, he saw that in very truth it *was* Weber. His relief and joy were great. He did not know until then how anxious he was that the stranger should prove to be Weber, in whose skill and resource he had so much confidence.

"Weber! Weber!" he cried again. "It's Scott. Don't you know me, or am I so clothed in snow that nobody can recognize me?"

"I recognize you now, Mr. Scott," said Weber, "and glad am I to see that it's you. I was afraid that I was being followed by a German scout. I could have disposed of him, but it would not have saved me from his comrades."

"Comrades!" exclaimed John, as he shook his hand. "Why, are Germans about?"

"I think they are. At least, I've come out here to see. You'll forgive my jest, Mr. Scott, in writing my name under that of your party on the register, won't you? As Mademoiselle Lannes has doubtless told you, I carried the letter from her brother, directing her to join him in Chastel, and, as my duties permitted, I came here also to see that my work was effective. I'd have gone at once, but I heard suspicious sounds in front of the hotel, and I came out at once to investigate."

"What did you find?"

"Near the cathedral I saw footprints which the falling snow had covered but partially. No, it's not worth while to go back and investigate them. They're under an inch of snow now."

"Why did you think Germans had made them?"

Weber opened his gloved hand and disclosed something metallic, a spike from a German helmet.

"This," he said, "had become loosened and it fell from the cap of some careless fellow. It could have been there only a few minutes, because the snow had not yet covered it. I think a considerable party has got behind the French lines under cover of the storm and has passed through Chastel."

"But they must have gone on. Why would they remain in a ruined town like this?"

"I see no reason for their doing so, unless to seek shelter for a while in some buildings not wholly wrecked, just as you and Mademoiselle Lannes' party have done."

John felt a throb of alarm.

"Has the Hôtel de l'Europe escaped their observation?" he asked.

"I think so. I did not notice any light myself when I approached it. But I had been in Chastel before, and of course knew of the house and its location. I went there at once, hoping that it had escaped destruction, and found my hopes justified. Has Mademoiselle Lannes heard anything from her brother? I did not see his name on the register?"

"He has not come, but the weather has made it impossible. Aeroplanes can't dare such snowstorms as this."

"That's true, but he's so wonderfully skillful and bold that he might get here in some fashion. Now I think we ought to make a good search among these ruins, Mr. Scott. It's more than likely that the Germans have passed on, but there's a chance that they will linger. You're armed, of course?"

"I've an automatic handy."

"So have I. Suppose we take a look in the wood here, and then we can search among those houses on our right."

The snow and the night, now at hand, biding them, they entered the little wood with confidence that they would fall into no trap. But it was empty, and returning to the edge of the town, they scouted cautiously all the way around it, finding no sign of either a friend or an enemy.

"We alone hold Chastel," said John, "and I think we'd better go back to the Hôtel de l'Europe. I've been away a full two hours and Mademoiselle Lannes may be worried about my long absence, not about me personally, but because of what it might possibly signify."

"That's our obvious course," said Weber, "and as I've registered I'll sleep at the hotel also."

"You'll certainly be welcome," said John, as he led the way back to the Hôtel de l'Europe. But as they were on the far side of the town, and the snow had grown deeper, it took them another half-hour to reach the building.

They stood just inside the door, brushing off the snow and shaking themselves. John glanced toward the door of the smoking-room but it was dark there. He was somewhat surprised. Julie had doubtless gone to bed, but Antoine, the grim and faithful, would be on watch.

"I expected Picard to meet us," he said.

"Probably they're all worn out, and anticipating no danger, have gone to sleep," said Weber.

The candle was still burning in the bureau, and John, picking it up, hurried into the smoking-room. A sudden, terrible fear had struck like a dagger at his heart. The silence, and the absence of Picard filled him with alarm. In the smoking-room he held the candle aloft, and then he uttered a cry.

The room was in a state of utter disorder. Chairs, tables and writing-desks were overturned, and glass was smashed. It was evident to both that a mighty struggle had taken place there, but no blood was shed. John's keen mind inferred at once that Picard had been set upon without warning by many men, but they had struggled to take him alive. Nothing else could account for the wrecked furniture, and the absence of red stains.

His fears now became a horrible certainty, and without a thought of Weber, rushing up the stairway, candle in hand, he knocked at the door of Julie's room, the room that she and Suzanne were to occupy together. There was no answer. He knocked again, loud and long. Still no answer and his heart froze within him. He threw the door open and rushed in, mechanically holding his candle aloft, and, by the dim light it shed, looked about him, aghast.

This room also was in disorder. A chair had been overturned and a mirror had been broken. There had been a struggle here too, and he had no doubt that Suzanne had fought almost as well as her father. But she and Julie were gone. To John the room fairly ached with emptiness.

He put the candle upon the dresser, sat down, dropped his face in his hands and groaned.

"Be of good courage, Mr. Scott," said Weber. "No great harm can have happened to Mademoiselle Lannes."

"It was the Germans whom you saw. They must have come here while we were looking for them on the outskirts of the town."

"It would seem so. But don't be downhearted, Mr. Scott. Doubtless they've made captives of Mademoiselle Lannes and her attendants, but they have not done any bodily harm even to the big Picard. The absence of all blood shows it. And the Germans would not injure a woman like Mademoiselle Lannes. A prisoner, she is safe in their hands, she can be rescued as she was once before or more likely be sent back to her own people."

"But, Weber, we do not know what will happen in a war like this, so vast, so confused, and with passions beginning to run so high. And I was away when she was taken! I who should have been on guard every moment! How can I ever meet Philip's look! How can I ever answer my own reproaches!"

"You have nothing with which to reproach yourself, Mr. Scott. You did what anyone naturally would have done under such circumstances. It has been a chance, the one dangerous possibility out of a hundred, that has gone against us."

John stood up. His despair was gone. All his natural courage came flowing back in a torrent, and Weber saw in his eyes the glow of a resolution, stern, tenacious and singularly like that of Lannes himself.

"I mean to get her back," he said quietly. "As you said, the one dangerous chance in a hundred has gene against us, and to offset it the one favorable chance in a hundred must come our way."

"What do you mean to do?"

"I don't know yet. But we can't remain in this hotel. It's no time to be seeking our comfort when our duty lies elsewhere."

He took the candle again, holding it in a hand that was perfectly steady, and led the way down the hall and the stairway to the little lobby. He did not speak, because he was trying to think rapidly and concisely. If he followed the strict letter of command he would return that night to the hospital camp, and yet he could remain and say that he was delayed by the enemy. He was willing to be untrue to his military duty for Julie's sake, and his conscience did not reproach him.

"Is the snow diminishing, Weber?" he asked, as they came again into the little lobby.

"Somewhat, I think, Mr. Scott," replied Weber as he went to the window. "Are you thinking of pursuit?"

"Such an idea has been in my mind."

"But where and how?"

"My thought is vague yet."

"It's like an Arctic land outside. All footsteps, whether of men or horses, have been hidden by the snow. There is certainly no trail for us to follow."

"I know it, Weber, but it seems to me that Mademoiselle Lannes is calling to me. She tells me to bring her back."

The Alsatian glanced at John, but the young man's face was earnest. It was evident that he believed what he said.

"Mademoiselle Lannes may be calling to you," he said, "but how can you go, and where?"

"I don't know," repeated John obstinately, "but I mean to find her."

He walked irresolutely back and forth and his eye fell upon the register again. Certainly it had been moved once more. He had remembered just how it lay after he saw Weber's name there, and now it was turned much further to one side. He snatched up the candle and held it over the open pages. Then he saw written in a heavy hand just beneath Weber's name:

Prince Karl of Auersperg, Zillenstein, Tyrol.

Luitpold Helmuth Schwenenger,   "   "

Captain Max Sanger, Dantzig, Prussia.

Suite of His Highness, twenty persons.

John understood thoroughly. He uttered a fierce cry of anger and grief, and Weber looked eagerly over his shoulder.

"We know now who has come," he said.

"Yes, we know," exclaimed John, "and I could wish that it had been anybody else! I hate this man! To me he represents all that is evil in the Old World, the concentrated wickedness of feudalism and I fear him, though not for myself! Weber, I can't bear to think of Julie Lannes in his hands! If it were von Arnheim or that young Kratzek or any normal German it would be different, but this man, Auersperg, is not of our time! He belongs to an older and worse age!"

"He is very hard and determined," said Weber. "In my secret work for France I have seen him more than once, and I know his character and family history thoroughly. An immense pride of birth and blood. Great courage and resolution and a belief that he, as a prince of the old stock, entitled to what he wishes."

"Out of place in our day."

"It may be. But war favors his beliefs, and now he holds the whip hand. The beautiful Mademoiselle Julie was his prisoner for a short time before, and you will pardon me for telling you, what you must have surmised, Mr. Scott, that her youth, her marvelous beauty and her courage and spirit, so befitting one who bears the name of Lannes, have made a great appeal to His Highness. That is why, under the cover of storm and battle, he has carried her away."

"The monster!"

"Not so bad as that, Mr. Scott. There are some things that even a prince would not dare in this comparatively mild age of ours. The Prince of Auersperg is a widower with no children. He will offer her a morganatic marriage."

"A morganatic marriage! And what is that? Neither the one nor the other. It's a disgrace for any woman! A mere halfway marriage!"

"It would be legal, and she'd have a title."

"A title! What would that amount to?"

"I've heard that you Americans are fond of titles, and that your rich women bring their daughters to Europe to marry them!"

"An infinitesimal minority, Weber. It's true that we have such foolish women, but the rest of us regard them with contempt."

"He could offer her vast wealth and even as a morganatic wife a great position."

"I think you're testing me. Weber, trying to see what I will say. Well, I will say this. I don't believe that Julie would accept Auersperg on any terms, not if he were to make her a real princess of the oldest princely house in the world, not if he were to lay the fortunes of the Rothschilds at her feet. She is of good French republican stock, and she is a thorough republican herself."

Weber smiled a little.

"Your faith in Mademoiselle Lannes is great," he said, "and I can see that it proceeds, in part at least, from a just and pure emotion."

John reddened. He saw that he had laid bare his soul, but he was not ashamed. Once more he strengthened his heart and now he resolved upon a plan.

"The snowfall is decreasing fast," he said. "Auersperg and his troop can't be far from here. The traveling is too hard for them to travel swiftly, even if they have automobiles. I shall go to the hospital camp, raise a force and search the country. The commandant will give me soldiers readily, because it would be worth while to capture such a man as Auersperg—behind our lines, too."

"I don't wish to discourage you," said Weber, "but I doubt whether you can find him."

"Maybe so and maybe not," said John, and then he remembered the automobile in which Julie and the Picards had come. Doubtless it was safe behind the cathedral where they had left it, and he could force it through the snow much faster than he could walk.

"Come!" he exclaimed to Weber. "I know of a way to save time."

He rushed through the snow to the rear of the cathedral and Weber, without question, followed him. The automobile was there, well supplied, and John sprang into the front seat. He was no skillful driver, but he had learned enough to manage a machine in some fashion, and powerful emotions were driving him on.

"Up, Weber!" he cried.

"Which way are you going?"

"To the hospital camp, of course, and we'll just touch the top of the high-arched bridge over the river! The snowfall is decreasing fast, and soon we'll be able to see a long distance."

"We can do so now, and the moon is coming out, too. Heavens, Mr. Scott, it's come too soon, because it shows us to the enemy!"

He pointed with a long and shaking finger. At the far end of the street a massive German column was emerging into view. John was startled.

"These are no raiders!" he exclaimed. "They must have broken through a portion of our lines and are attempting to flank other positions! But Chastel's hospitality for us is ended."

He put on full speed and drove the machine rapidly through the snow toward the river.

"We've another reason now why we should reach the camp!" he exclaimed. "Our people must be warned of the presence of the Germans in force in Chastel!"

There was a crash of rifle fire and bullets struck all about them. Two or three glanced off the side of the machine itself, which a moment or two later ran into a deep drift and stuck there, panting.

Weber sprang out and threw himself flat in the snow. John instinctively did the same, and the second volley fired with better aim riddled the machine. There was a heavy explosion, it turned on its side, its wheels revolving for a moment or two, and then it lay still, like a dying monster.

John sprang to his feet and rushed for the shelter of a building only a few yards away. He saw Weber's shadow flitting by his side, but when he reached cover he found that he had lost him. Doubtless in the excitement of the moment the Alsatian had found hiding elsewhere. He was sorry that they had become separated, but Weber had a great ability to take care of himself, and John was quite sure that he would escape. The task that lay upon him now was to make good his own flight.

The building, the shelter of which he had reached, was a low brick structure, already much damaged by shells and shrapnel. But the walls were thick enough to protect him for the moment from bullets, and flinging himself down in the deep snow he crouched in the shadow until he could regain sufficient breath for further flight. He heard more shots fired, but evidently random triggers only had been pulled, as no bullet struck near him.

The fall of snow ceased almost entirely, and the moon grew brighter and brighter. Chastel was a vast white ruin, tinted with silver, and as such it had an uncanny beauty of its own. But John, thankful that the snow was so deep, lay buried in it, where it had drifted against the wall. The Germans in a town so near the French lines were not likely to make a diligent search for a single man, and he felt that he was safe if he did not freeze to death.

Peeping above the snow he saw about fifty German infantrymen walk down the road toward the river, their heavy boots crunching in the snow. They were stalwart, ruddy fellows, boys of twenty-one or two—he knew now that boys did most of the world's fighting—and he liked their simple, honest faces. He felt anew that he did not hate the German people; instead he felt friendship for them, but he did hate more intensely than ever the medieval emperors and the little group of madmen about them who, almost without warning, could devote millions to slaughter. An intense democrat in the beginning and becoming more intense in the furnace of war, he believed that the young German peasants coming down the road would have much more chance before the Judgment Seat than the princes and generals who so lightly sent them there.

The soldiers went on a little distance beyond the edge of the town. The cessation of the snow and the brilliant moonlight enabled them to see far into the plain below, where the hospital camp lay. John, looking in the same direction, saw little wisps of smoke rising above the blur of the camp, but the distance was too great for him to detect anything else.

The low note of the trumpet called to the young troops, and they turned back into the town. John rose from his covert, brushed the snow from his clothing, beat his chest with his fists, and increased the circulation which would warm his body anew. Then he stood against the wall listening. He had no doubt that the Germans would go away presently—there was nothing to keep them in Chastel—and he made a sudden shift in his plans. He would go back to the Hotel de l'Europe, and stay there until day. Lannes would surely come in the morning. He had no doubt that at daybreak he would see the lithe and sinuous figure of the *Arrow* shooting down from the blue depths, and then he and her brother would go away in search of Julie. Looking down from the air and traveling at almost unbelievable speed, their chances of finding Auersperg's party would be a hundred times better than if he merely prowled along on the ground.

The thought was a happy one to him, and again there was a great uprising of youth and hope. But the hosts of the air were already at work to defeat his plan. The invisible powers which war could now use were ready when the storm died. Far away the wireless stations sputtered and crackled, and words carried on nothing, were passing directly over him. They made no mention of John Scott, but he was vitally involved in what they were planning. Down under the horizon little black dots that were aeroplanes had begun to rise and to look cautiously over a field, where wireless had already told them that something was done. Further away telephone and telegraph wires were humming with words, and all the hosts of the air were concentrating their energies upon Chastel.

John, having left the shelter of the wall, stepped into the road, where the snow had been trodden deep by the young Germans. From that point he could not see into Chastel, but a deep solemn note came from a far point to the east. It was the voice of a great gun carrying an immense distance in the night, and it struck like a hammer upon his heart. It seemed to him a warning that the path that way, the way Auersperg had undoubtedly gone with Julie, was barred.

He walked up the newly trodden road into Chastel, and then he darted back again to cover. He saw the gleam of many gray uniforms and he heard a clank which he knew could be made only by the wheels of cannon. The new forces of the enemy were coming and evidently they were now in great strength in Chastel and beyond it. John's heart leaped in alarm. It was a powerful flank movement, a daring and successful attempt under cover of the storm, and he recognized at once all his dangers.

Keeping as well under cover as he could, he turned and raced toward the bridge. He saw the misty smoke hovering over the hospital camp, and he did not believe that any adequate force to meet the Germans could be found there, but alarms could be sent in every direction.

He expected that more than one shot would be sent after his flying figure, but none came and his swift flight took him far toward the river. Then he saw a long line of dark forms before him and the flashing tips of bayonets. Holding his arms high above his head he shouted in French over and over again that he was a friend, and then ran almost directly into the arms of a short muscular man in the uniform of a French colonel.

"Bougainville!" he cried.

"Aye, Mr. Scott, it is I! My regiment is here and many others."

"Then look out. Chastel is full of Germans."

"It is for them that we've come!"

CHAPTER VI
JOHN'S RESOLVE

John stood weakly, and with heart palpitating, but it was only for a few moments. Strength poured back in a full tide, and he said to Bougainville:

"You'll let me go back with you?"

"Of course, but there's heavy fighting ahead. Messages warned us in the night that the Germans had broken through, and ever since the storm stopped the wireless has been talking to us, giving us the exact details. We've been marching for hours. My regiment was the first to cross the river but, as you see, others are close behind."

"And you command them all?"

The eyes of the former Apache of Montmartre glittered.

"Yes," he replied. "It was an honor that General Vaugirard assigned to me. I lead the vanguard."

Except the radiance from his eyes he showed no emotion. John noticed that his features were cast in the antique mold. The pallor and thinness of his face accentuated his powerful features, and once more John was reminded of the portraits of the young Napoleon. Could there be such a thing as reincarnation? But he remembered that while a new mind like Napoleon's might be possible a new career like Napoleon's was not. Then all thoughts of any kind upon the subject were driven from his mind by the flash of firing that came from Chastel.

The rifles were rattling fast, and with them soon came the heavy crash of artillery. Bougainville ran up and down his lines, but, to John's surprise, he was holding his men back, rather than urging them on. But he quickly saw the reason. He heard the hissing and shrieking of shells over his head and he saw them bursting in Chastel.

The fire increased so fast and became so tremendous in volume that all the French lay down in the snow, and John put his fingers in his ears lest he be deafened.

He understood the purpose of the French commander. It was to hurl a continuous shower of steel upon the enemy, and then when it ceased the French were to charge. Raising his head a little he saw the ruined buildings of Chastel melting away entirely under the tremendous fire of the great French field guns. House after house was springing into flames and wall after wall was crumbling down in fragments. German guns were replying fast, but their position amid falling masonry was much worse than that of the French in the open.

John was lying in the snow near Bougainville, with the shells from both sides hissing and shrieking in a storm over their heads. He was used to being under fire and he knew that none of these missiles was intended for them, but he could not restrain a quiver of apprehension now and then, lest some piece of shrapnel, falling short, should find him. It was always the shrapnel with the hideous whine and shriek and its tearing wound that they dreaded most. The clean little rifle bullet, which if it did not kill did not hurt much, was infinitely more welcome.

"How long will this go on?" John asked of Bougainville; his voice could be heard as an undertone in the roar of the battle.

"Not long, because at present we have the advantage. The Germans know that they're worse off in the town than they would be outside. Our guns are bringing tons and tons of brick and stone about their ears. Hark to our splendid artillery, Mr. Scott! See how it sweeps Chastel!"

The French fire always increasing in volume was most accurate and deadly. The famous seventy-five-millimeter gun was again proving itself the most terrible of mobile field weapons. As walls fell, pyramids of fire shot up in many places, casting a sinister glow over the snowy earth. But above everything rose the lofty and beautiful spire of the Gothic cathedral, still untouched.

All the time the moonlight had been steadily growing more brilliant. Save where the burning houses and the flashing of the cannon cast a red glow a veil of silver mist, which brightened rather than obscured, hung over the snow. John distinctly saw Germans in the town and often, too, he saw them fall.

A man with a bugle was lying in the snow near Bougainville and the little colonel reached over and touched him. John saw the soldier put the instrument to his lips, as if he would make ready, and he knew that an important movement was at hand. He tautened his own figure that he might be ready. The artillery fire behind them ceased suddenly. The air there had been roaring with thunder, and then all at once it became as silent as the grave. The bugler leaped to his feet and blew a long and mellow note. The Bougainville regiment and other regiments both right and left sprang up and, with a short, fierce shout, rushed upon the town. John, his automatic in his hand, charged with them, keeping close to Bougainville.

A scattering fire of bullets carried away many, but John knew that he was not touched. Neither was Bougainville, who, like Bonaparte at Lodi or Arcola, was now leading his men in person, waving aloft a small sword, and continually shouting to his children to follow him. The French fell fast, but they reached the first line of the houses, and then they sent a deadly hail of their own bullets upon the defenders.

Every street and alley in Chastel was swept by the fire of the French. John heard above the crash of the rifles the incessant rattling of the machine guns, and then, as they opened out, the roar of the seventy-five-millimeters added to the terrible tumult. The Germans, withdrawing to the far edge and taking what shelter they could, replied, also with cannon, machine guns and rifles.

John saw Chastel already in ruins fairly melting away. Caught as it must have been in the former action it came tumbling, stone and brick walls and all to the ground. Detached fires were burning at many places, and a great pyramid of flame leaped up from a point where the Hôtel de l'Europe stood. The cathedral alone, as if by some singular chance, seemed to be untouched. The lofty Gothic spire shot up in the silver moonlight, and towered white and peaceful over fighting Gaul and Teuton. John looked up at it more than once, as he fired a rifle, that he had picked up, down the street at the fleeting shadows.

He was filled with an unreasoning rage. He did not hate any one of the Germans who were fighting on the other side of Chastel, but the anger that seized him when he found Julie missing was still heavy upon him. Before, whenever he had fired at an enemy he had usually felt a secret hope that the bullet would miss, but now he prayed that every one would hit. Bougainville pulled him down. "Not too fast!

Not too fast!" he said. "You're worth more alive than dead. We'll soon drive them from Chastel anyhow. The seventy-fives are doing the work."

Bougainville had read the story of the battle aright. The great seventy-five-millimeter guns were too much for the German force. As the houses of Chastel were swept away the enemy on the other side was left exposed, and the Germans, despite their courage and energy, were cut down fast. Aid for the French was coming continually. New regiments rushed up the snowy slopes. John heard a shout behind him, and Captain Colton and the Strangers coming from afar rushed into the battle. As they were about to swing past John joined Wharton and Carstairs.

"We thought you were gone forever this time," shouted Carstairs. "There seems to be a special Providence for you Yankees!"

"It's skill, not luck, that counts!" exclaimed Wharton.

John joined them, and Bougainville, taking command of the whole battle, directed the charge upon the town. The spirits of the French were at the highest, and shouting tremendously they soon passed through Chastel and drove the enemy beyond it, headlong into the forest. Having superior numbers now, a better knowledge of the ground and led by a man of genius like Bougainville, they soon broke up the German force, capturing a part of it, while the rest fleeing eastward, burst through the French trenches, and, after further heavy losses, succeeded in getting back to the main German army.

The pursuit was carried on some time by the French cavalry which had appeared as the last charge was made, but Bougainville, with the clear note of trumpets, recalled the infantry. He was satisfied with the victory that had been won in Chastel, and he did not wish to exhaust his troops with vain rushes in the deep snow.

The Strangers halted with the rest, and John, coming out of the red rage that had possessed his soul, saw that Captain Colton was uninjured and that Carstairs and Wharton, who stood near him, had only scratches.

"Grazed four times," said Carstairs happily. "The bullets knew a good man when they saw him, and turned aside just in time to give him slight but honorable wounds."

"Two scratches for me, too," said Wharton.

"Which proves what I told you," said Carstairs, "that it was often luck, not skill, that saved you."

"Both count," said Captain Colton, tersely. "Napoleon had immense skill. Suppose bad luck had sent a bullet into his heart in his first battle in Italy. Would have been forgotten in a day. And if no bullet had ever touched him, wouldn't have amounted to much, without immense skill."

"Do we go back to Chastel, sir?" asked John.

"Back to what's left of it. Not much, I think. See nothing but Gothic tower!"

John looked up. The great Gothic spire hung over a scene of desolation and ruin, now complete save for the cathedral itself. Otherwise not an undamaged house remained in Chastel. Fires still smoldered, and the largest of them all, marked where the Hôtel de l'Europe had stood. The firing had ceased save for a distant murmur where the cavalry still pursued, and John choked as he gazed at ruined Chastel. He looked most often at the burning Hôtel de l'Europe where he had spent such happy hours, the happiest, in truth, of his life, hours that glowed. He could see as vividly, as if it were all real again, Julie and himself at the little table by the window, and Antoine and Suzanne serving. He choked, and for a little while he could not reply to Wharton's question:

"Why, Scott, what's struck you? You look as if you had lost your last friend!"

"Wharton," replied John at last, "I found Mademoiselle Lannes and her servants, Antoine and Suzanne Picard here, come as requested by letter, to meet her brother Philip. I found them in the cathedral waiting, and we went to the Hôtel de l'Europe, where she and I dined together."

"Good Heavens! You don't mean to say she was there under the awful fire of our guns?"

"No, else I should not have been with you. Weber, the trusty Alsatian, of whom you know, came to us in the town. It was he who had borne the letter from Philip to Mademoiselle Julie. We thought we saw Germans in the outskirts of Chastel. We did not find any, but when we came back to the Hôtel de l'Europe, where we left them, Mademoiselle Julie and her servants, the Picards, were gone."

"Perhaps they were alarmed by the German advance and have taken refuge somewhere in the woods. If so, it will be easy to find them, Scott."

"No, they're not there. They're in the hands of the enemy. I shouldn't mind it so much if she were merely a captive of the Germans, but that man Auersperg has taken her again."

"How can you possibly know that to be true, Scott?"

Then John told the story of the register, and of the successive writing of the names. Cotton heard him, too, and his face was very grave.

"It's a pity Bougainville couldn't have come earlier," he said. "We might not only have saved Mademoiselle Julie but have captured this Prince of Auersperg as well. Then we should indeed have had a prize. But the wireless could not talk through all the storm and we had no warning of the German movement until the snowfall died down."

"What are we going to do?" asked John.

"We'll stay on the site of Chastel at least until morning, which can't be far away."

John looked at his watch.

"It will be daylight in two hours," he said.

"Oh, by the way," exclaimed Carstairs, "what became of Weber?"

"We were making our escape in Mademoiselle Lannes' automobile when we ran into a detachment of Germans. Our car was riddled; we both dodged for shelter and that was the last I saw of him."

"He escaped. I wager a pound to a shilling on it. The Alsatian not only has borrowed the nine lives of a cat, but he has nine original ones of his own."

"I feel sure, like you, Carstairs, that he has escaped and I certainly hope so. He's a clever man who has the faculty of turning up at the right time."

"It promises to be a clear dawn," said Wharton. "You may not believe it, Carstairs, but I'm a fine weather prophet in my own country, and if I can do so well there I ought at least to do as well with the low-grade weather supplied by an inferior continent like Europe."

"It's no wonder they call you a mad Yankee, Wharton. Low-grade weather! Have you any fog that can equal our London variety?"

"It's quality, not quantity that counts with a superior, intellectual people such as we are."

"Intellect! It's luck! I don't remember his name, but he was a discerning Frenchman, who said that a special Providence watched over drunken men and Americans."

"A special Providence watches over only those who have superior merit."

"I think," said John, "that I'm bound to take a little rest, if Captain Colton will let me."

"Oh, he'll let you if you ask him," said Carstairs. "You're a particular favorite of his, although I can't understand why. Wharton and I are much more deserving. But you do look all played out, old fellow."

John had sustained a sudden collapse. Intense emotion and immense physical exertion, continued so long, could be endured no longer, and he felt as if he would fall in the snow. But a portion of the victorious force was to remain at Chastel, and some tents had been pitched. Captain Colton readily gave John permission to enter one of them and roll himself in the blankets.

It was still an hour of dawn, but the night was light. Fires yet burned here and there in Chastel, where not a single building now stood unharmed, save the cathedral. The mutter of the cannon came from the vast front both to east and to west.

John looked into the great misty world and his face was turned toward the east. He had no doubt that Auersperg had gone in that direction with Julie, and he meant to find her. But how? He prayed silently for the coming of Lannes with the *Arrow*. For such a search as this the swift aeroplane could serve while one might plod in vain over the ground. Lannes would come before the next night! He must come! If he had made an appointment for such a meeting nothing could delay him more than a day.

He did not have any great fear for Julie's present safety. The modern civilized world had suddenly broken loose from many of its anchors, but so conspicuous a man as Auersperg could not stain his name with a deed that would brand him throughout Europe. Weber, however, had spoken of a morganatic marriage, and fearful pressure might be brought to bear. A country so energetic and advanced as Germany had clung, nevertheless, to many repellent principles of medievalism. A nation listened with calm acceptance and complacency, while its Kaiser claimed a partnership, and not altogether a junior partnership either, with the Almighty. Much could be forgiven to an Auersperg, the head of a house that had been princely more than a thousand years. John shuddered.

He had not gone to the tent at once as he intended. His nerves were yet leaping and he knew now that they must become quiet before he could sleep. Men were moving about him, carrying the wounded or helping with the camp, but they were only misty forms in the white gloom. Looking again toward the east he saw a silver bar appear just below the horizon. He knew it was the bright vanguard that heralded the coming sun, and his imaginative, susceptible mind beheld in it once more an omen. It beckoned him toward the east, and hope rose strong in his heart.

"Wharton," he said, "I suppose we'll stay awhile in Chastel."

"So I hear. Until noon at least."

"Then you wake me three hours from now. It will be enough sleep at such a time, and I want to be up when Lannes comes. You promise?"

"Certainly, Scott, I'll do it, though you'll probably swear at me for bothering you. Still, I'm ready to do any unpleasant duty for a friend when he asks it."

John laughed, went into the tent, rolled himself in the blankets and in a minute was fast asleep. In another minute, as it seemed, Wharton was pulling vigorously at his shoulder.

"Get up, Scott!" exclaimed Wharton. "Your three hours, and a half hour's grace that I allowed you, have passed. Didn't I tell you that you'd be ungrateful and that you'd fight against me for fulfilling your request! Open your eyes, man, and stand up!"

John sprang to his feet, shook his head violently several times, and then was wide awake.

"Thanks, Wharton," he said. "You're a true friend but you're a wretched reckoner of time."

"How so?"

"You said it was three hours and a half when in reality it was only three minutes and a half."

But a clear wintry sun was shining in at the door of the tent, and he saw its gold across the snow. Beyond was a kitchen automobile at which men were obtaining coffee and food.

"Has Lannes come?" asked John.

"Not yet, but of course he'll be here soon; by noon, I fancy."

John went out and took his breakfast with his comrades of the Strangers. The morning was uncommonly bright. There was not a trace of cloud in the heavens, which had turned to the soft, velvety blue that one sometimes sees in winter, and which can make a man fancy that it is summer when he looks up, rather than winter when he looks down.

While John ate and drank, he continually scanned the skies looking for the coming of the *Arrow*. He saw aeroplanes hovering here and there over the French and German lines, but none coming toward Chastel.

He had expected, too, that Weber might return in the morning, but he did not reappear and John felt a distinct disappointment. Many had been killed, but Wharton and Carstairs had reported that no body had resembled Weber's. Then it was certain that he had not fallen. Perhaps the Germans had driven him ahead of them, and he would rejoin the French at some distant point.

The morning passed, slow and bright, but it did not bring Lannes. General Vaugirard himself came about noon, a huge purring man in a huge puffing automobile. He cast an approving eye over Bougainville's work, and puffing his cheeks still wider whistled a low, musical note.

"It could not have been done better," he said. Then he caught sight of John and exclaimed:

"Ah, here is our young American, he who has been transformed into a good Frenchman! Glad am I to see you alive and unhurt, but I bring you news which is unpleasant. Ah, well, such is life! It must be expected in a war like this."

Alarm leaped up in John's heart. He felt instinctively that it concerned Lannes! Was he dead? But he steadied his voice and said:

"May I ask what it is, General?"

"That young friend of yours and great servant of his nation, Philip Lannes, the famous aviator. He has been wounded. No, don't be alarmed, it's not mortal, but it will keep him in hospital for some time. It happened two days ago, nearly a hundred miles west of here. He had just landed from his aeroplane, and he was fired at by some German skirmishers hidden in a wood. Fortunately French cavalry were near and drove off the Germans. Lannes is so young and so healthy that his recovery will be complete, though slow."

"What a misfortune at such a time!" exclaimed John.

"What do you mean by 'at such a time'?"

Then John related the presence of Julie Lannes in Chastel and the manner of her capture by Auersperg. He told, too, why she had come there.

General Vaugirard puffed out his huge cheeks and whistled a note or two.

"I can't understand why Lannes should have wanted her to come to such an exposed place," he said. "But youth is daring and doesn't always count the risks."

Youth *was* daring and John resolved that he would help to prove it.

"General," he said, "could I ask your aid in a little matter that concerns me?"

"If it is not to betray our army to the Germans I think you can."

"I want you to help me to become a spy. I'll make the request to Captain Colton, and then, if it's indorsed, I'll go eastward and see what I can find out about the Germans."

"But I understood that she was not a German."

John reddened from brow to chin.

"I admit that much," he said, "but at the same time I intend to serve France all I can. I might be of more help that way than as a mere minor officer in the trenches."

"If you're successful, yes; if caught, all's lost. Hard trade, that of spy."

"But I want to go, sir. I never wanted to do anything so much before in my life. You'll help me, won't you?"

"But how can you go among the Germans? Your German is not the best in the world."

"It's better than you think. I've been devoting most of my leisure to the study of it in the last six months. Besides there are subjects of Germany who do not speak German at all. I shall claim to be a native of French Lorraine. I learned French in my infancy and I speak it not like an American or an Englishman but like a Frenchman."

"That helps a lot. What's to be your new name?"

It was not a matter to which John had given any thought, but as he glanced at the ruined town the question solved itself.

"Chastel, Castel," he said. "I shall drop the 'h' and call myself Jean Louis Castel, born in French Lorraine in 1893, after that region had enjoyed for more than twenty years the glorious benefits of German military rule."

"Very well," said the General. "Now go and see Captain Colton."

Captain Colton's lips twisted into a crooked smile when he heard John. His glance was a mingling of sympathy and apprehension. He knew the great dangers of the quest, but he liked John Scott and he could understand.

"John," he said, calling him by his first name, "I would not send anybody upon such an errand as yours. You recognize the fact that the chances are about ten to one you'll find a bullet at the end of your search."

"I think I'll get through."

"It's a good thing to hope. I think I can procure this commission for you from General Vaugirard. But we'll go to him at once. We'll not let the grass grow—or rather, the snow melt under our feet while we're about it."

John did not tell him that he had already spoken to the general, as he wished the whole proceeding to be in perfect order.

General Vaugirard was by a fire which had been built in the Place near the shattered fountain. Wrapped in a huge overcoat he looked truly gigantic as he walked up and down thinking.

"Let me speak with him first," said Captain Colton.

John held back and saw the two talk together earnestly a minute or two. Then the big general beckoned to him and as John approached he said:

"The request that you have made through Captain Colton is granted. In a war like this is may be the good fortune of a spy to render a very great service."

John bowed.

"Thank you, sir," he said simply.

"I understand that you wish to start at once," continued the general. "Dress like a peasant, and look with all your eyes and listen with all your ears. And don't forget while you're seeking the enemy's secrets that all France loves a lover."

John flushed a deep red, and Vaugirard and Colton laughed. The general put his hand in the most kindly fashion upon John's shoulder.

"You are one of the bravest of my children," he said, "and I have an affection for thee, thou stalwart American youth. See to it that thou comest back again. Thy hand, Monsieur Jean Castel, for such, I hear, is to be your name."

John's hand was engulfed in the huge palm. General Vaugirard gave it a great shake and turned away. Then John and Captain Colton walked back to the place that had been allotted to the Strangers, where it soon became known to Wharton and Carstairs that their comrade would depart that night upon a quest, seemingly hopeless. They drew John aside:

"Scott," said Carstairs, "are you really going? It's certain death, you know."

"A German bullet or a German rope," said Wharton, "and you'll never be seen or heard of again. It's an ignominious end."

"As surely as the night comes I'm going," replied John to both questions. "I understand the risks and I take them."

"I knew the answer before I asked you," said Carstairs. "You Americans are really our children, though sometimes you're not very respectful to your parents. They call us prosaic, but I think we're really the most romantic of the races."

"It's proved," said Wharton, "when sober fellows like Scott go away on such errands. I think you'll win through, Scott, in the way you wish."

John knew that the good wishes of these two friends, so undemonstrative and so true, would follow him all the time and he choked a little. But when the lump in his throat was gone he spoke casually, as if he were not venturing into a region that was sown thick and deep with dragon's teeth.

At the advice of Captain Colton he slept several hours more that afternoon, and in the darkest part of the night, clothed simply like a peasant, but carrying a passport that would take him through the French lines, he said good-by to his friends, and, taking his life in his hands, departed upon his mission. Lest he be taken for a *franc-tireur* he was entirely unarmed, and he wore a thick blue blouse, gray trousers equally thick, and heavy boots. He also carried, carefully concealed about his person, a supply of gold and German notes, although there would not be much use for money in that region of the dragon's teeth into which he was venturing.

He re-crossed the little river on the same high-arched bridge by which he had come, skirted the hospital camp, and then bore off toward the east. It was past midnight, the skies were free from snow, but there were many low, hovering clouds which suited his purpose. He was still back of the French lines, but his pass would take him through them at any time he wished. The problem was how to pass those of Germany, and the difficulty was very great, because for a long distance here the hostile trenches were only three or four hundred yards apart.

He discerned to the eastward a dim line of hills which, as he knew, rose farther on into mountains, and it occurred to him that he might find it easier to get through in rough country than in the region of low, rounded hills, where he now stood. He carried a knapsack, well filled with food, a blanket roll, and now he resolved to push on all night and most of the following day, before passing the French lines.

Keeping a watchful eye he pursued his steady course across the hills. The depth of the snow impeded speed, but action kept his heart strong. The terrible waiting was over, he was at least trying to do something. Fresh interests sprang up also. It was a strange, white, misty world upon which he looked. He traveled through utter desolation, but to the east, inclining to the north was a limitless double line, which now and then broke into flashes of flame, while from points further back came that mutter of the big guns like the groanings of huge, primeval monsters.

It seemed to John barbarous and savage to the last degree. He knew that he was in one of the most densely populated and highly cultivated portions of the world, but the dragon's teeth were coming up more thickly even than in the time of old Cadmus.

He walked until it was almost morning without seeing a human being, and then, the snow having dragged on him so heavily, he felt that he must take rest. Crawling into a hole in the snow that he scraped out under a ledge, he folded himself between his blankets and went to sleep.

CHAPTER VII
THE PURSUIT

John Scott would not perhaps have slept so well in a hole in the snow if he had not been inured to life in a trench, reeking in turn with mud, slush, ice and water. His present quarters were a vast improvement, dry and warm with the aid of the blankets, and he had crisp fresh air in abundance to breathe. Hence in such a place in the Inn of the Hedge and the Snow he slept longer than he had intended.

His will to awake at the rising of the sun was not sufficient. The soothing influence of warmth and the first real physical relaxation that he had enjoyed in three or four days overpowered his senses, and kept him slumbering on peacefully long after the early silver of the rising sun had turned to gold on the snow.

He had dug so deep a hole and he lay so close under the hedge that even a vigilant scout looking for an enemy might have passed within a dozen feet of him without seeing him. Another drift of snow falling after he had gone to sleep had covered up his footsteps and he was as securely hidden as if he had been a hundred miles, instead of only a scant two miles, from the double French and German line.

No human being noticed his presence. A small brown bird, much like the snowbird of his own land, hopped near, detected the human presence and then hopped deliberately away. Nobody was in the snowy fields. They were within range of the great German guns, and the peasants were gone. Had John been willing to search longer he could easily have found an abandoned house for shelter. As he had made mental notes before, Europe was now full of abandoned houses. In some regions rents must be extraordinarily low.

While he slept, firing was resumed at points on the long double line. Rifles flashed, and incautious heads or hands were struck, and somewhere or other the cannon were always muttering. But it was all in the day's work. Months of it had made his whole system physical and mental so used to it that it did not awaken him now.

Nevertheless the hosts of the air were uncommonly active while he slept. The wireless, sputtering and crackling, was carrying the news from general to general that a smart little action had been fought at Chastel, where another smart little action had been fought not long before, that the Germans had been overly daring and had paid for it.

Yet it was only an incident on a gigantic battle front that extended its mighty curving line from Switzerland to the sea, and soon the wireless and its older brother the telephone, and its oldest brother the telegraph, talked of other plans which would cause a much greater slaughter than at Chastel. Chastel itself, unless its beautiful Gothic cathedral brooding unharmed over the ruins could win it a word or two, would have no place at all in history. John himself was only one among eight or ten million armed men, and not a single one of all those millions knew that he lay there in the snow under the hedge.

The aeroplanes came out in the clear frosty blue, and both German and French machines sauntered lazily up and down the air lanes, but they did not risk encounters with one another. They were scouting with powerful glasses, or directing the fire of the batteries. One French machine circled directly over John, not more than two or three hundred feet away, but the man in it, keen of eye though he was, did not dream that one of the bravest of the Strangers lay asleep under the hedge beneath him.

The fleets of flyers were larger than usual, as if they were anxious to take the fresh air, after days of storm. But the most daring and skillful of all the airmen, Philip Lannes, was not there. He still lay in a hospital a hundred miles to the west, with a bullet wound in his shoulder, and while the time was to come when the *Arrow* under his practiced hand would once more be queen of the heavens, it was yet many days away.

The sun rose higher, suffusing the frosty blue heavens with a luminous golden glow, but John slept heavily on. He had not known how near to exhaustion was his nervous system. Perhaps it was less physical exhaustion than emotion, which can make huge drains upon the system. Now he was in the keeping of nature which was restoring all his powers of both mind and body, and keeping him there until he should again have all his strength and all the keenness of his faculties, needful for the great work that lay before him.

It was halfway toward noon when he awakened, remembered dimly in the first instant, and then comprehending everything in the second. He unrolled the blankets, slipped out of his lair and knew by the height of the sun that he had slept far beyond the time appointed for himself. But he did not worry over it. Barring a little stiffness, which he removed by flexing and tensing his muscles, he felt very strong and capable. The fresh air pouring into his lungs was so different from the corruption of the trenches that he seemed to be raised upon wings.

He resumed his walk toward the hills, and ate breakfast from his knapsack as he went along. Presently he noticed a large aeroplane circling over his head, and he felt sure that it was observing him. It was bound to be French or other French machines would attack it, and, after one glance, he walked slowly on. The machine followed him. He did not look up again, but he saw a great shadow on the snow that moved with his.

The knowledge that he was being watched and followed even by one of his own army was uncomfortable, and he felt a sensation of relief when he heard a swish and a swoop and the aeroplane alighted on the snow beside him. The man in the machine stepped out and asked:

"Who are you and where are you going?"

John did not altogether like his manner, which in his own idiom he styled "fresh."

"I've a name," he replied, "but it's none of your business, and I'm going somewhere, but that's none of your business either."

"They're both my business," said the man, drawing a revolver.

"Read that," said John, producing his passport.

The document stated simply that Jean Castel was engaged upon an important mission for France, and all were commanded to give him what help they could. It was signed by the fat and famous general of brigade, Vaugirard, and therefore it was a significant document.

"I apologize for brusqueness," said the aviator handsomely, "but the times are such that we forget our politeness. What can I do for you,

Monsieur Jean Castel, who I am sure has another and more rightful name at other times."

"Just now Castel is my right name, and all friends of mine will call me by it. Thank you for your offer, but you can do nothing—"

John stopped suddenly as he glanced at the aeroplane poised like a huge bird in the snow.

"Yes, you can do something," he said. "I notice that your plane is big enough for two. I want to reach the mountains to the eastward without all this tremendous toiling through the snow. You can carry me there in an hour or two, and besides this passport I give you a password."

"What's the password?"

"Lannes!"

"Lannes! Philip Lannes, do you know him?"

"I have been up with him in the *Arrow* many times. I've fought the Taubes with him. I helped him destroy both a Zeppelin and a forty-two-centimeter gun."

"Then I know you. You are his friend John Scott, the American. I thought at first that you had the accent of North America. Oh, I know of you! We flying men are a close group, and what happens to one of us is not hidden long from the others. Your password is sufficient."

"You know then that Lannes is in a hospital with a bullet wound in his shoulder?"

"I heard it two days ago. A pity! A great pity! He'll be as well as ever in a month, but France needs her king of the air every day. My own name is Delaunois, and I'll put you down in those hills at whatever point you wish, Monsieur Jean Castel of America."

John smiled. Delaunois was a fine fellow after all.

"I can't give you an extra suit for flying," said Delaunois, "but your two blankets ought to protect you in the icy air. I'll not go very high, and an hour or a little more should put us in the heart of the hills."

"Good enough, and many thanks to you," said John.

They gave the machine the requisite push, sprang in and rose slowly above the snowy waste. It was a good aeroplane, and Delaunois was a good aviator, but John missed the *Arrow* and Philip. He knew that the heavens nowhere held such another pair. Alas! that Lannes should be laid up at such a time with a wound!

But he quickly called himself ungrateful. Delaunois had come at a most timely moment, and he was doing him a great service. It was very cold above the earth, as Delaunois had predicted, and he wrapped the blankets closely about himself, drawing one over his head and face, until he was completely covered except the eyes.

To the westward several other planes were hovering and to the eastward was another group which John knew to be German. But the flying machines did not seem disposed to enter into hostilities that morning, although John saw the double line of trenches blazing now and then with fire, and, at intervals, the heavy batteries on either side sent a stated number of shells at the enemy.

Seen from a height the opposing trenches appeared to be almost together, and the fire of the hostile marksmen blended into the same line of light. But John did not look at them long. He had seen so much of foul trenches for weary months that it was a pleasure to let the eye fill with something else.

He looked instead at the high hills which were fast coming near, and although covered with snow, with trees bare of leaves, they were a glorious sight, an intense relief to him after all that monotony of narrow mud walls. He knew that trenches or other earthworks ran among the hills also, but the nature of the ground compelled breaks, and it would be easier anyhow to pass through a forest or a ravine.

"Where do you wish me to put you down?" asked Delaunois.

"At some place in those low mountains there, where the German lines are furthest from ours."

"I think I know such a point. You won't mind my speaking of you as a spy, Mr. Jean Castel of America, will you?"

"Not at all, because that's what I am."

"Then don't take too big a risk. It hasn't been long since you were a boy, and I don't like to think of one so young being executed as a spy."

"I don't intend to be."

"It's likely that I may see Philip Lannes before long. I go westward in two or three days and I shall find a chance to visit him in the hospital. If I see him what shall I tell him about a young man whom we both know, one John Scott, an American?"

"You tell him that his sister, Mademoiselle Julie Lannes, came to the village of Chastel to meet him, in accordance with his written request, and while she was waiting for him with her servants, Antoine and Suzanne Picard, not knowing that he had been wounded since the writing of his letter, she was kidnapped and carried into Germany with the Picards by Prince Karl of Auersperg. Prince Karl is in love with her and intends to force her into a morganatic marriage. Otherwise she is safe. The American, John Scott, in addition to his duties as a spy for France, a country that he loves and admires, intends, if human endeavor can achieve it, to rescue Mademoiselle Lannes and bring her back to Paris."

Delaunois took one hand from the steering rudder and turned glistening eyes upon John.

"It's a knightly adventure," he said. "It will appeal to Frenchmen when they hear of it, and yet more to Frenchwomen. I should like to shake the hand of this American, John Scott, and since he is not here, I will, if you will let me, shake the hand of his nearest French relative, Jean Castel."

He opened his gloved palm and John's met it in a strong grasp.

"I'm glad," said Delaunois, "that I saw you, and that I am able to give you this lift. We're over the edge of the mountains now, and presently we'll cross the French lines. I think I'd better go up a considerable distance, as they won't know we're French, and they might give us a few shots."

The machine rose fast and it grew intensely cold. John looked down now upon a country, containing much forest for Europe, and sparsely inhabited. But he saw far beneath them trenches and other earthworks manned with French soldiers. Several officers were examining them through glasses, but Delaunois sailed gracefully over the line, circled around a slender peak where he was hidden completely from their view, and then dropped down in a forest of larch and pine. "So far as I know," he said, when the plane rested on the snow, "nobody has seen our descent. We're well beyond the French lines here, but you'll find

German forts four or five miles ahead. As you see, this is exceedingly rough ground, not easy for men to occupy, and so the French stay on one side of this little cluster of mountains while the Germans keep to the other. And now, Monsieur Jean Castel, I leave you here, wishing you success in your quest, success in every respect."

Again the two strong hands met. A minute later the aeroplane rose in the air, carrying but one of the men, while Jean Castel, peasant of Lorraine, was left behind, standing in the snow, and feeling very grateful to Delaunois.

John watched the aeroplane disappear over the peak on its return journey, and then he walked boldly eastward toward the German lines. Modesty kept him from accepting Delaunois' tribute in full, but it had warmed his heart and strengthened his courage anew. Delaunois had considered it not a reckless quest, but high adventure with a noble impulse, and John's heart and spirit had responded quickly. Great deeds come from exaltation, and that mood was his.

He followed what seemed to be a little path under the snow, leading along the side of the mountain toward the eastward, the way he would go. Here portions of the earth were exposed, where the snow had already melted much under the heat of the high sun. Three or four hundred feet below a brook ran noisily over stones, but that was the only sound in the mountains. He felt though that the Germans must be somewhere near. Men with glasses might be watching him already.

He decided at once upon his rôle. In Europe peasants were often heavy and loutish. It was expected of them, and none would be heavier or more loutish than he. He thrust both hands in his pockets, and began to whistle familiar German songs and hymns, varying them now and then with a chanson or two that might have been sung for centuries in Lorraine.

The path led on across a little valley and then along the slope of another ridge. Under the increasing heat of the sun the snow was now melting much faster, and streams ran in every ravine. But the stalwart young peasant, Jean Castel of Lorraine, was sure of his footing, and he advanced steadily toward his goal.

Germans in rifle pits saw the figure coming their way, and several officers examined it critically with their glasses. All pronounced the stranger obviously a peasant, and they were equally sure that he could do them no harm. He was coming straight toward their pits and so they awaited him with some curiosity.

John presently caught the shimmer of sun on bayonets, and he knew now that he would soon reach the German earthworks. His first care after Delaunois left him, had been to destroy the passport that General Vaugirard had given him and there was not a scratch of writing about him to identify him as John Scott.

Whistling louder than ever, and looking vacant of countenance, he walked boldly toward the first rifle pit, and, when the sharp hail of the German sentry came, he promptly threw up his hands. An officer whom he took to be a lieutenant and four or five men came toward him. All wore heavy gray overcoats and they were really boys rather than men; not one of them, including the officers, seeming to be more than twenty. But they were large and muscular, heavily tanned by wind and snow and rain.

John had learned to read character, and as he walked carelessly toward them he nevertheless watched them keenly. And so watching he judged that they were honest youths, ready to like or hate, according to orders from the men higher up, but by nature simple and direct. He did not feel any fear of them.

"Halt!" said the officer, whom John judged to be a Saxon—he had seen his kind in Dresden and Leipsic.

John stopped obediently, and raised his hand in a clumsy military fashion, standing there while they looked him over.

"Now you can come forward, still with your hands up," said the officer, though not in any fierce manner, "and tell us who you are."

John advanced, and they quickly searched him, finding no weapon.

"You can take your hands down," said the officer. "Unarmed, I don't believe you'd be a match for our rifles. Now, who are you?"

"Jean Castel, sir, of Lorraine," replied John in German with a strong French accent.

"And what have you been doing here between our lines and those of the French?"

"I took some cattle across the mountains for the army and having sold them I was walking back home. In the storm last night I wandered through the lines into this very rough country and got lost."

"You do look battered. But you say you sold your cattle. Now what have you done with your money?"

The officer's tone had suddenly become suspicious, but John was prepared. Opening his heavy blouse he took from an inside pocket a handful of German gold and notes. The young lieutenant glanced at the money and his suspicions departed.

"It's good German," he said, "and I don't think a peasant like you could have got it unless he had something valuable to sell. Come, you shall go back with us and I'll turn you over to a higher officer. I'm Lieutenant Heinrich Schmidt, and we're part of a Saxon division."

John went with them without hesitation. In fact, he felt little fear. There was nothing to disprove his statements, and he was not one of those who looked upon Germans as barbarians. Experience had shown him that ordinary Germans had plenty of human kindness. He sniffed the pleasant odors that came from the kitchen automobiles near by, and remarked naïvely that he would be glad to share their rations until they passed him on.

"Very well, Castel," said Lieutenant Schmidt, "you shall have your share, but I must take you first to our colonel. He will have important questions to ask you."

"I'm ready," said John in an indifferent tone. But as he went with the men he noted as well as he could, without attracting attention to himself, the German position. Rifle pits and trenches appeared at irregular intervals, but the mountains themselves furnished the chief fortifications. In such country as this it would be difficult for either side to drive back the other, a fact which the enemies themselves seemed to concede, as there was no firing on this portion of the line. But at points far to the west the great guns muttered, and their faint echoes ran through the gorges.

The path led around one of the crests, and they came to a little cluster of tiny huts, which John knew to be the quarters of officers. Snug, too, they looked, with smoke coming out of stovepipes that ran through the roofs of several of them. A tall man, broad of shoulder, slender of waist, blue of eye, yellow of hair, and not more than thirty, came forward to meet them. John recognized at once a typical German officer of high birth, learned in his trade, arrogant, convinced of his own superiority, but brave and meaning to be fair.

"A peasant of Lorraine, sir," said Lieutenant Schmidt. "He says that his name is Jean Castel, and that he has been selling cattle. We found him wandering between the lines. He was unarmed and he has considerable money."

"Come closer," said the officer to John. "I'm Colonel Joachim Stratz, the commander of this regiment, and you must give a thorough account of yourself."

John advanced willingly and saluted, feeling that the glance Colonel Stratz bent upon him was heavy and piercing. Yet he awaited the result with confidence. It was true that he was American, but he had been with the French so much now that he had acquired many of their tricks of manner, and his French accent was impeccable.

"You are a seller of cattle?" said Colonel Stratz, suddenly in English.

The words of reply began to form, but John remembered himself in time. He was a French peasant who understood no English, and giving Colonel Stratz a puzzled look he shook his head. But he wondered what suspicion had caused the German to ask him a question in English. He concluded it must be a mere chance.

Colonel Stratz then addressed him in German, and John replied to all his queries, speaking with a strong French accent, repeating the tale that he had told Lieutenant Schmidt, and answering everything so readily and so convincingly that Colonel Joachim Stratz, an acute and able man, was at last satisfied.

"Where do you wish to go now, Castel?" asked the German.

"To Metz, if it please you, sir."

"Wouldn't it be better for you to stay, put on a uniform, take up a rifle and fight for our Kaiser and Fatherland?"

John shook his head and put on the preternaturally wise look of the light-witted.

"I'm no soldier," he replied.

"Why weren't you called? You're of the right age."

"A little weakness of the heart. I cannot endure the great strain, but I can drive the cattle."

"Oh, well, if that is so, you serve us better by sticking to your trade. Lieutenant Schmidt, give him food and drink, and then I'll prepare for him a pass through the lines that will take him part of the way to Metz. He'll have to get other passes as he goes along."

John saluted and thanked Colonel Stratz, and then he and Lieutenant Schmidt approached one of the great German kitchen automobiles. It was easy to play the rôle of a simple and honest peasant, and while he drank good beer and ate good cheese and sausage, he and Lieutenant Schmidt became quite friendly.

Schmidt asked him many questions. He wanted to know if he had been near the French lines, and John laughingly replied that he had been altogether too near. Three rifle bullets fired from some hidden point had whizzed very close to him, and he had run for his life.

"I shall take care never to get lost again," he said, "and I intend to keep well behind our army. The battle line is not the place for Jean Castel. Why spoil a first-class herder to make a second-class soldier?"

He winked cunningly at Schmidt, who laughed.

"You're no great hero," said the German, "but if a man wants to take care of his skin can he be blamed for doing so? Still, you're not so safe here."

"How's that?" asked John in assumed alarm.

"Now and then the French send shells over that mountain in front of us and when one is fired it's bound to hit somewhere. We haven't had any at this point yet, but our time is sure to come sooner or later."

"Then I think I'll be going," said John, willing to maintain his new reputation as a timid man.

Schmidt laughed again.

"Oh, no, not yet," he said. "Your passport isn't ready, and without it you can't move. Have another glass of this beer. It was made in Munich, and puts heart into a man."

John drank. It was really fine beer, and the food was excellent, warm and well cooked. He had not realized before how hungry and thirsty he was. It was a hunger and thirst that the cold meat and bread in his knapsack and snow water would not have assuaged. Many

Germans also were refreshing themselves. He had noticed that in both armies the troops were always well fed. Distances were short, and an abundance of railways brought vast quantities of supplies from fertile regions.

While he was still eating he heard a shriek and a roar and a huge shell burst two or three hundred yards away. Much earth was torn up, four men were wounded slightly and an empty ambulance was overturned, but the regular life of the German army went on undisturbed.

"I told you that we had French messengers now and then," said Lieutenant Schmidt, holding a glass of beer in his right hand and a sausage in his left, "but that message was delivered nearer to us than any other in three days. I don't think they'll fire again for a half-hour, and the chances are a hundred to one that it will fall much further away. So why be disturbed?"

Lieutenant Schmidt was beginning to feel happy. He had a sentimental German soul, and all the beer he wanted brought all his benevolence to the surface.

"I like you, Castel," he said. "Your blood is French, of course, or it was once, but you of Lorraine have had all the benefits of German culture and training. A German you were born, a German you have remained, and a German you will be all your life. The time is coming when we will extend the blessings of our German culture to all of France, and then to England, and then maybe to the whole world."

Lieutenant Schmidt had drunk a great deal of beer, and even beer when taken in large quantities may be heady. His tongue was loose and long.

"And to that distant and barbarous country, America, too," said John.

"Aye, and to the Americans also," said Lieutenant Schmidt. "I hear that they don't love us, although they have much of our blood in their veins. There are many people among them bearing German names who denounce us. When we finish with our enemies here in Europe we'll teach the barbarous Americans to love the Kaiser."

"A hard task," said John, with meaning.

"So it will be," said Lieutenant Schmidt, taking his meaning differently, "but the harder the task the better we Germans love it.

And now, Castel, here comes your passport. Its little winged words will bear you safely to the headquarters of General Osterweiler thirty miles to the north and east, and there you'll have to get another passport, if you can. *Auf wiedersehen,* Jean Castel. Your forefathers were French, but you are German, good German, and I wish you well."

Lieutenant Schmidt's cheeks were very red just then, not altogether with the cold, and his benevolence had extended to the whole world, including the French and English, whom he must fight regretfully.

"Oh," said John, as an afterthought, although he was keenly noting his condition, "while I was wandering in the snow of the big storm, I heard from a sentinel that one of our great generals and beloved princes. Prince Karl of Auersperg, had passed this way with his train."

Perhaps if Lieutenant Schmidt had not taken so much good Munich beer after a long fast he might have become suspicious, because it was not the question that an ordinary peasant and cattle-herder would ask unless the previous conversation had led directly to it. But as it was he fairly exuded trust and kindness.

"Not here," he replied, "but at a point further toward the west and north. So great a figure as Prince Karl of Auersperg could scarcely go by without our hearing of it. Colonel Stratz himself spoke of it in my presence."

"I saw him once in Metz before the war. A grand and imposing figure. Perhaps I shall behold him there again in a few days."

"I think not. It was said that the prince was going to his estates in the east. At least, I think I heard something of the kind, but it probably means that he was on his way to the eastern frontier. Prince Karl of Auersperg is not the man to withdraw from the war."

John's heart dropped suddenly. Would he be compelled to follow the prince halfway across Europe. Oh, why had he left the Hôtel de l'Europe even for a moment? With Picard's help he might have been able to hold off Auersperg and his followers, or a lucky shot might have disposed of the prince. He felt it no crime to have wished for such a chance. But strengthening his heart anew he took up the burden that had grown heavier.

"*Auf wiedersehen*, Lieutenant Schmidt," he said, and whistling softly to himself he began his passage through the German lines, showing his passport more than a dozen times before he passed the last trench and rifle pit, and was alone among the hills behind the German lines. He might have reached the railroad and have gone by train to Metz, but he preferred, for the present at least, to cling to the country, even at the risk of much physical hardship and suffering.

He still carried his blankets, and he was traveling through a region which had been much fought over in the earlier stages of the war. Since the German lines were still in France some peasants had returned to their homes, but many houses were yet abandoned, their owners probably thinking that the tide of battle would roll back upon them, and that it was better to wait.

He turned presently from the hilly path into a good road, paved almost like a street, and breaking from a bush a stout stick, which he used peasant fashion as a cane, he walked briskly along the smooth surface, now almost clear of the snow which had fallen in much smaller quantities in the lowlands.

He met a battery of four twenty-one-centimeter guns with their numerous crews and an escort of cavalry, advancing to the front, and he stepped to one side of the road to let them pass. The leader of the cavalry hailed him and John's heart gave a sudden alarming throb as he recognized von Boehlen. But his courage came back when he saw that he would not have known the Prussian had he remained twenty feet away. Von Boehlen was deeply tanned and much thinner. There were lines in his face and he had all the appearance of a man who had been through almost unbearable hardships.

John had no doubt that a long life in the trenches and intense anxiety had made an equal change in himself. The glass had told him that he looked more mature, more like a man of thought and experience. Moreover, he was in the dress of a peasant. After the first painful heartbeat he awaited von Boehlen with confidence.

"Whence do you come?" asked the colonel of Uhlans—colonel he now was.

John pointed back over his shoulder and then produced his passport, which Colonel von Boehlen, after reading, handed carefully back to him.

"Did you see anything of the French?" he asked glancing again at John, but without a sign of recognition.

"No, sir," replied John in his new German with a French accent, "but I saw a most unpleasant messenger of theirs."

"A messenger? What kind of a messenger?"

"Long, round and made of steel. It came over a mountain and then with a loud noise divided itself into many parts near the place where I stood. One messenger turned itself into a thousand messengers, and they were all messengers of death. Honored sir, I left that vicinity as soon as I could, and I have been traveling fast, directly away from there, ever since."

Von Boehlen laughed, and then his strong jaws closed tighter. After a moment's silence, he said:

"Many such messengers have been passing in recent months. The air has been full of them. If you don't like battles, Castel, I don't blame you for traveling in the direction you take."

John, who had turned his face away for precautionary measures, looked him full in the eyes again, and he found in his heart a little liking for the Prussian. Von Boehlen seemed to have lost something of his haughtiness and confidence since those swaggering days in Dresden, and the loss had improved him. John saw some signs of a civilian's sense of justice and reason beneath the military gloss.

"May I pass on, sir?" he asked. "I wish to reach Metz, where I can obtain more horses for the army."

"Why do you walk?"

"I sold my last horse and the automobiles and trains are not for me. I know that the army needs all the space in them and I ask nothing."

"Fare on then," said von Boehlen. "Your papers are in good condition and you'll have no trouble in reaching Metz. But be sure you don't lose your passport."

The injunction was kindly and John, thanking him, took up the road. Von Boehlen and his Uhlans rode on, and John looked back once. He caught a single glimpse of the colonel's broad shoulders and then the long column of horsemen rode by. There was no military pomp about them now. Their gray uniforms were worn and stained and many of the men sagged in their saddles with weariness. Not a few showed wounds barely healed.

The cavalry were followed by infantry, and batteries of guns so heavy that often the wheels sank in the paved road. Sometimes the troops sang, pouring forth the mighty rolling choruses of the German national songs and hymns. The gay air as of sure victory just ahead that marked them in the closing months of summer the year before had departed, but in its place was a grim resolution that made them seem to John as formidable as ever. The steady beat of solid German feet made a rolling sound which the orders of officers and the creaking of wagons and artillery scarcely disturbed. The waves of the gray sea swept steadily on toward France.

John showed his passport twice more, but all that day he beheld marching troops. In the afternoon it snowed a little again and the slush was everywhere, but he trudged bravely through it. Having escaped from the trenches he felt that he could endure anything. What were snow, a gray sky and a cold wind to one who had lived for months on a floor of earth and between narrow walls of half-frozen mud? He was like a prisoner who had escaped from a steel cage.

Toward dark he turned from the road and sought refuge at a low but rather large farmhouse, standing among trees. He modestly made his way to the rear, and asked shelter for the night in the stable, saying that he would pay. He learned that the place was occupied by people bearing the German name of Gratz, which however signified little on that borderland, which at different times had been under both German and French rule.

Nor did the proprietor of the house himself, who came out to see him, enlighten him concerning his sympathies. If he liked France obviously it was no time for him to say so when he was surrounded by the German legions. But John could sleep on the hay in the stable, and have supper and breakfast for certain number of marks or francs which he must show in advance. He showed them and all was well.

John, after carefully scraping all the mud and snow from his boots was allowed to go in the big kitchen and sit on a stone bench beside the wall, while two stout women cooked at a great furnace, and trim maids came for the food which they took upstairs.

When he sank down upon the bench he realized that he was tired through and through. It was no light task even for a hardened soldier to walk all day in bad weather. One of the cooks, a stout middle-aged woman whom the others called Johanna, gave him a glance of sympathy. She saw a young man pale from great exertion, but with a singularly fine face, a face that was exceedingly strong, without being coarse or rough. Johanna thought him handsome, and so did the other cook, also stout and middle-aged, who bore the French name of Nanine.

"Poor young man!" said one and, "Poor young man!" repeated the other. Then they filled a plate with warm food and handed it to him. While he ate he talked with them and the passing maids, who were full of interest in the handsome young stranger. He told them that he was a horse-trader, and that he had been in no battle, nor would he be in any, but he saw that he was not believed, and secretly he was glad of it. These were trim young maids and a young soldier likes admiration, even if it comes from those who in the world's opinion are of a lower rank than he.

They asked him innumerable questions, and he answered as well as he could. He told of the troops that he had seen, and they informed him that German forces had been passing there at times all through the winter. Princes and great generals had stopped at the farmhouse of Herr Gratz or Monsieur Gratz, as he was indifferently called. The war had ruined many others, but it brought profit to him, because all the guests paid and paid well.

John in a pleased and restful state listened, and he was soothed by the sound of their voices. He had often heard old men at home, veterans of the Civil War, tell how grateful to them was the sight of a woman after months of marching and fighting. Now he understood. These were only cooks and housemaids, but their faces were not roughened like those of soldiers, and their voices and footsteps were light and soft. Moreover, they gave him food and drink—for which he would pay farmer Gratz, however—and made much over him.

"We had royal guests last night," said the youngest of the maids, whom they called Annette, a slender blond girl.

"Going to the battle front?"

"Oh, no. They were going the other way, toward Metz, and perhaps only one was a real prince."

"Maybe this prince had seen enough of battles?"

"I cannot say. I saw him only once. He was a large man, middle-aged, and he had a great brown beard."

John's whole body stiffened. Questions leaped to his lips, but he compelled his muscles to relax and by a great effort he assumed a tone of indifference.

"What was the prince's name?" he asked with apparent carelessness.

"I don't know, but the people around him were as respectful to him as if he were a king. There were two women with him, but the master himself served these two alone in their room."

"But you caught a glimpse of one of the women, the younger, Annette?" said Johanna.

"So I did, but it was only a glimpse."

"What did she look like?" asked John, who was trying to keep down the beating of his heart.

"It was only a second, but I saw a face that I will never forget. She was very pale, but she had beautiful blue eyes like stars, and the most lovely golden hair that ever grew in the world."

"Julie! My Julie!" groaned John under his breath.

"What did you say?"

"I was merely wondering who she was."

"I wondered, too, and so did all of us. We heard a tale that she was a princess, a niece or a daughter, perhaps, of the great prince, with whom she traveled, and we heard another that she and the woman with her were French spies of the most dangerous kind who had been captured and who were being taken into Germany. And the face of the beautiful young lady, which I saw for only a moment, was French, not German."

John felt hot and then cold from head to foot. Julie a spy! Impossible! Spies were shot or hanged, and sometimes women were no exceptions. How could such a charge be brought against her? And yet anything could happen in such a vast confused war as this.

Julie, his Julie of the starry blue eyes and the deep gold hair to be condemned and executed as a spy! A cold shiver seized him again.

Then came sudden enlightenment. Auersperg was medieval. In his heart he arrogated to himself the right of justice, the upper, the middle and the low, and all other kinds, but he had ability and mingled with it an extreme order of cunning. Julie of the Red Cross, a healer of wounds and disease, would not be held a prisoner, but Julie, a spy, would be kept a close captive, and her life would be in the hands of the general commanding those who had taken her. Oh, it was cunning! So cunning that its success seemed complete, and he thrilled in every vein with pain and anger.

"Are you ill?" asked the good Johanna, who had noticed the sudden deepening of his pallor.

"Not at all, thank you," he replied, forcing himself to speak in a level tone. "I feel splendidly. All of you are too kind to me. But that was an interesting story about the prince and the girl whom he brought with him, who might be either a relative or a captive."

"I'm thinking she must have been his niece," said romantic Annette, "but I'm sure she didn't love him. Perhaps she wanted to run away with some fine young officer, and he caught her and brought her back."

"When did they leave?"

"Very early this morning. They came in automobiles, but neither when they arrived nor when they departed was the lady in the machine with the prince. She and the woman with her, who must have been her servant, were in a small machine alone, except for the chauffeur."

"It's a strange tale. Which way did they go?"

"Toward Metz. We know no more. The prince did not look like a man who would tell his intentions to everybody."

"The story has in it the elements of romance," said John. "I think with you, Annette, that the young lady who must certainly have been of high birth, was being carried away from some young man who loved her well."

A lively discussion followed. John's voice had decided the opinion of the kitchen. It had been divided hitherto, but it was not now. The beautiful young lady with the starry eyes and the golden hair had certainly been torn away, and the sympathy of cooks and maids was strongly for her. While they talked John tried to collect his thoughts. After the first shock, he was convinced that Julie's life was in no danger, but her liberty certainly was. Auersperg would use the charge that she was a spy to hold her, and he was a powerful man. The pressure upon her would grow heavier and heavier all the time. Could she resist it? He might make her think that the fate of a spy would be hers, unless she chose to marry him.

In all the world, since Philip would lie long in the hospital with a wound, there was but one man who could help her. And it was he, John Scott. Out of the depths of his misery and despair a star of hope shot up. His own strong heart and arm, and his only, would rescue her. Some minds gather most courage when things are at the worst, like steel hardening in the fire, and John's was markedly of this type. Since chance had brought him on this road, and to the very house in which Julie had slept, the same kindly chance would continue to guide him on the right way. It was a good omen.

The twilight outside, cold and gray, was deepening into night. His appetite was satisfied and he felt buoyant and strong. Had he obeyed his impulse he would have started on the road to Metz in pursuit. But he knew that it was folly to exhaust himself in such a manner for nothing. Instead he told Johanna that he would go to the stable now and sleep. Jacques, a stalwart hostler, was called to show him his quarters, and he departed with all their good wishes.

Jacques was a large brown peasant, and as he led the way to the stable he said:

"They told me your name was Jean Castel from Lorraine?"

"Yes, back of Metz."

"And the house is full of German officers."

He pointed to the windows of the dining-room, which were ruddy with light. Young men in tight-fitting uniforms, their blond hair pompadoured, were outlined vividly against the glow.

"Will they go forward or will they come back?" asked Jacques in a hoarse whisper. "Is the work of Bismarck to stand or is it to undo itself?"

John believed Jacques to be a French sympathizer, anxious for an opinion that would agree with his hopes, but one could not be sure in such times, and it behooved him above all, with Julie at the end of his journey, to be careful. So he merely shrugged his shoulders and replied:

"I know not. I'm a simple buyer and seller of horses. I'm a much better judge of a horse than of an army. I've no idea which side is the stronger. I don't love war, and I'm going away from it as fast as I can."

Jacques laughed.

"Perhaps it will follow you," he said. "There is war everywhere now, or soon will be. I hear that it's spreading all over the world."

John shrugged his shoulders, and followed Jacques up a ladder into a loft over the horses. But it was not a bad room. It had two small iron beds and it was secure from wet and cold.

"You take that," said Jacques, pointing to the bed on the right. "It belonged to Fritz who was the hostler here with me. He went to the army at the first call and was killed at Longwy. Fritz was a German, a Saxon, but he and I were friends. We had worked together here three years. I'd have been glad if the bullets had spared him. The horses miss him, too. He had a kind hand with them and they liked him. Poor Fritz! You sleep in the bed of a good man."

"My eyes are so heavy that I think I'll go to bed now."

"The bed is waiting for you. It's always welcome to one who has walked all day in the cold as you have. I have more work. I have the tasks of that poor Fritz and my own to do now. It may be an hour, two hours before I'm through, but if you sleep as soundly as I do I'll not wake you up."

John sank into deep slumber almost at once and knew nothing until the next morning.

CHAPTER VIII
INTO GERMANY

A frosty dawn was just beginning to show through the single window that lighted up the little room. It opened toward the east, where the light was pink over the hills, but the upper sky was yet in dusk. John sat up in bed and rubbed the last sleep out of his eyes. A steady moaning sound made him think he was hearing again the thunder of great guns, as he had heard it days and nights at the Battle of the Marne.

The low ominous mutter came from a point toward the north, and glancing that way, although he knew his eyes would meet a blank wall, he saw that it was only Jacques, snoring, not an ordinary common snore, but the loud resounding trumpet call that can only come from a mighty chest and a powerful throat through an eagle beak. Jacques was stretched flat upon his back and John knew that he must have worked extremely hard the night before to roar with so much energy through his nose while he slept. Well, Jacques was a good fellow and a friend of France, the nation that was fighting for its existence, and if he wanted to do it he might snore until he raised the roof!

John sat up. He saw the pink on the eastern hills turning to blue and then spreading to the higher skies. The day was going to be clear and cold. He walked to the window and looked up at the skies, seeking for aeroplanes, after the habit that had now grown upon him. But the sky was speckless and no sounds came from the Gratz farmhouse. Doubtless the German officers quartered there were sleeping late, knowing that they had no need to hurry to the front, since the fighting in the hills and mountains was desultory.

But the crisp clear blue of the cold morning was wonderfully suitable to the hosts of the air and they were at work. Along a battle front of five hundred miles in the west and of seven or eight hundred in the east messages were flashing, on wires by telephone and telegraph and then on nothing but the pulsating air.

John, who had been compelled to deal so much with these invisible agencies felt them now about him. He had a highly sensitive mind like a photographic plate that registered everything, and when he opened the window that he might see better and admit the fresh air, he did not have to reach out for knowledge. It came, and registered itself upon that delicate and imaginative mind. He had thought so much and he had striven so hard to see and to divine what lay before him that he felt almost able to send messages of his own through the air, messages of hope winging their way directly to Julie.

The mind of man is a strange thing. It may be a godlike instrument, the powers of which are yet but little known. John did not believe in the least in anything supernatural, but he did believe in the immense and unfathomed power of the natural. Alone, and in the early dawn with silence all about him it seemed that he heard Julie calling to him. Her voice traveled like the wireless on the pulsating air. She needed him and she turned to him alone for aid. She had divined in some manner that only he could help her and he would come, no matter what the risk. The cry was registered again and again upon his sensitive soul, and always he sent back the answer that he was coming. His mind, like hers, had become a wireless, and both were working.

He became unconscious of time and place. He no longer saw the blue sky, but he stretched out his arms and called:

"I am coming!"

"Coming? What do you mean by coming? Who is it you're telling?"

John came out of his dream, or the misty region between here and nowhere, and turned to Jacques, who in the process of awakening at that moment had heard his words which were spoken in French.

"I was just talking to the air," replied John a little uncertainly. "Fine mornings appeal to me, and I was telling this one that I'd soon come out into it"

Jacques continued to awaken. He was a big man who worked hard and who slept heavily. Rousing from sleep was a task accomplished by degrees and it took some time. He had heard John with one ear and now he heard with the other. His right eye opened slowly and then the left. The blood became more active in his brain and in a minute or two he was awake all over.

"Telling the morning air that you're coming out into it, eh Castel?" he said as he put one foot on the floor. "You're a poet, I see. You don't look it, but being French, as you Lorrainers are, it makes you fond of poetry."

"I do believe you have it right, Jacques," said John, "but if I can get my breakfast now I mean to go upon the road at once."

"Oh, you can get it, Castel. The whole kitchen has fallen in love with you. I found that out last night after you had gone away. That little Annette told me so."

"It was to tease you," said John, who understood at once and who was willing to fib in a good cause. "I saw her watching through a window a fine big fellow, exactly your size, age and appearance, and with the same name. I said something about his being a hulking hostler and she turned upon me like a hawk."

"Now, did she?" exclaimed Jacques, a great smile spreading slowly across his face.

"She did. Told me it was a poor return for their kindness to criticize a better man."

"Ah, that Annette is bright and quick. She can see through a man at one look. Castel, I like you, and I hope you'll get to Metz without trouble. But keep a civil and a slow tongue in your mouth. Don't speak until the Germans speak to you, and then tell the truth without stammering. I'll go to the kitchen with you, as my work begins early."

John knew that he had a friend, and the two left the stable together. But he was not thinking much then of the Gratz farm or of anybody upon it. He had sent his soul on before, and he meant that his body should catch up with it.

Johanna, Annette and the master, Gratz himself, were in the kitchen. He ate a good breakfast with Jacques, paid Gratz for food and lodging, and putting his blankets and knapsack upon his back, took once more to the road. Jacques repeated his good advice to be polite to men to whom it paid to be polite, and Annette, standing by the side of the stalwart hostler, waved him farewell.

The slush, frozen the night before, had not yet melted, and John walked rapidly along the broad firm highway, elated and bold. Julie had called to him. He would not reason with himself, and ask how or why it had been done, but he felt it. He liked to believe that wireless signals had passed between them. Anyway he was going to believe it, and hence his heart was light and his spirit strong.

He passed sentinels posted along the road, but his passport was always sufficient, and his pleasant manner bred a pleasant manner in return. Soon there was nothing but a line of smoke to mark where the Gratz farm stood, but he carried with him good memories of it. He hoped that the romance of Jacques and Annette would end happily. In truth he was quite sure that it would, and he began to whistle softly to himself, a trick that he had caught from General Vaugirard.

John had no certainty that he would enter Metz, which must now be less of a city than a great fortress with a powerful garrison. But he felt sure that he could at least penetrate to the outskirts and there find more trace of Auersperg. A prince and man of his social importance could scarcely pass through the city without being noticed, and there would be gossip among the soldiers. Fortunately he had been in Metz twice and he knew the romantic old city at the confluence of the Moselle and the Seille, dominated by its magnificent Gothic cathedral. After all he might overtake Auersperg there and in some manner achieve his task. Chance took a wide range in so great a war and nothing was impossible.

He was now approaching the line between France and Germany, and Metz lay only eleven miles beyond. The beauty of the clear cold day endured. There was snow on the hills, but the brilliant sun touched it with a luminous golden haze, and the crisp air was the breath of life.

He swung along at a great gait for one who walked. Life for months without a roof had been hard, but it had toughened wonderfully those whom it did not kill, and John with a magnificent constitution was one of those who had profited most. He felt no weariness now although he had come many miles.

About one o'clock in the afternoon he sat on a stone by the roadside and ate with the appetite of vigorous youth good food from his knapsack. While he was there a German sergeant, with about twenty men in wagons going toward Metz, stopped and spoke to him.

"Hey, you on the stone, what are you doing?" asked the sergeant.

John cut off a fresh piece of sausage with his clasp knife and answered briefly and truthfully:

"Eating."

The sergeant had a broad, red and merry face, and facing a man of good humor he was not offended.

"So I see," he said, "but that wasn't what I meant."

John, without another word, took out his passport, handed it to him and went on eating. The sergeant examined it, handed it back to him and said:

"Correct."

"I show it to everybody," said John. "When a man speaks to me I don't care who he is, or what he is, I hand it to him. I, Jean Castel, as you see by the name on the passport, don't want trouble with anybody."

"And a wise fellow you are, Castel. I'm Otto Scheller, a sergeant in the service of his Imperial Majesty and the Fatherland."

"You look as if you had seen much of war, Sergeant Scheller, but I am a dealer in horses and I am happiest where the bullets are fewest."

"It's an honest confession, but it does not bespeak a high heart."

"Perhaps not, but sometimes a horse-dealer is more useful than a soldier. For instance, the off horse of the front wagon has picked up a stone in his left hind foot, and if it's not taken out he'll go lame long before you reach Metz."

"Donnerwetter! But it's true. You do know something about horses and you have an eye in your head. Here you, Heinrich, take that stone out, quick, or it won't be good for you!"

"And the right horse of the third wagon has glanders. The swelling is just beginning to show below the jaw. It's contagious, you know. You'd better turn him loose, or all your horses will die."

"Donner und blitzen! See Fritz, if it's true. It's so, is it? Then release the poor animal as Castel says, and put in one of the extras. See, you Castel, you're a wizard, you hardly glanced at the horses, and you saw what we didn't see, although we've been with them all day."

"I've grown up with horses. It's my business to know everything about them, and maybe your trade before the war didn't bring you near them."

Scheller threw back his great head and laughed.

"If a horse had approached where I worked," he said, "much good beer would have been spilt. I was the head waiter in a restaurant on the Unter den Linden. Ah, the happy days! Oh, the glorious street! and here it's nothing but march, march, and shoot, shoot! Three of my best waiters have been killed already. And the other lads are no horsemen either. That big Fritz over there made toys, Joseph drove a taxicab, August was conductor on a train to Charlottenberg, and Eitel was porter in a hotel. We're all from Berlin, and will you tell us, Castel, how soon we can take Paris and London and go back to the Unter den Linden?"

John shook his head.

"There are about fifteen hundred million people in the world who are asking that question, Otto Scheller," he replied, "and out of all the fifteen hundred millions not one can answer it. But I will ask you a question in return."

"What is it?"

"Will you give me a ride in one of your wagons to Metz?"

"Why, certainly," replied Scheller. "Your passport is in good order, and we can take you to the first line of fortifications. There you'll meet high officers and you'll have to make more statements, because Metz, as you know, is one of the most powerful fortresses in Europe."

"I know; why shouldn't I, a Lorrainer, know? But my passport will take me in. Meanwhile, I thank you, Otto Scheller, for the kindness you're showing me."

"All right, jump in, and off we go."

It was a provision wagon, drawn by stout Percherons, which John felt sure had been bred in France, and which he also felt sure had never been paid for by German money. The wagon was empty now, evidently having delivered its burden nearer the battle lines, and John found a comfortable seat beside the sergeant, while a stout *Pickelhaube* drove.

"Looks like peace, Castel," said the sergeant, waving his hand at the landscape, "but things are not always what they seem."

"How so?"

"See the hills across there. The French hold part of them, and often the artillery goes boom! boom! They threaten an attack on Metz. We shall hear the cannon before long."

John looked long at the hills, high, white and silent, but presently they began to groan and mutter as Scheller had predicted they would. Flashes of flame appeared and giant shells were emptied like gusts of lava from a volcano. One burst in the road about three hundred yards in front of them, and tore a hole so deep that they were compelled to drive around it.

"The French are good with the guns," said Scheller, regarding the excavation meditatively, "but of course it was by mere chance that the shell struck in the road."

John felt a light and momentary chill. It would certainly be the irony of fate if on his great quest he were smitten down by a missile from his own army. But no others struck near them, although the intermittent battle of artillery in the hills continued.

Sergeant Scheller paid no attention to the distant cannon fire, to which he had grown so used long since that he regarded it as one of the ordinary accompaniments of life, like the blowing of the wind. He was in a good humor and he talked agreeably much about battle and march, although he betrayed no military secrets, chiefly because he had none to betray.

"I march here and I march there," he said, "I and my men shoot at a certain point, and from a certain point we're shot at. That's all I know."

"And that, I take it, is the cathedral in Metz," said John, pointing toward the top of a lofty spire showing against the blue.

"So it is, Castel, and here you'll have to show your passport again. We're approaching the fortifications. I couldn't tell you about them if I would. We drive along a narrow road between high earthworks and we see nothing."

Their entry into Metz was slow and long. John was compelled to show his passport again and again, and he answered innumerable questions, many searching and pointed, but again he was thrice lucky in knowing the town and something about Lorraine.

Now that he was inside, with a powerful German army all about him, he must decide soon what to do. Fortunately he had made a friend of Scheller who advised him to go to a little Inn near the Moselle, much frequented by thrifty peasants, and John concluded to take his advice.

"Good-by, Castel," said Scheller, reaching out a huge fist. "I like you and I hope we'll meet in Paris soon."

John took the fist in a hand not as large as Scheller's, but almost as powerful, and shook it.

"Here's to the meeting in Paris," he said, but he added under his breath, "may it happen, with you as my unwounded prisoner."

He left Scheller after thanks for the ride, and found his way to the Inn of the Golden Lion, which was crowded with stout farmers and peasants. It was old-fashioned, with a great room where most of the men sat on benches before a huge fire, which cast a cheerful glow over ruddy faces. Some were eating sausage and drinking beer, and there was plenty of talk, mostly in German.

John modestly found a place near the fire for which he was very grateful, and ordered beer and cheese. Apparently he was nothing but a peasant going about his own humble business, but he listened keenly to everything that was said, reckoning that someone ultimately would mention the Prince of Auersperg, or could be drawn into speaking of a man of so much consequence who might be present in Metz.

He attracted little attention, as he sat warming himself before the fire and listening. People of French sympathies might be in the crowd, but if so they were silent, because nearly all the talkers were speaking of German success. It was true that they had been turned back from Paris, but it meant a delay only, they would soon advance again, and this time they would crush France. Meantime, von Hindenburg was smashing the Russians to pieces. John smiled as he gazed into the crackling fire. After all, the Germans were not supreme. They knew a vast deal about war, but others could learn and did learn. They were splendid soldiers, but there were others just as good and they had proved it.

Men came and went through the Inn of the Golden Lion. Sometimes soldiers and officers as well as civilians sought its food and fire. The day had turned darker, full of raw cold, and a light hail was falling. John was glad to have a place in the inn. He reflected that a man's good luck and bad luck in the long run were about even, and, after so much bad luck, the good luck should be coming his way. He would certainly remain in the inn that night if he could, and a bench before the fire would be a sufficient bed for the peasant he seemed to be, at such a time, with the city full of troops, and the French batteries almost near enough to be heard.

More officers were coming in now. Some of them stood before the great fire, warming themselves and drying their uniforms, the hail having begun to drive harder. He thought he might see some one whom he knew. It was possible that von Arnheim, the young prince of whom he had such pleasant memories, was in Metz, and it was possible also that he might come to the Inn of the Golden Lion. And there was young Kratzek, who he knew had been exchanged. Some chance might make him, too, enter the inn, but John's second thought told him the fulfillment of his wish would be folly. They were his official enemies and must seize him if he made himself known to them. He was merely lonesome, longing for the sight of a familiar face.

His own appearance had been changed greatly by a stubby young beard that called aloud for a razor. Clad in a peasant's garb, and with a cap drawn down over his face Carstairs and Wharton themselves might have passed without knowing him.

Although the young Germans did not appear, one whom John expected least came. A man of medium size, built compactly, and with a short brown beard, trimmed neatly to a point, walked briskly through the room, and spread out cold hands before the flames. John was dozing in his chair, but the man's walk and manner roused him at once. They seemed familiar, and a glance at the face showed him that it was Weber.

He resisted a powerful impulse to call to him or to signal to him in some manner. The impulse was strong to recognize the appearance of a friend, but he understood the deadly danger of it. He was a spy and so was Weber. By recognition each might betray the other, and it was best that he should not attract the Alsatian's attention in any way. So he pretended to doze again, although he was really watchful.

Weber stood by the fire a little while, until he was warm. Then he sat down in one of the chairs and called for beer and sausage, which he drank and ate slowly and with evident relish. His eye roved about the room and once or twice fell upon John, but did not linger there. Evidently he did not recognize the peasant with the stubby growth of young beard. Nor did he appear to know anyone else in the room, and, after a few inquiring glances, he seemed to be busy with his own thoughts.

A half-hour or so later Weber went into the street, and John, muttering that he wished a little fresh air, rose and followed. He had in mind only a vague idea of speaking with Weber, and of finding out something about Auersperg, of whose movements the Alsatian was likely to know. But when he was outside Weber had vanished. He walked up the street, only a little distance in either direction, because the soldiers were thick everywhere, and their officers wanted explanations. Moreover, he recognized the futility of search. Weber was gone as completely as if he had been snatched up into the air by an invisible hand, and John felt that he had missed an opportunity.

He took courage, nevertheless, and dismissing Weber from his mind, he made a renewed effort. The precious passport once more came into play, and gradually, he made his way toward the finest hotel in Metz. If Auersperg was still in the city it was likely that a man of his temper and luxurious habits would be at this hotel.

There were sentinels about the building and it was crowded with guests of high degree. The assemblage here was altogether different from that of the Inn of the Golden Lion. Generals and colonels were passing, and John learned from a soldier that a prince of the empire was inside. His heart beat hard. It could be none other than Auersperg, and using every possible excuse he remained in the vicinity of the hotel.

At last while he stood there he saw a face appear at an upper window, and his heart gave a great leap. Despite the falling dusk, the strangeness of the place and the distance, the single faint glimpse was sufficient. It was Julie. He could not mistake that crown of wonderful golden hair in which slight coppery tints appeared, and the face, pale now.

John impulsively reached out his arms, but she could not see the young peasant who stood afar, watching her. He dropped his arms, caution again warning him, but he stood gazing. Perhaps it was a powerful, mysterious current sent from his heart that drew her at last. She looked in his direction. John knew that she could not recognize him there in the gloom, but, snatching off his cap, and, reckless of risk he waved it three times about his head. It was a signal. He did not know whether she could see it, nor if, seeing, could she surmise what it meant, but he hoped vaguely that something might come of it. In any event, it was a relief to his feelings and it brought hope.

After the signal he forgot to put the cap on his head, but stood with it dangling in his hand.

"Hey, you fool!" said a rough German voice, "why do you stand there staring, with your cap in your hand, and your head bare, inviting the quick death of pneumonia that an idiot like you deserves?"

Although the voice was rough it was not unkindly, and as John came out of his dreams and wheeled about he saw again the rubicund face of Sergeant Scheller.

"I was looking at the hotel," he replied with perfect composure, as he replaced his cap, "and I saw one of our great generals pass in at the door. At least I thought him such by his uniform, and taking off my cap to honor him I forgot to put in back again."

Scheller burst into a roar.

"Why, it's our Castel once more!" he exclaimed. "Good, honest, simple, patriotic Castel! You can take off your cap when a general passes, but you needn't keep it off after he's gone."

"I thought it might be our great Kaiser himself."

"I don't think he's in Metz, although he may be near, but your act does credit to your loyalty, Castel."

John glanced up at the window. Julie was gone and the twilight was coming over city and fortress. Yet he had seen her, and he felt that he would be able to follow Auersperg wherever he might go. He had no doubt that the prince would leave in the morning, traveling swiftly by automobile, but he, plodding on foot, or in any way he could, would surely follow. It gave him courage to remember the old fable of the tortoise and the hare, a fable which doubtless has proved a vain consolation to many a man, far behind in the race.

"Come to the Inn of the Golden Lion," he said to Scheller, for whom he had a genuine friendly feeling, "and take a glass of beer with me. I was wandering about, and it interested me to see the great people go into the hotel or come out."

"A half-dozen of our famous generals are there," said Scheller, who seemed to be both well informed now and talkative.

"Some one told me that the great Prince Karl of Auersperg was there, too," said John at random.

"So he is," replied Scheller, seeing nothing unusual in the question, "and he has with him under close guard the two French women spies. It's quite certain that he will carry them into Austria, perhaps to Salzburg or some place near there."

It was precious information, given casually by a chance acquaintance, and John believed that it was true. It was in the region of Salzburg that his great Odyssey had begun, and now it seemed that chance, after many a curve through the smoke of battle, was taking him back there.

"I'm off duty, Castel, and I'll be glad to go with you," he heard Scheller saying. "Beer is always welcome and I think you're a good fellow. It's too bad the blood of your forefathers was French, but it's had a German stiffening under our rule."

"The German spirit is strong and the Kaiser's armies are mighty," said John sincerely. "Now we'll hurry to the inn and have our beer."

Scheller was not loath, and before the great fire John toasted his health in a huge foaming mug, and Scheller toasted back again. Then the sergeant gave him a grip of his mighty hand and told him good-by.

"I like you, Castel, lad," he said, "and whatever you want I hope you'll get it."

John, imaginative at all times, but with his nerves keyed to the highest pitch now, took it as an omen. The kindly Scheller little dreamed what he sought, but the good wishes of a sergeant might have as much effect as those of a general or a prince with the Supreme Power.

"Farewell, lad," said Scheller again, and, "Farewell," John responded.

When he was gone John sank back into his chair. He had not been able to secure for the night more than a bench in the great room, but with his blankets he could do very well. Besides, there was a certain advantage in the place, as a dozen others would be sleeping in it, making it a news center.

He bought a supper of cheese and sausage, and continued to watch the people who came to the Inn of the Golden Lion. He thought Weber might return, and if so he meant to speak with him, if a possible chance should occur, but there was no sign of the Alsatian.

The heat and the smoke made him doze, by and by, and knowing that it would be long before the room could be cleared, he resigned himself at last to sleep, a circumstance that attracted no attention as others also were sleeping in their chairs.

When he awoke it was past midnight, and only those who were to make it a bedroom remained. Then he stretched his hardy form, wrapped in his blankets, on a bench beside the wall and fell promptly into the deep slumber of the young and just.

He awoke once or twice in the night and heard healthy snores about him. German civilians and Lorrainers were asleep on the benches and they slept well. The fire in the great, ancient fireplace had burned low, but a fine bed of coals glowed there and cast quivering lights over the sleepers. John thought he beard from afar that mutter of the guns, with which he was so familiar, but he did not know whether it was fancy or reality, as he always returned quickly to his deep slumber.

CHAPTER IX
THE GREAT CASTLE

John himself the next morning saw the departure of Prince Karl of Auersperg and his suite, and it was not altogether chance that brought it about. He was aroused as the other sleepers were by the waiters who were preparing the room for the day. The Inn of the Golden Lion was doing a rushing business in a town full of German troops, who ate well and drank well and who paid.

His night's rest was refreshing to both mind and body, and, after a good breakfast, he went once more toward the hotel which was frequented by the highborn and the very highborn. He had no plan in mind, but he knew that the magnet drawing him was Julie.

The morning was clear and cold, the streets slippery, but vivid with life, mostly military. He carried his knapsack full of food, and his blankets in a pack on his back, which his passport showed to be his right as a peasant trading in horses, and returning from the front to his home for a fresh supply. But there was little danger to him at present, as there were many other peasants and farmer folk in Metz on one errand or another.

He walked about the hotel, and presently noticed signs of bustle. Several automobiles, one of much magnificence, drove up to the entrance and halted there, obviously awaiting a company of importance. John had no doubt from the first that it was the equipage of the Prince of Auersperg. No one else would travel in such state, and he would stay to see him go with his prisoners. Others drawn by curiosity joined him and they and the young peasant stood very near.

John saw the door open, and a porter of great stature, clad in a uniform, heavy with gold lace, appear, bowing profoundly. It was often difficult to tell a head porter from a field marshal, but in this case the man's deferential attitude not only indicated the difference, but the fact also that Auersperg was coming.

The prince, preceded by two young men in close-fitting blue-gray uniforms, came out. John was bound to confess once more that he was a fine-looking man, large, bearded magnificently, and imposing in appearance and manner. His effect at a state ball or a reception would be highly decorative, and many a managing American mother would have been glad to secure him as a son-in-law, provided the present war did not make such medieval survivals unfashionable.

Auersperg entered his automobile, a very dark red limousine of great size, and he was shut from John's view, save only his full beard glimmering faintly through the glass. More men came, soldiers or attendants, and among them was Antoine Picard, gigantic and sullen. His arms were unbound and he went with the others willingly. Perhaps Auersperg had divined that he would not attempt to escape, as long as Julie was in his hands.

Then came the two women, Julie first, and John heard about him the muttered exclamation: "The French spies!" He knew that this belief had taken strong hold of the soldiers and people who stood about. Women, when they chose to be, were the most dangerous of all spies and the watchers regarded them with intense curiosity.

Neither was veiled. Julie was erect, and her chin high. John saw that the girl had become a woman, matured by hardship and danger, and she looked more beautiful than ever to him that morning. Her cheeks were pale and tiny curls of the deep golden hair escaped from her hood and clustered about her temples. John's heart swam with pity. Truly, she was a bird in the hands of the fowler.

She gave a glance half appealing and half defiant at the people, but the stalwart Suzanne who followed her was wholly grim and challenging. Then something strange occurred. John had the most intense anxiety for her to look at him. He had no belief whatever in anything supernatural, but sound, intelligible words were made to travel on waves of air, and it was barely possible in this unexplored world that thought too might be propelled in the same way.

Almost unconsciously he kept his eyes upon Julie's and he poured his very soul into the gaze. It was only a little distance from the door to the automobile which she was to take, and he had time. His gaze became concentrated, burning, a thing more of the spirit than of sight, and as her eyes glanced once more about the circle of idle spectators they met his own and rested there.

John looked straight into their dark blue depths and he saw a startled flash leap up. Chance or a power yet unknown had drawn her gaze and made her vision keen. He saw that she knew him, knew him even in that peasant's dress and under the new stubble of beard. The flash became for a moment a fire, and her figure quivered, but he was not afraid. He had an instinctive confidence that she would understand, and that she would not betray him by any impulsive act.

"I am here to save you," his eyes said.

"I know it," hers replied.

"I will follow you across the world to help you."

"I know that, too."

"Don't betray the fact that you've seen a friend."

"I will not."

Thus the eyes spoke to one another and understood what was said. Julie's glance passed on, and with unfaltering step she entered an automobile, the German chauffeur standing by the side of it and respectfully holding the door. Suzanne followed, the chauffeur closed the door, sprang into his seat and the little train moved majestically through the streets of Metz. Comment was plentiful and it was not unkind to Julie.

"Too handsome to be executed as a spy," said a burly German almost in John's ear. "A girl with a face like that should never feel the touch of a bullet or a rope. It's a face to be kissed and a neck to fit into a man's arm."

The man's phrasing was rough, but both his admiration and his pity were sincere, and John felt no resentment toward him.

"Some of the French girls are wonderful for looks," said another and younger German, "but they're the most dangerous kind. If it's proved on the one the prince has caught she'll expect her blue eyes and all that hair of gold to pull her through."

Him, John hated and would have been glad to strike, but he could help neither Julie nor himself by resenting it. Instead, he watched the automobiles, four in number, disappear on the road leading from

Metz toward Stuttgart, a small body of hussars following as a guard, and then, pack on back, he trudged on foot behind them.

The invaluable passport carried him through the fortifications, and along the great highway into the country. He was glad that Auersperg had not gone by train, as it would have been harder to trace him then. Now, although far behind, he could hear of him at inns and little towns by the way. Yet he was compelled to recall to himself again and again the ancient and worn fable of the hare and the tortoise.

He knew well enough that the tortoise did not often overtake the hare. Hares were cunning little animals, riot able to fight and almost wholly dependent upon speed for survival in the battle of life. Hence, they never went to sleep, and in only a single instance recorded in history had a tortoise won a footrace from a hare. Yet an old proverb, even if based upon a solitary exception, is wonderfully consoling, and John was able to use it now as comfort.

After he had passed the fortifications and was well behind the German interior lines, travel became easier. The Germans, considering their army a wall before them, were less suspicious and the interruptions were few. John, moreover, was a cheerful peasant. He had a fair voice, and he sang German hymns and war songs in a mellow baritone as he strode along. The road was really not so bad, after that long and hideous life in filthy trenches. The heat of Sahara would be autumn coolness after a return from Hades, and now John enjoyed the contrast.

There were many tracks of automobiles in the light snow and hail that covered the road, and one broader than the rest John felt sure was made by the great limousine of Auersperg. It was like a trail to lead him on, and he was a trailer who could not be shaken off.

Rejoicing in his new possession of German—thankful now that he had studied it so hard—although he spoke it with a strong accent of Lorraine, John saluted such German soldiers as he passed and wished them good day. Invariably the salute was returned in pleasant fashion. His nature was essentially friendly and therefore he bred friendliness in others. Although he was in a hostile land he was continually meeting people who seemed to have an instinctive wish to help him.

As he walked on he overtook a stout man of middle age dressed heavily in brown who appeared to be a priest, and who turned upon him a benign countenance.

"Why do you travel so fast for one on foot?" asked the man.

"Because I feel strong and my errand takes me far, Father."

"If it takes you far, my son, the less speed in the beginning the greater at the end."

"True, Father," said John, slackening his pace, and glancing at the shrewd face which was also both ruddy and kindly. "The Church can give good advice in temporal as well as spiritual matters."

"Even so, my son," said the priest, who had noted John's frank countenance, his width between the eyes. "One of my vocation cannot go through life merely looking inward. Come, walk with me. The world is mad, gone wholly mad, but let us try to be two sane beings in it for a little while."

"Thanks, Father," said John. "I can wish no better company. I agree with you that the world has gone mad. I have seen its madness at its height."

"And at such a time the Church, Protestant or Catholic, must do the best it can. But we are so few, while so many souls are leaving their bodies. And yet I tell you, young sir, that not one man in a hundred of this great European peasantry knows why he fights. I, a priest, may speak freely, and I do so because my mind is full of indignation this morning."

"I do not love war, either. You see I walk away from it. But why are you on foot, Father?"

"By preference. I might have gone in one of the automobiles with the soldiers, but they are a part of the war madness, and I wished to be alone. You will learn with years that it's well to be alone at times, when one may take the measure of himself and those about him. I have chosen to walk this morning, because it makes my blood run better, and the winds at least are pure."

"I find the case the same with me, sir. My best thoughts usually come when I'm walking and alone."

The priest threw out his hands in a wide gesture.

"We agree, I see," he said. "You appear to be a peasant, but your voice is that of another kind. No, do not protest or say anything. It is no business of mine that you're not the peasant you claim to be, nor do I ask the nature of your errand behind the German army."

"I could not tell it to you, Father, but it is an errand of peace. I think it the highest and holiest I could undertake, and, in undertaking it, I believe myself to be animated by such a spirit as the knights felt in the first flush of the Crusades."

"I believe your words. When I first looked into your eyes I said they were those of an honest young man. We of the cloth learn to know. We feel instinctively the presence of honesty or dishonesty. Young sir, I hope that your quest, although it may take you far, will take you to success."

John's heart beat hard. He knew that the man was only a village priest, but good wishes carry. They might even travel upon waves of their own, and send to a happy goal those for whom they were intended.

"Father," he said, "you and I have never met before this day, and we may never see each other after it. As I told you, mine is a long quest and it's full of danger. Will you give it your blessing without asking what it is?"

"Willingly," said the priest as he spread out his hands, and murmured rapid words in Latin. John, Protestant though he was, felt a curious lightening of the soul. The Crusaders always sought a blessing before going into battle, and a spiritual fire that would uphold him seemed to have passed from the mind of this humble village priest to his.

They went on now for a little while in silence. Uhlans, hussars, infantry and cannon passed them, but few questions were asked of them. The day remained cold, and the heavens were a brilliant blue. It was fine weather for walking and the middle-aged man and the young man kept pace with each other, stride for stride.

By and by they drank from a brook and then ate together. The priest also carried a knapsack under his heavy brown overcoat and they shared their food, finishing it with a sip or two from a flask of light wine.

"We come to a crossroad a mile further on," said the priest, "and there I think we will part. I turn into the crossroad, and you, I take it, keep the road to Stuttgart."

"I shall be sorry."

"The way of the world, my son. All through life we are meeting and parting. The number of people who travel with us all the road is very small. It may be that I have surmised somewhat of your quest. No, say nothing! I would not know more, but a far greater power than mine will help you in it."

They parted at the crossroad and John felt as if he left an old friend. When he looked back he saw the priest on a little hill gazing after him, and he felt again as if the good wish that would count was coming on a wave of air. Then his own road dipped into a valley and at nightfall he came to a village which had a little inn, humble but neat and clean. Here he procured a razor and shaved the stubble from his face. He no longer had a fear of meeting anyone whom he might know, save possibly Weber, and Weber was a friend.

John's frank face and cheerful manner again made friends for him. The stout innkeeper and his stout wife favored him with the food, and hearing that he had come from Metz they wanted to know all the gossip, which he told them as far as he knew. He had noted the broad track of the great limousine in the road before he entered the inn, and thinking it must have stopped there for a little while, he spoke casually of those who passed.

"Aye," said the innkeeper, "many go by, many of whom will never come back. They go mostly toward Metz, but a great prince traveling in the other direction came today, before noon, and we served him refreshment."

"Perhaps it was the Prince of Auersperg," said John. "He was in Metz when I was there, and I saw him leave."

"They did not tell me his name, but that must have been the man."

"He was in a great, dark red automobile."

"Then it was surely he. One could not mistake that automobile. I take it that only kings and princes travel in its like."

"He carried with him two Frenchwomen, dangerous spies, intended for imprisonment in Germany."

"So I heard, and we saw the face of one of them, very young and with the most marvelous golden hair. I never saw a fairer face. But, as all the world knows, the most beautiful women are often the most wicked. I suppose there wasn't a woman among the Philistines who could compare with Delilah in either face or figure."

"I suppose not," said John, scarcely able to restrain a smile. "Did the women come into the inn?"

"Oh, no. My wife took food to them in the automobile. She saw them much better than I did. She says that the younger one—and she was but a girl—spoke softly and did not look wicked at all. But then, my wife is fat and sentimental."

The stout hausfrau smiled.

"It is Hans who has the heart full of sentiment," she said. "When he saw that the French spy was a girl of such beauty and such youth he believed that she should not be punished, and he a good German! Ah, all men are alike!"

Hans filled his pipe and wisely made no reply. But John smiled also.

"Is it wicked in a man to have an eye for beauty?" he said. "I know that my host's heart has thrilled many a time when he caught a glimpse of the lady who is now his wife and the very competent head of his household."

It was obvious, but both smiled.

"Hans is not so bad," said the hausfrau complacently, and John's compliment won him an unusually good room that night. Hans told him also that he could probably secure him a place in an empty supply wagon the next morning, and John was grateful. Walking was good, and it had done much to maintain his strength and steady his nerves, but one could not walk all the way across Germany.

He was aware that he was surrounded by dangers but he felt that the omens remained fair. Perhaps the good wishes that had been given to him still clothed him about and protected him from harm. In abnormal times the human mind seeks more than an ordinary faith.

He would have slept well, but in the night an army passed. For hours and hours the gray legions trod by in numbers past counting, the moonlight casting gleams upon the spiked helmets. Then came masses of Uhlans and hussars and after them batteries of great guns and scores and scores of the wicked machine guns. Truly, as the priest had said, the whole world had gone mad. He remembered those days in Vienna when the gay and light-head ed Viennese had marched up and down the streets all night long, singing and dancing, and thinking only of war as a festival, in which glorious victory was sure and quick. Torrents of blood had flowed under the bridges since then, gay Austria, that had set the torch, had been shaken to its foundation, and no victory was yet in sight for anybody.

Nevertheless the German legions seemed inexhaustible. John had seen them turned back in those long days of fighting on the Marne, and more than a million had been killed or wounded since the war began, but that avalanche of men and guns still poured out of the heart of Germany. He felt more deeply than ever that the world could not afford a German victory, and the sanguinary spectacle of a Kaiser riding roughshod over civilization. The fact that so many German people were likable and that Germany had achieved so much made the case all the worse.

He took the road the next morning, not on foot this time but in an empty provision wagon, returning eastward, drawn by two powerful horses and driven by Fritz, a stout German youth. Both Hans and the hausfrau wished him well, and he soon made a friend of Fritz, who was a Bavarian from a little village near Munich. John knew Munich better than any other German city, and he and the young German soon established a common ground of conversation, because to Fritz Munich was the greatest and finest of all cities.

That was one of the pleasantest mornings he experienced on his long and solitary quest. His heavy clothing kept him warm, his seat was comfortable, the pace was good and Fritz was excellent company. Fritz was a simple peasant, though, in his belief that Germany was right in everything and omnipotent, that the other nations through jealousy had conspired to destroy her, but she, instead, would destroy them all, and rule a conquered world.

John saw readily that the poison had been instilled into him from his birth by the men higher up, and he blamed Fritz very little for his misguided beliefs. Besides, it was pleasant to have the company of one somewhat near his own age, and to listen to human talk. There was a girl, Minna, in the village near Munich whom Fritz was going to marry as soon as the war was over.

"And that won't be long now," said Fritz. "It's true that we were halted before Paris last year, but we came again more numerous and more powerful than ever. The Kaiser will make a finish of it all in the spring, and I shall marry Minna. We shall go into Munich, see the beautiful city, and then go back to our home in the village."

"A fine place, Munich," said John. "In my dealing in horses I've been there more than once. Do you remember the Wittelsbach Fountain in the Maximilienplatz?"

"Aye, and a cooling sight it is on a warm day."

"And the green Isar flowing through the Englischer Gardens!"

"And the ducks swimming down to the edge of the little falls, swimming so close that you think they're going over and then swimming away again."

"Yes, I've seen them, and once I went into the gallery and saw the strange pictures they called Futurist, which I think represent the bad dreams of painters who have gone to bed drunk."

"You're a man of sense, you Castel, even if you do have a French name. I went in there myself once, and then I hurried away to the Hofbrau and drank all the beer I could that I might forget it."

John laughed, and Fritz laughed with him.

"How far do you go?" asked John.

"Only to Stuttgart. I wish it was Munich. Then I might see Minna again before returning to the war."

But they had a placid journey to Stuttgart, sleeping by the way in the wagon. Arriving in the city John paid Fritz for his ride and parted from him with regret. He spent a night here in a humble inn, and discovered that Auersperg and his party were now two days ahead of him. The automobiles were moving with speed, and John surmised that the prince did not intend to remain long at his castle over the Austrian border. Perhaps he would have to return to the war, leaving Julie and Suzanne there. He hoped so.

Two days later John was in Munich, and he learned that Auersperg had not increased his lead. It was easy enough to trace him. He had secured an extensive suite of apartments at the large hotel, the

Bayerischer Hof, although Julie and the Picards had been secluded in another part of the hotel. Auersperg had gone to the palace and had held a long conference with the old King of Bavaria, but on the second day he had left, still going eastward, escorted by hussars.

John departed again and on foot. The weather was balmier now, with touches of spring in it. Faint shades of green appeared in the grass and the foliage, and his pursuit was sanguine. Fortune had certainly favored him in a remarkable manner, so far. He had been able to answer all questions in a convincing way, and here in Bavaria the people were not so suspicious, and perhaps not so stern as they were in Prussia. Nor did he doubt for a moment that Julie knew he was following them. She had recognized him and their eyes had spoken in the language of understanding to each other. It was easy enough to re-create for himself, almost as vivid as reality, her beautiful face with the golden hair showing under the edges of the hood, and the startled look of the dark blue eyes when they first met his own. Relief and joy had been in that look too. He could read it.

John had learned in Munich the location of Auersperg's principal castle. It was Zillenstein in a spur of the Eastern Alps just inside Austria, where for centuries the Auerspergs had held great state, as princes of the Holy Roman Empire. Now when they were princes of both the German and the Austro-Hungarian empires with their greater fealty for the former, they often went there nevertheless, and John's information in Munich made him quite sure that the prince had gone directly toward the ancient stronghold.

Auersperg could cover the distance quickly in his powerful automobiles, but it would take John a long time on foot, helped by an occasional ride in a peasant's cart. Nevertheless he hung on with patience and pertinacity. He was but a single man on a quest in the heart of Germany, but in the old days men had gone alone through a world of dangers to the Holy Sepulchre and had returned. He was not far from the path taken by those from Western Europe, and he was uplifted by the knowledge. The feeling that he, too, was a crusader grew strongly upon him, and by night and day was his support.

He crossed the border at last and came to Salzburg in the mountains, where the gray-green Salzach flows down from the glaciers and divides the town. The place was thronged with soldiers, and the summit of the frowning Muenchburg was alive with activity.

Here in the very heart of the Teutonic confederation, far from hostile frontiers, travelers were not subjected to such rigid scrutiny. It was deemed that everything was safely German, and John could travel at ease almost like an inhabitant of the land.

Salzburg looked familiar to him. There had been much to photograph it upon his mind. He remembered the uneasy night he and his uncle had passed there before his flight with Lannes, which had taken him into such a train of vast events. It had been only seven or eight months before but it seemed many times as long. He had felt himself a boy in Vienna, he felt himself a man now. He had been through great battles, he had seen the world in convulsion, his life a dozen times had hung on a hair, and since it is experience that makes a man he was older than most of those twice his age.

He was stopping after his custom at an obscure inn, and in the moonlight he strolled through the little city. In its place among the mountains on both sides of the gray-green river it was full of romance to him, romance colored all the more deeply by memory. Off there among those peaks the *Arrow* had first come for him and Lannes, while here the great Mozart had been born and lay buried. In remoter days Huns had swept through these passes, coming from Asian deserts to the pillage of Europe.

John sat down on a bench in the little square before the cathedral and looked up at the mountains. He knew the exact location in which lay Zillenstein, the ancient seat of the Auersperg race, and he calculated that in two days he could reach it on foot, the lone youth in peasant's garb, pursuing the powerful prince and general, surrounded by retainers and hussars and in the land of his ancestors.

John wondered what had become of his comrades. Was Lannes well, and had he got his message? Were Carstairs and Wharton still alive, and where was Weber? They were questions the solution of which must wait upon the success of his quest, and therefore the answer might never come. But he fiercely put away such a thought. He would succeed! He must succeed!

He was not walking in the dark. He had learned that Auersperg and his people had arrived at Salzburg two days before, and had left after a few hours for Zillenstein. The prince was in excellent health and would not remain at his castle more than a week. Then he would return to the western front, where he was one of the great generals around the Kaiser. He had brought with him two Frenchwomen, spies, who would be imprisoned in the dungeons of Zillenstein until the war was over, if, indeed, they were not shot before. One, it was said, was very young, and beautiful, but she was the more dangerous of the two.

Poor Julie! there was a conspiracy of fate against her, but John shook himself and felt his courage rising anew, powerful, indomitable, invincible. He had come so far alone, and he would rescue her with his single hand! He went back to the inn and sat for a while among peasants and listened to their talk. They knew little of what was passing beyond the Teutonic empires. As usual in Germany and Austria, they accepted what the men higher up told them. They were always winning victories everywhere, and it would be but a short time before the treacherous English, the wicked French and the ignorant Russians were crushed.

John yawned after a while and went to his room. He intended to be fresh and strong the next morning when he started on the last stage of his search, and when the dawn came he was glad to see that it was clear and bright. By noon he was deep among the hills, and so far had answered all questions without arousing any suspicion. But he knew that trouble about his identity was bound to come in time. He could not go on forever, playing the rôle of Jean Castel, a horse-buyer from Lorraine. Lorraine was far away now, and he was beyond his natural range.

And yet his frank young face and smiling eyes were continually making him friends where he expected none. Explanations that might have seemed doubtful coming from others were convincing when he spoke them, and here in this hostile land, where he would have been executed as a spy, his identity known, he was instead helped on his way.

Late in the afternoon, when he was high up on the shoulder of a mountain he came to one of the little wayside shrines that one sees in the Catholic countries of the Old World. A small stream of clear, green water ran almost at the feet of the image, and he knelt and drank. Then he sat down to eat a little bread and sausage from his knapsack, and, while he was there, a middle-aged woman with two young boys also came to the shrine, before which they knelt and prayed. When they rose John politely offered them a portion of his bread and sausage, but they declined it, thanking him, and bringing forth food of their own, ate it.

John saw that the woman's face was very sorrowful, and the boys were grave and thoughtful beyond their years. He knew that they were under the shadow of the war, and his sympathy drew him to them.

"You have other sons, perhaps," he said gently, "and they are with the armies?"

"Alas, yes," she replied. "I have two others. One went to the east to fight the Russians and the other was sent to the west to meet the French. I have not heard from either in three months. I do not know whether they are alive or dead. We go into Salzburg tomorrow to get news of them, if we can."

"I hope they may come back to you," said John simply.

"And you? You are not of Austria."

"No, I came from a land that was French before I was born but which is now German, and under the beneficent rule of the great Kaiser—Lorraine."

"You have indeed made a great journey."

"But it's to help one who needs help. I'd go if it took me to the other side of the world. The errand is sacred."

"Then I wish you Godspeed upon it. You are young, and you have a good face. What you say must be true. I shall pray for you and the happy end of your search."

She uttered words rapidly under her breath. She was a middle-aged and uneducated Austrian woman, but as she prayed and the shadows deepened on the mountains he received an extraordinary impression. A priest had prayed, too, for his success, and the second prayer could not be a mere coincidence. It was one of a chain. His will to succeed was so powerful, and so many others were helping him with the same wish that he could not fail.

CHAPTER X
THE FAIR CAPTIVE

The woman gathered up the remains of the food, crossed herself again before the shrine, and she and her sons prepared to resume the descent of the mountain.

"I thank you for your good wishes," said John. "They may go far."

"And so may yours," she said. "Farewell!"

"Farewell!"

He watched them, walking down the slope, until a turn in the road hid them, and then he resumed his own ascent, slow now, because he had been climbing all day, and he wished to conserve his strength. The night was coming fast, and, if it had not been for the smooth-paved road over which he was walking, he might have fancied himself in a primeval wilderness. The sun was sinking in a sea of red light and peaks and ridges were outlined against it, clear and sharp. Old and thickly inhabited Europe melted away, and the young crusader stood alone and solitary among the mountains.

The road led around a cliff, and far across a valley on the other side he saw Zillenstein, that nest from which the Auerspergs had first ruled and raided. The red light of the setting sun fell upon it, magnifying every battlement and tower, and making them all glow with color. Vast as it was, it seemed even vaster in the red light and in the fire of John's own imagination.

His mind was filled with history and old romance, and it made him think of Valhalla. Here certainly was the dusk of the gods. Auersperg was one of the last representatives of the old order that troubled Europe so much in its going, for to John, a keen and intense lover of freedom and of the career open to all the talents, the present war was in its main feature a death struggle between autocracy and democracy.

He stared at the gigantic ramparts of Zillenstein, as long as the sun endured. He would have given much then to have had a powerful pair of glasses, but no horse-buying peasant could carry such equipment without arousing suspicion.

The day sank into the night and the last tower of Zillenstein was hid by the dusk. Just before going, and, when all the red light had faded, the castle showed huge, black and sinister. But John's soul was not cast down by it. Uncommon situations bred uncommon feelings and impulses. His imaginative mind still retained the impression that all the signs and omens were in his favor, and that the prayers of the righteous availed.

He came out of his dreams, and began to think of his night's lodging. The air was turning cold on the mountain and an unpleasant wind was trying to strike through his clothing, but he still carried his pair of blankets, and he had become hardened to all kinds of weather. He had a good supply, too, of the inevitable bread and sausage, and there was water for the taking.

He turned from the road and walked through a wood higher up the side of the mountain, having caught a gleam of white through the trees and being anxious to ascertain its nature. He found the remains of a small and ancient marble temple—temple he took it to be—and he was sure that it had been erected there perhaps fifteen centuries ago by the Romans. He knew from his reading that they had marched and fought and settled throughout all this region and in almost all of Austria. Marcus Aurelius might have been here, he might even have built the temple itself, and other Roman emperors might have stood in the shadow of its shattered columns.

It was a round temple, like those to Ceres that he had seen in Italy, and while some of the columns had fallen others stood, and a portion of the roof was there. He saw for himself a place under this fragment of a roof and against a pillar.

But he devoted his attention first to supper. A small cold stream flowed from under a rock fifty feet away, and drinking from it now and then he ate his bread and sausage in comfort, and even with a sense of luxury. He was a crusader and he was upborne more strongly than ever by his faith. Alone on the mountain in the darkness everything else had melted away. America was an immeasurable distance from him and the figures of his uncle, Mr. Anson and his young friends of the army became thin shadows.

The moon, full and dominant, came out after a while and silvered the skies. Stars in myriads trooped forth and danced. John felt that they were friendly, that they were watching over him, and once more he saw happy omens. Despite his long walk he was not tired and he enjoyed the deep peace on the mountains. He might have been awed at another time, but now he was not afraid.

Zillenstein, too, came out, bathed in silver, an immense threatening mass set solidly in the shoulder of the opposite mountain, more sinister even in the moonlight than in the sunlight. He wondered how many hundreds of innocent human beings had perished in its dungeons. He had not the slightest doubt that Julie was there, but she at least was safe from everything, save a long imprisonment and a powerful pressure that might compel her to become the morganatic wife of Auersperg. It might be the old story of the drop of water wearing away the stone.

Clouds began to trail slowly up the valley, and Zillenstein faded away again. The long columns of mist and vapor seemed so near that John felt as if he could reach out his hand and touch them.

His day's exertions began to tell now, and the chill of the night deepened. He sought his chosen shelter within the old temple, and lying down on the stone floor wrapped in his blankets, sank fast into sleep. Morning dawned, sharp and clear, and the red sun came out of Asia, turning the huge pile of Zillenstein once more into a scarlet glow, a vast blood-red splotch in the side of the mountain.

He drank at the little stream, then bathed his face, ate breakfast, and, knapsack on back, returned to the road that led down the far side of the mountain. His courage was still high. The crusader of the day before was none the less the crusader this morning, and he whistled soft and happy airs as he descended. He knew that it was a trick that he had caught from General Vaugirard and he wondered where that fat old hero might be now.

But as he walked along he formed his plan. Every general who intends to attack an enemy must choose a method of approach, and the crusader's plan to assail Zillenstein was now quite clear in his mind. His decision brought him the usual relief, following the solution of a doubt, and he intended that his journey that day through the great valley should resemble somewhat a stroll of pleasure.

He whistled at times and at times he sang. He remembered the story, of the faithful troubadour, Blondel, who sought his master, Richard of the Lion Heart, imprisoned somewhere in a castle in Austria, and who, finding him, sang under his window to let him know one loyal friend was there. But Richard, under the light of history, had become merely a barbarous king, cruel to his enemies and unjust to his friends. John felt that his own quest was higher and better.

Toward noon he was in the middle of a valley down which a swift little river flowed. Old men, women and children were at work in the fields preparing for the new crop, and again John's frank eyes and hearty voice won him a welcome. He was a man of Lorraine who had been on the far western front and they welcomed Ulysses on his travels. They said that he was going to Zillenstein at a fortunate time, as the prince had just returned for a space and the great castle was full of people. When so much of the youth of the land was gone away a handy man with horses might obtain work there. The prince used automobiles chiefly, but many horses were employed also.

Once John was compelled to show the German passport. It was of no use in Austria, except as a proof of identity, and good faith, and as such it served him well.

In the afternoon he began to ascend the slope that confined the southern side of the valley, and toward night he drew near to Zillenstein. The view of the castle here was less clear than from the other side of the valley. Patches of pine on the slopes beneath hid many of the towers and battlements, but he saw lights shining from lofty windows, and about the castle were many small houses. He surmised that Zillenstein and its surroundings had not changed much since the Middle Ages. Here was the castle, and below it were the cottages and huts of the peasants and retainers who might be as loyal as ever to the prince whose lineage was more ancient than that of either Hohenzollern or Hapsburg.

Two young hussars riding down the road, their horses' hoofs ringing on the stones, brought back the modern world. They were gay young fellows, smoking cigarettes, their Austrian caps tipped back to let the cool breeze blow upon their foreheads, and they called cheerfully to the strong young peasant who walked slowly up the road. John lifted his cap and answered in a tone that was respectful but not servile.

"You look like one who has traveled far," said the younger of the two, a mere boy.

"From Lorraine," answered John. "My name is Jean Castel, which is French, but I, its owner, am not. My family became German before I was born, and has been so ever since."

"Ah, I see, made German by strength of arms."

"And growing more German every day by will and liking."

"You speak well for a peasant."

"I was a dealer in horses, which took me much over the land and everyone who travels learns. See, here is my passport."

"Why should I look at your passport?"

"Everyone else does. Then why not you?"

"No, I don't want to see it. I take your word for it You couldn't have come so deep into Germany, unless you were one of us. What do you seek at the castle?"

"My trade is gone and I want work with the horses. There must surely be a place on the estate of so great a prince."

"There is, but he wants good men, the very best."

"Let him try me."

"I'll try you now."

The hussar leaped from his horse and asked John to get into the saddle. John had noticed that it was a big brute with a red eye, and every other indication of a wicked temper, but in his earlier youth he had spent a year on a great ranch belonging to his uncle in Montana, and the cowboys had taught him everything. He was quite aware that a dramatic effect would be useful to him now, and he decided to temporize a little in order that the culmination might be greater.

"It has been my business," he said, "to try and sell horses, not to ride them."

Both officers laughed derisively.

"Prince Karl of Auersperg likes bold men around him," said the one who had dismounted, "and he would not care for a hostler who was afraid of his own horses."

John, despite the fact that he had invited it, was stung somewhat by the taunt.

"While I said it was not my business to ride horses I didn't say I couldn't ride them," he replied.

"Then up with you and prove it."

John seized the bridle, and as the great black horse, feeling the touch of an unfamiliar hand, pulled away from him, he made one leap and was in the saddle. He felt in an instant from the fierce quiver running through the mighty frame that he had a demon beneath him. The Austrians, who doubtless had not expected him to accept the challenge, were alarmed and the younger, whose name John afterward learned to be Pappenheim, shouted:

"Jump off! He'll kill you!"

John had no notion of leaving the saddle, either willingly or unwillingly. He believed that after his training by the cowboys he could ride anything, and when he felt the great frame draw itself together he was ready. He saw too that he could make capital. He would impress these volatile Austrians and at the same time he would recommend himself as an expert horsemen to Prince Karl of Auersperg.

The black horse made a series of mighty jumps, any one of which would have sent a novice flying, but the trained rider on his back knew instinctively which way he was going to leap, and swayed easily every time. Then panting, and mad with anger and fury, the horse rushed down the road. John pulled hard on the bridle to keep him from stumbling. He heard the two Austrians behind him shouting, and the one on horseback pursuing, but he did not look back.

When the horse had gone three or four hundred yards he pulled harder on the bit, and gradually turned him about in the road. Then he raced him back up the hill, a most exhausting proceeding for any animal however strong. Then the horse began to jump and kick again, but he could not shake off his incubus. A side glance by John showed that young Pappenheim was standing among the trees by the roadside well out of the way and that the mounted officer had also drawn back among the trees.

He felt that now was the time for his stroke. He knew that the horse was conquered, overcome chiefly by his own struggles, and letting him breathe a little he urged him straight forward in the road toward the castle, which was only a few hundred yards away.

As he emerged from the woods he saw that the road led through the remains of an ancient wall, and across a bridge over a moat which was partly filled up. In the cleared space in front of the wall several soldiers were standing and near them were two hussars. The hussars rode forward, as if they would prevent the flight of the horse, but John urged on his waning spirit and he dashed over the moat and through the wall into the inner precincts of the castle yard, where the animal stopped dead beat and covered with foam.

He slipped from the horse, as a man, who had been sitting in a camp chair in the shadow of a great pine, rose in surprise, and stood looking at him. It was Prince Karl of Auersperg himself, in a uniform of gray and silver, his great brown beard forked and spreading out magnificently. John took off his cap, saluted and despite the fierce beating of his heart stood calmly before him.

"What does this mean?" demanded the prince.

John was saved a reply by young Pappenheim, who came up running.

"It was my fault, Your Highness," he said. "We met him in the road coming to the castle, where he said he wished to be employed as a hostler. I told him to prove his skill by riding my horse, which hitherto has tolerated no one but myself on his back. He rode him like a Cossack, and here he is! The fault, sir, was mine, and I crave the pardon of Your Highness, but this man has proved himself a horseman."

The prince combed his great forked beard with his fingers, and looked at the young peasant with a contemplative eye. John surmised that Pappenheim stood well with him, and would be forgiven.

"The test was, perhaps, severe," he said, "but the young man seems to have endured it well. I might say that in his own little world he has achieved a triumph. Send him to the stables, and tell Walther, the head groom, to give him work."

After the one examining glance he no longer looked at John who had now disappeared from his own world. John had no fear of detection. He had let his semblance of a young beard grow again, and Prince Karl of Auersperg would not dream of his presence there in the mountains of Austria.

"Thanks, Your Highness," he said, again bowing respectfully. A groom took the horse and Pappenheim went with him to the stables, where he recommended him specially to Walther, a stalwart Tyrolean, who was evidently glad to have him, as he was short of help.

"Treat him well. Walther, because he will be of use," said Pappenheim. "He has ridden my own horse and no one but myself has ever done that before."

The Tyrolean's eyes gleamed with wonder and approval.

"Then you must know horses," he said, and put him to work at once in the stables. John toiled with a will. All things still moved as he could wish them to go. The blessings upon his errand that he had received were not without effect. It was true that he was but a stable boy, but he was within the precincts of the castle of Auersperg, and Julie was but a few hundred yards away. He recalled an old line or two, from Walter Scott, he thought;

> And he bowed his pride
> To ride a horse-boy in his train.

As he remembered it, the service had a motive somewhat similar to his own, and he was glad to "bow his pride," because he believed that he would have ample chance to raise it up again. As he went about his work singing and whistling softly to himself, he cast many a glance up at the huge castle.

Truly Zillenstein had been a great fortress. In the old days it must have been impregnable. Much of it was still standing in its ancient strength. John saw that the walls were many feet thick, and that in the older parts the windows were mere slits through which a human body could not pass.

A much more modern addition to the right wing had been built, and John surmised that Prince Karl and his suite lived there. Auersperg might have medieval notions of caste, but he was certain to have modern ideas of luxury.

He worked hard through all the rest of the day. What a lucky thing it was that he had always liked horses, and had spent that year on the western ranch of his uncle! Horses were the same everywhere, and as far as he could see they responded as readily to kind treatment in Europe as in America. The same friendly disposition that won him the favor of people was now winning him the favor of animals, and Walther, who had spent fifty years in the stables, complimented him on his soothing touch. John saw that he had made a new friend, and he meant to use him as a source of information.

He soon learned that Prince Karl would not stay long at Zillenstein. He had come there, partly, to meet several great officers of Austria and confer with them. His position as a Prussian general and a prince of both empires made him the most suitable person for the duty, and Zillenstein, in the heart of Austria, was the best place for the meeting.

Walther, a taciturn man, volunteered so much, but he went no farther, and John, despite his great anxiety, did not ask any questions. He knew that he was a too recent arrival at Zillenstein to be making inquiries without arousing suspicion, and it was better anyhow to go slowly. Late in the afternoon, Walther directed him to saddle and bridle a fine young horse and lead him to the front of the castle.

"One of the young noblemen who was wounded in a great battle in the west has been recovering from his wound at Zillenstein," he said, "and he has been riding every day toward evening. You will hold the horse until he comes, but he is always prompt."

John led the horse, a fine young bay, along a curving road, until he stood before the entrance of the castle. There he waited in silence, but he was using his eyes all the time. He admired the great size and strength of Zillenstein, even in its decayed state, and he was confirmed in his belief that the prince and his suite inhabited the extension of the right wing. Doubtless Julie and Suzanne should be sought there.

While he stood holding the horse one or two soldiers passing gave him scrutinizing looks, and a couple of trim Austrian maids did likewise, smiling at the same time, because John was very good looking, despite his fuzzy young beard. He smiled back at them, as became one of his lowly station who had met with approval, and whispering to each other they passed on. Now, he had two more new friends, and it occurred to him that these maids also might be of use to him in his great quest. He had formed his plan and like a good general he was marshaling every possible force for its success.

While he was thinking about it, the convalescent came, a young officer, trim, slender, in a fine uniform of blue and silver. It was none other than that same lad, Leopold Kratzek, whom he had saved in the fight at the trench. In his surprise John came very near to greeting him by name, but luckily he controlled himself in time.

He noticed that Kratzek was almost entirely recovered. The color in his face was fresh, his walk was firm and elastic, and John was glad of it. He liked the lad whose life he had saved. He recalled, too, that his presence there was not strange. Kratzek was the relative of Auersperg, and it was natural that he should be sent to Zillenstein to recover.

The young Austrian glanced at the new groom, but there was no sign of recognition on his face.

"I have not seen you before," he said.

"No, sir," replied John, "I've just come today. I've been wandering eastward from Lorraine, where I was born, and the Herr Walther has been kind enough to give me work."

"You're the man of whom I heard Pappenheim speak so well. He has been telling us all how a wandering peasant rode that black devil of his."

"I am fortunate in understanding horses."

"Well, you've made a friend in Pappenheim."

John gave him the reins and Kratzek, drawing himself a little stiffly into the saddle, cantered away. John, although not recognized, felt as if he had met a friend again, and Zillenstein seemed less lonely to him.

He watched Kratzek riding down the mountain until the firs and pines hid him, and then, as he turned to go back to the stables, he found the two maids near him, a little forward, and yet a little shy, but wholly curious about the handsome young stranger.

Bearing in mind that the news of the household, even of a huge castle, filtered most often through women, he smiled back at them and said pleasantly in his new German:

"Good morning. May I ask your names?"

One was blond and the other brunette, and the brunette answered:

"We're Ilse and Olga, maids of the household of His Highness, Prince Karl of Auersperg."

"And very pretty maids, too," said John gallantly, as he took off his cap and bowed. "When I look at Ilse I think she is the more beautiful, when I look at Olga I think she is the more beautiful, but when I see them together I think they are equally beautiful."

They giggled and nudged each other.

"You are the man who rode the young count's horse," said Ilse, who took the lead in talk as brunettes usually do, "and I hope you will pardon our forwardness in wishing to look at so wonderful a person."

There was a wicked little glint in her eye, but John only smiled again.

"I was lucky," he said.

"We saw you," said Olga. "We were standing on the edge of the lower terrace when you sprang into the saddle. We were sure you would be killed."

"But we were glad you were not," said Ilse. "We were pleased when we saw you riding the great black horse directly back to the castle. Do you mean to stay here all the time?"

"Where there is so much beauty and wit I should like to remain," replied John with increasing gallantry, still holding his cap in his hands, "but who can tell where he will be a week hence in times like these?"

Again they laughed and nudged each other. Ilse had a shrewd and observant mind.

"Your German has a French accent," she said.

"I was born in a land that was once French—Lorraine—so my blood is French by descent, although I am wholly German in loyalty and in feeling. But I'm not the first person of French blood that you ever saw, am I?"

He asked the question in a careless tone, but he awaited the answer with anxiety.

"Oh, no," replied Ilse. "Many people come to the great castle of Zillenstein. Two Frenchwomen are here now, spies, terrible spies they say, but I can scarce believe it, at least of the young one, Mademoiselle Julie, who is so beautiful, and who speaks to us so gently."

"But it may be true of the other of low degree, the surly Suzanne," said blond Olga.

"At least, they're where they can't get back to France as long as this war lasts," said John, looking up at the formidable castle. "It seems a sad thing to me that women should be spies. It isn't right."

He spoke in his most engaging manner. Again his frank look and attractive smile were winning him friends where he needed friends most. He saw, too, that he was on a subject that interested the maids. Once more fortune was favoring him who wooed her so boldly.

"But," said the blond and substantial Olga, "I think the beautiful Mademoiselle Lannes is in no danger. The prince himself loves her and would marry her. We can see it, can we not Ilse?"

"At least we think it."

"We know it. And His Highness might search Europe and not find a woman more beautiful. She has the most wonderful hair, pure gold, with little touches of copper, when the firelight or the sunlight is deep upon it, and when loosed it falls to her knees. I have seen it."

"And marvelous blue eyes," said Ilse. "A dark blue like the waters of our mountain lakes. Oh, no, the Prince of Auersperg can never punish her!"

John laughed.

"This French spy seems more dangerous as a captive than free," he said.

"That is so," said Ilse, seriously. "If Prince Karl of Auersperg, powerful as he is, were disposed to punish her, the others would not let him."

"What others?"

"The young Count Kratzek, the relative of the prince. He loves her, too, and he scarcely seeks to hide it. And Count Pappenheim, who is of kin to the emperor, worships her beauty."

"The lady must be Psyche herself," said John.

But not knowing who Psyche was, they shook their heads.

"And that is not all," continued Ilse. "A Prussian prince was here, a fine and gallant man, tall and young. He, too, is at the feet of the lovely Mademoiselle Julie. I heard him say that he had seen her before she was brought to Zillenstein."

John's pulses suddenly beat hard. He knew instinctively the identity of the Prussian prince, but he asked quietly:

"What was the man from Prussia called?"

"Prince Wilhelm von Arnheim. I was present when he first saw here the beautiful Mademoiselle Julie. He bent before her and kissed her hand, as if she were a princess herself. The look that he gave her was full of love, and it was also most respectful. I, Ilse Brandt, know."

"I've no doubt of it, because you've received many such looks yourself, beautiful Ilse," said John.

"There she is now! At the window!" exclaimed Olga.

John looked at once, and his heart leaped within him. Julie stood framed in a window, high up in the new part of the castle. The light seemed to fall upon her, as one turns it in a flood upon a picture, and her figure was in the center of a glow that brought out the coppery touches in the wonderful golden hair, that was the marvel of everybody. She seemed to be gazing wistfully over the misty mountains, and John's heart was full of yearning.

"I can't believe," said Ilse, "that she is a spy or has ever been a spy. She has not the look, nor the manner. When the Prince von Arnheim was here they gave a great dinner, and Prince Karl bade her come to it. I took her a beautiful dress of his niece, who is away in Vienna. I thought she would refuse, but she said that she would come as Prince Karl requested. I was her maid, I dressed her and she was very beautiful. She went to the dinner, and the aged Lady Ursula, the cousin and dependent of the prince, sat with her."

"What happened?" asked John in a low voice.

"I think it was their intention at first to remind her that she was a prisoner. Prince Karl is a hard and stern man, and he would bend her to his will, but the Prince Wilhelm frowned upon them all, and the Count Kratzek was also most respectful."

"They had brought her to complete their triumph and instead the triumph was hers," John could not keep from saying.

"It is so," admitted Ilse. "They were abashed before her, and at the last when they drank a toast to the glorious victory of our German race, she withheld her glass, and then, taking a sip of the wine, she said she wished with all her heart, as long as it should beat in her body, for the triumph of France. That, too, I saw, and while I do not wish for the triumph of France it was thrilling to see but one and a girl defying so many strong men."

"I wish I had been there to see," murmured John.

"What did you say?" asked Olga.

"That only a very brave woman could have done such a thing."

"She is brave. She does not fear any of them, and the woman Suzanne with her has a tiger's temper."

"But she loves the young mademoiselle. One can see that," said Ilse, "and she will guard her."

John wished to know what had become of Antoine, but he did not dare ask pointed questions. Julie left the window presently and the light went with her. The sunlight was dying now on the eastern mountains, but a great happiness came to him. He had found her. The footsteps of the crusader had been guided aright. His star had led him on through many dangers, and his spirit was high with hope.

It was, perhaps, well that the growing twilight kept Ilse and Olga from seeing the glow in his eyes, but it was time for the two to go, and, laughing and supporting each other in what they considered a mild flirtation, they disappeared within the castle. John sent a smile after them. They were good girls and he knew that he had made two valuable friends who would tell him all that was happening to Julie in Zillenstein.

He went back to the stables and plunged anew into his work with a zeal and skill that aroused the admiration of Walther. His knowledge of horses was most useful to him now, and, as he had also learned much about automobiles in his campaigning, he volunteered to help with them too. He saw the great limousine in which the prince himself had traveled, and he helped two of the hostlers to clean it. Walther growled as he looked on.

"When I was a lad," he said, "the magnificent, living horse was king at Zillenstein. Now it's a machine that can't either think or feel."

"We can't fight the times, Herr Walther," said John, cheerfully. "The automobile like the railway has come to stay."

"I suppose so, but the noble Count Kratzek returns. Take his horse."

John went forward and held the bridle after the young Austrian had dismounted. Kratzek had a fine color from his ride, and he seemed to John to be completely well of his wound. He handed the young peasant who was holding his horse half a krone, and then walked briskly into the castle.

John put the little silver piece in his pocket, after having touched his cap, and led the horse into the stable. He did not feel humiliated. He found something humorous in receiving a tip of ten cents from the man whose life he had saved. He unsaddled the horse, put him in his stall, rubbed him down, and came forth to receive the unqualified praise of Walther.

"You, Castel," he said, "you're a fiend for work. I can see that. Most of my men look upon work as an enemy. They run from it and hide from it. Now, come you to the kitchen and you shall eat well in reward."

The great kitchen for the servants and retainers, who were many, was in the basement of the castle and John, his appetite sharp from the day's work, ate bountifully. The obvious fact that he had already won the regard of Walther, a man of importance, inspired respect for him, and once the brunette Ilse, flitting through the kitchen, gave him a glance of approval.

He slept that night in a little room above the horses, but first he saw the moon rise over Zillenstein, the valley and the mountain, a vast panorama, white and cold. He did not know what his next step was to be. He did not know how he was to communicate with Julie, but he had an implicit confidence in the Providence that had guided him so far and so well.

Three days went by and he did not yet find the way, but he saw Julie once more at the window and yet another time walking on the terrace in front of the castle accompanied by Suzanne. He was walking Pappenheim's restive horse back and forth and he was not a hundred feet from her, but he knew no sign to make. The air was cold then, and she was wrapped in the long, dark red cloak that he knew. A hood also of dark red covered her head, but tiny curls of the marvelous golden hair escaped from it, their glowing color deepening by contrast the pallor of her lovely face. Again John's heart, overflowing with pity and love, yearned for her.

The crusader worships that which he seeks. John had come to the end of his search, but apparently the way of rescue was as hard as ever. He saw her, but he could not speak to her, and there was no way to let her know that he was near. Suzanne, dark, grim and powerful, walked a step or two behind her, watching over her with a love that was ready for any sacrifice. John felt a deep respect for this faithful and taciturn woman of Normandy, and he was devoutly glad that she was there to be a comfort and support to Julie in these trying days.

As John walked the horse up and down, the maid, Ilse, passing on an errand, stopped and spoke to him.

"It's the French spy and her maid," she said. "They allow her to take the air twice a day upon the terrace. I can't think that she is merely a spy. It must be something political, too high for such as you and me to understand. Perhaps she is a great French lady who is held as a hostage. Do they do such things in war now, Jean Castel?"

"I think so."

"Prince Karl sends her flowers this morning. See, Olga comes with them, but she does not speak French, nor do I. She will not know from whom they come."

Often the great opportunity appears when it is least expected. A trifle may open the way and John, quick as lightning, saw and seized his chance. Throwing the reins of the now quiet horse over a pillar he said:

"I know French, as I come from Lorraine. Let me take them."

Without waiting for her assent he took the flowers from the hand of the willing Olga and walked boldly across the terrace to Julie, who was looking over the valley. Bending the knee he offered the flowers, saying:

"Prince Karl sends you these, Mademoiselle Lannes."

She started a little at the sound of his voice and he continued in a lower tone:

"Julie, I've come across Germany for you. Make no sign. I'm here to save you. I'm a groom in the prince's stables!"

He saw the delicate color like the first flush of dawn overspread her face, and a light that had never shone for any other spring into her eyes. All the hardships that he had endured, all the dangers that he had run were as nothing now.

"John," she exclaimed, in a voice tremulous with fear for him, not for herself, "you must leave Zillenstein at once! Your life is not safe here for a moment!"

"When I go you go with me," he said.

They had spoken rapidly in whispers and not even Suzanne had noticed. Accustomed now to the servants in the castle she had merely seen a young peasant bringing flowers from the prince to her mistress. They had been brought before and there was nothing unusual about it.

"Tell the prince that I thank him," said Julie, aloud, but in indifferent tones.

John bowed and walked back toward the horse, his heart beating hard with triumph and joy.

CHAPTER XI
THE EFFICIENT HOSTLER

When John Scott returned to the stables his pulses were still throbbing with joy and he trod the grass of the Elysian Fields. Young love is pure and noble, a spontaneous emotion that has nothing in it of calculation, and the wild and strange setting of his romance merely served to deepen his feelings.

He was the young crusader again, a knight coming to rescue his lady from the hands of the infidels. He had made the impossible possible. He had seen her and spoken with her, and despite his peasant clothes and his position of a menial that he had willingly taken, she had known him at once. He had seen the deep color flushing into her face and the light like the first arrow of dawn spring into her eyes, and he knew that he had not come in vain.

He put so much vigor into his work, and he whistled and sang, low but so joyously that the stolid Walther took notice.

"Why are you so happy, you Castel?" he asked.

"I've seen the sun, Herr Walther."

"There is nothing uncommon about that. The sun has risen every morning for a million years and more."

"But not this sun, Herr Walther. It never rose before and it's the brightest and most glorious of them all."

Walther looked up at the sun. It was in truth bright, casting a golden glow over all the mountains, but he saw nothing new about it.

"It's a fine sun, as you say," he said, "but it's the same as ever. Ah, you're French after all — in blood, I mean, I don't question your loyalty — and you see things that are not. Too much imagination, Castel. Quit it. It's not wholesome."

"But I'm enjoying it, Herr Walther. Imagination is a glorious thing. You see the same sun that I do in so far as our eyes are able to look upon it, but you do not see it in the same way. It appears far more splendid and glorious to me than it does to you. Our eyes are mirrors and mine reflect today with much more power and much more depth of color than yours do."

Walther stared at him, comprehending but little of what he had said, and shook his head slowly.

"Your French blood is surely on top now, Castel," he said. "I should call you a little mad if you didn't work so hard and with such a good heart."

"Ah, well, if we enjoy our madness, pray let us remain so."

Walther shook his head again, and walked away some distance where he stopped, and looked long at his new helper who toiled with uncommon diligence but who whistled and sang in a low but happy manner as he toiled. A new thought was slowly making its way into his stolid brain. A man might have a madness, and be none the worse for it. Well, every one to his own madness.

John had heard from Ilse that Julie walked on the terrace twice every day, once in the morning and once in the afternoon, and he strove so to arrange his work that he might see her again that afternoon. Knowing that he was already a favorite with Walther he made many suggestions. This horse or that needed exercise, and one that had been a favorite with the prince before he had taken to the automobile, and that even now was often ridden by him, would be all the better for sun and air. Walther agreed with him and John deftly postponed the time until about four o'clock, the warmest and brightest part of the afternoon, when he thought it most likely that Julie would come again.

He led the horse back and forth along a road that led from the stables to a forest hanging on the slope, being in sight of the terrace about half the way. But the terrace was bare and it was not until he had made three or four turns that Julie with her following shadow, Suzanne, appeared. Again John's heart beat heavily, and the hand that held the bridle trembled. He could not help it. His mind, highly sensitive and imaginative, was nevertheless powerful and tenacious to the last degree. And he was there in the heart of old romance. The vast castle, gray and sinister, loomed above him, but beyond was the golden light on the mountains.

He did not try to attract her attention, but, walking calmly on with the horse, poured all his soul into the wish that she would look his way. He had not the remotest belief in the supernatural as he told himself again, but he continued to wish it with all his power and strength, and presently her gaze turned toward the young peasant and the horse who were walking slowly up and down the road. He was too far away to read her face, but his fond fancy told him that she rejoiced again to see him there.

She looked at him a little while, but she made no sign or signal. He expected none. She would know too well that it might create suspicion and from some one of the many windows of the castle jealous eyes might be watching.

She advanced to the edge of the terrace with her faithful shadow still close behind her, and then the prince came. He was in a white and silver uniform of Austria, a magnificent figure of a man, despite his middle years, and his great brown beard gave him a majestic aspect. But John knew that his eyes were set close together and that the soul behind them was unscrupulous and cruel.

He saw Auersperg take off his gorgeous hat and bow low before the young Julie. Then they walked together on the terrace, the dark shadow of Suzanne following, but further behind now.

John's heart was filled with a fierce and consuming rage. The presence of Auersperg, magnificent, triumphant, powerful, a medieval baron here in the most medieval of all settings, a very monarch indeed, brought him back to earth. What could he do alone in the face of so much might? What could Julie herself do, helpless, before so much pressure? And, after all, from his point of view and from the point of view from his class, Auersperg was making her a great offer, one that nobles in the two empires would hold to be most honorable. For the first time he felt a tremor of doubt, and then he stilled it as base and unworthy. The very word "morganatic" was repulsive to him. It implied that the man stooped, and that the woman surrendered something no real wife could yield. Julie, whose blood was the blood of the great republican marshal, would never submit to such a wrong.

John presently saw someone standing on the steps of the terrace, and as he turned with the horse, he beheld a wild and jealous face. It was young Kratzek, and he was watching Auersperg and Julie. He was only a lad, this Austrian noble, but John's heart felt a touch of sympathy. A common love made them akin and he knew that Kratzek's love like his own was the love of youth, high and pure. He felt neither hate nor jealousy of the Austrian.

His eyes went back to Julie and Auersperg. Their faces were turned toward him now and he could see that it was the prince who talked and that Julie listened, saying but little. The thud of hoofs on the road into the valley came to him and Pappenheim, on his great black horse, galloped into view. But he pulled to a walk when he saw the two on the terrace, and John smiled to himself in grim irony. Pappenheim also loved the ground upon which the young Julie walked. Von Arnheim and von Boehlen should be there, too, and then the jealous circle would be complete.

Kratzek presently walked away, and Pappenheim rode slowly past the castle and out of sight. Julie turned from the prince and looked fixedly for a little while in John's direction. He felt that she meant it as a sign, and he was eager to reply in some way, but prudence held him. Then she went into the castle and Auersperg was left alone on the terrace.

John saw that Prince Karl of Auersperg was very thoughtful. He walked slowly back and forth, his figure magnified in the sun's glow, and now and then he thoughtfully stroked his great brown beard. He seemed to John more than ever out of place. His time was centuries ago among the robber barons. In such a group he would not have been the worst, but in his soul John wished that the hour for all such as he had come. If the great war struck that dead trunk from the living body of the human race it would not be fought wholly in vain.

He went into the castle after a while, his walk slow and thoughtful, and John returned with the horse to the stables. All the rest of the day, he worked with such diligence and effect that Walther bade him rest.

"You may go about the castle as much as you please," he said, "and you may enter the part set aside for the servants, but you must stop there. Nor can you go beyond the immediate castle grounds. If you try it you risk a shot from the sentries."

"I've no wish to be shot and so I'll not risk it," said John, with the utmost sincerity, and after bathing his face and hands, he strolled through the grounds of Zillenstein, his course soon and inevitably leading him toward the addition to the right wing from the windows of which lights were shining. Yet the grounds outside were heavy with shrubbery, and, keeping hidden in it, he advanced farther and farther, eager to see.

He was not yet twenty yards from the walls and he saw human figures passing before the windows. Then a dark form presently slipped from a small door and stood a moment or two on the graveled walk, as if undecided. John felt the pulses beating hard in his temples. He knew that stalwart figure. It was none other than the grim and faithful Suzanne and, daring all, he went to the very edge of the shrubbery, calling in a loud whisper:

"Suzanne! Suzanne!"

She stood attentive, glanced about, and, seeing that no one observed her, came to the edge of the deep shadow.

"Suzanne! Suzanne!" called John again. "It is I, John Scott! Have you any message for me from Mademoiselle Julie?"

She looked again to see that none was near, and then stepped boldly into the shrubbery, where John seized her arm half in entreaty and half to hurry her.

"O, Suzanne! Suzanne!" he repeated, with fierce insistence. "Have you any word for me?"

They were completely in the heavy shadow now, between the short clipped pines, where no one, even but a few feet away, could see, and before replying she looked at him, her grim face relaxing into a smile. She had always watched him before with a sort of angry jealousy, but John believed that he now read welcome and gladness in her eyes.

"Suzanne! Suzanne!" he repeated, his insistence ever growing stronger. "Is there no word for me?"

"Aye," she said, "my mistress bids me tell you that she is grateful, that she understands all you have risked for her sake, that she can never repay you sufficiently for your great service, and that she feels safer because you are near."

"Ah," breathed John, "it is worth every risk to hear that."

"But she fears for you. She knows that you are in great danger here. If they discover who you are, you perish at once as a spy. So she bids me tell you to go away. It is easy to escape from here to the Italian frontier. She would not have you lose your life for her."

"Is it because my life is of more value to her than that of any other man? Oh, tell me, I pray you?"

Another of her rare smiles passed over the grim face of the woman.

"It is a question that Mademoiselle Julie alone can answer," she said. "But when she went to her room she wept a little and her tears were not those of sorrow."

"Oh, then, Suzanne, she is indeed glad that I am here. Tell her that I came for her, and that I will not go away until she goes too."

"She is in no great danger here; she is a prisoner, but they treat her as a guest, one of high degree."

"Auersperg would force her to marry him."

Suzanne smiled once more, but gravely.

"The prince would marry her," she said, "and he is not the only one who wishes to do so. But fear not. Auersperg cannot force her to marry him. She is of the same tempered steel as her brother, the great Monsieur Philip. Were she a man as he is, she would dare as much as he does, and being a woman she will dare in a woman's way none the less."

"And the others, Kratzek and Pappenheim, and von Arnheim if he should come, they are young and brave and true! Might she not, as the only way of escape from the high-handed baron, marry one of them?"

For the fourth time Suzanne smiled. Never before had she permitted herself that luxury so many times in a month, but there was an odd glint in this latest smile of hers, which gave to her face a rare look of softness.

"Nor will she marry any of them," she said, "although they are brave and honest and true and love her. Mademoiselle Julie has her own reasons which she does not tell to me, but I know. She will not marry Prince Karl of Auersperg. She will not marry Prince Wilhelm von Arnheim, she will not marry Count Leopold Kratzek, she will not marry Count Maximilien Pappenheim. Do I not know her well, I who have been with her all her life?"

And once more that smile with the odd glint in it passed over her stern face. But John in the thickening dusk could not see it, although her low earnest voice carried conviction.

"Tell her for me, will you, Suzanne," he said, "that I think I can take her from the castle of Zillenstein. Tell her, too, that I am in little danger in my peasant's clothes. I have been face to face with the prince himself and he has shown no sign of recognition, nor has Count Kratzek who was my prisoner once. Tell her that I will not go. Tell her that my heart is light because she fears for my safety and, O Suzanne, tell her that I will watch over her the best I can, until all of us escape from this hateful castle."

"It is much to tell. How can I remember it alt?"

"Then tell her all you remember."

"That I promise. And now it's time for me to go back. We cannot risk too much."

She turned away, but John had another question to ask her. His heart smote him that he had not thought of Picard.

"Your father, Suzanne?" he said. "I have not heard of him. Is he here?"

"They left him a prisoner at Munich. Doubtless he will escape and he, too, will reach Zillenstein."

"Tell Mademoiselle Julie that her brother did not come to the appointed meeting at Chastel, because he was wounded. Not badly. Don't be alarmed, Suzanne. He'll be as well as ever soon."

"Then he, too, will come to Zillenstein. You are not the only one who seeks, Monsieur Scott."

"But I am the first to arrive. Nothing can take that from me."

"It is true. Now I must hasten back to the castle. If I stay longer they will suspect me."

She slipped from the shrubbery and was gone, and, John, afire with new emotions, strolled in a wide circuit back to the stables.

A week went by. Twice every day he saw Julie on the terrace, but no word passed between them, the chance never came. But the hosts of the air were at work. The invisible currents were passing between the girl on the terrace who was treated like a princess and the young peasant who walked the horses in the road.

"Be not afraid. I have a strength more than my own to save you," came on a wave of air.

"I fear not for myself, only for you lest they discover you," came the answering wave.

"I love you. You are the most beautiful woman in the world and the bravest. It's cause for pride to risk death for you."

"I know that you are here for me. I knew that you would come, when I saw you in Metz. I know that under your peasant's garb you are a prince, more of a real prince than any Auersperg that ever lived."

John was outside of himself. He felt sometimes as if he had left his body behind. The spirit of the crusader was still upon him, and in sight of his beloved, the prize that he had reached but not yet won, he cast aside all thought of danger or failure and awaited the event, whatever it might be, with the supreme confidence of youth. It is but truth to say that he was happy in those days, filled with a stolen delight, all the sweeter because it was stolen under the very eyes of the medieval baron, lord almost of life and death, who was master there.

He steadily advanced in the good graces of Walther. No other such industrious and skillful groom had appeared at Zillenstein in many a day, and he rapidly acquired dexterity also with the automobiles. None could send them spinning with more certainty along the curving mountain roads. He practiced with diligence because he had a vague premonition that all this knowledge would be of use to him some day.

Pappenheim went away, but returned after four days. John fancied that he had been in Vienna, but he knew the magnet that had brought him back. He saw the young Austrian's eyes flame more than once when Julie appeared in her favorite place on the terrace. And yet John neither hated nor feared him.

Kratzek was well enough to go back to the battle front, but he lingered. John did not know what excuses he gave, but he was there, and his eyes, too, burned when Julie passed.

Often in the evening he watched for the grim Suzanne and the word that she would bring, but she did not come. Day by day he saw her, the long black shadow behind her mistress, but she never looked toward him, however intensely he wished it.

The prince went forth occasionally, but he always used an automobile and he was never gone longer than a day. John wondered why he remained so long at Zillenstein, knowing that he was a general in the German army and a man of weight at the battle front. He concluded at last that he must be waiting there for a conference of some kind between important men of Germany and Austria. He had heard through the gossip in the castle that Italy was threatening war on Austria, and the Teutonic powers must now face also toward the southwest. Much might be decided at Zillenstein.

Ilse and Olga were still his best sources of information. Very little that passed in the castle missed their shrewd inquiring minds, and they had found in the handsome young peasant from Lorraine one with whom they liked to talk. He jested and laughed with them but there was a certain reserve on his part that they could not break down but which drew them on. He would not flirt with them. None was readier than he for light words and airy compliments, but nothing that he said permitted either of the trim young Austrian girls to think that he might become a lover.

"I think, Herr Johann," said Ilse, "that you have left behind in Lorraine a maid whom you love."

"It may be so," said John vaguely. "I saw one in Metz whom anybody could love."

"What was she like?" asked Ilse, eagerly.

"A skin the tint of the young rose, eyes like the dawn on a summer morning, hair a shower of the finest spun silk, and a walk like that of a young goddess."

"It's beautiful, but it doesn't describe; what was the color of her hair and eyes?"

"I don't know. They dazzled me so much that I merely remember their loveliness and glory."

"It can't be!" exclaimed Ilse, who did not walk in Elysian paths. "You jest with us. You recall her hair and eyes."

John shook his head impressively.

"The French prisoner, the one they call a spy, Mademoiselle Lannes, is the most beautiful woman I've ever seen," said blond Olga, "but no one could look at her without remembering the color of her hair and eyes, such a marvelous gold and such a deep, dark blue."

"His Highness, Prince Karl, remembers them well," said Ilse.

"But not better than the young Count Kratzek," said Olga.

"Nor better than Count Pappenheim."

"And yet they're going to send her away."

"It's because the generals and princes are coming for the great council and they wouldn't have more to fall in love with her."

"And it might give even Prince Karl trouble to answer questions why she is here."

John's pulses began to beat heavily despite all his efforts at calmness and he turned his face away that they might not see the eager light in his eyes. When he had mastered himself sufficiently to use a quiet voice he asked:

"When is this great council of which you speak?"

"In three or four days," replied Ilse. "We hear that many Serene Highnesses are coming from both Berlin and Vienna."

"And the French girl is to be carried away before they come?"

"She goes the day after tomorrow with the dark woman, Suzanne, to the hunting lodge of His Highness, higher in the mountains."

Then with a frightened gesture she clapped her hand upon her mouth.

"You will say nothing of it, Herr Johann?" she pleaded. "It is a secret from all but a few, and His Highness doubtless would punish us terribly if he knew that we told."

"You can trust me, Ilse," said John earnestly. "I would not bring trouble upon you or Olga. Besides, what is it to me?"

He sought by indirect questions to learn more from them, but they would not continue, seeming to be afraid that they had already said too much. Then he turned casually from the subject, lest he rouse suspicion, and spoke of his horses. But all the while he was searching his mind, as one looks for a treasure, to discover how he could follow Julie and Suzanne to their new abode.

He gathered from Walther that the hunting lodge was higher in the mountains in the depths of a great forest, about six leagues from

Zillenstein where there was much big game. In times of peace the prince frequently went there, and a good automobile road led to the lodge, although in winter the snow was often so deep that the place was inaccessible.

Late that afternoon the hoofs of horses beat steadily on the road leading from the valley up to Zillenstein. John from a coign of vantage saw approaching a young man in a gray German uniform, followed by four hussars, also in German gray. Anyone who came to Zillenstein was of interest, and as John looked the leading figure became familiar. Doubt soon changed to certainty. He knew the swing of the broad shoulders and the high pose of the head. It was the young prince, von Arnheim.

"And so they all gather," said John to himself.

He was swept by the little shiver that one often feels when influenced suddenly by a powerful emotion. Fate or chance had a wonderful way of bringing about strange things. He had seen it too often not to know. He was sure in his heart now that von Boehlen too would come some time and somehow.

He looked at the terrace. Julie and Suzanne had appeared there in the last few minutes, and they were gazing at the gallant figure of young von Arnheim who was now so near. The prince himself, when he saw Julie, sprang from his horse, ran lightly up the steps, and bending low over her hand, kissed it. Nor did John feel jealousy or hate of him.

He was glad that von Arnheim had come. He was sure that Julie did not love him and never would, but he was a brave and honest man who would do no wrong. Julie was safer from insult with him near. To the rank of Prince Karl of Auersperg he could oppose a rank the equal of his own.

He was too far away to hear their words or even to note their faces, but he saw the young prince talk with her for a little space and then go into the castle, doubtless to notify Auersperg of his arrival. Julie as her eyes roved about the great panorama of mountain and valley saw John, and the wireless messages of their eyes passed and repassed again.

"I know that you are watching and risking your life for me," hers said.

"Gladly," his replied.

"I like Prince Wilhelm von Arnheim, but it's liking, not love."

"I wish to believe it and do."

Then the little waves of air were stilled, as she went back into the castle, doubtless because she feared to arouse suspicion, and John returned to his work with Walther, convinced that he must form some plan now. Von Arnheim must merely be the vanguard of the council, and Julie might be sent away earlier than Ilse had announced. He must contrive a way to follow.

That night he lurked once more in the shrubbery. He had been there nearly every night, hopeful that Suzanne would pass again, but not until tonight did she come. The tall figure, swathed almost to the eyes in a heavy cloak, came down the terrace to the walk, and John whistled low a note of a French folksong. He had merely hoped that she would stop a moment or two to listen, and the little device succeeded. She paused and looked at the black mass of the shrubbery.

"Suzanne! Suzanne!" called John, his voice showing all the intenseness of his anxiety.

"Monsieur Scott," she said in a loud whisper.

"Yes, Suzanne, here behind the bushes! I must have word with you!"

Silently she stepped into the impenetrable shadows and John eagerly seized her hand.

"Your mistress, Mademoiselle Julie," he whispered eagerly, "she does not break down with the suspense and anxiety? She still hopes?"

"You need not fear for her courage, Monsieur Scott. Did I not tell you that she had a heart of steel, even the same as that of her great brother. I should not tell it to you, but she has never despaired since you came."

John's fingers closed convulsively upon the large muscular hand of Suzanne and in the darkness the woman's grim face relaxed into a smile.

"You are holding my hand not that of Mademoiselle Julie," she said.

"Your words bring me such joy, Suzanne, that I forgot, but I must speak to your mistress."

"You cannot. It is impossible. She is watched more closely than ever."

"But there is news that she must know! Then you must tell it to her!"

"What news? You surely don't mean that they will try her on this ridiculous charge of being a spy!"

"No, not that, Suzanne, but they're preparing to send her and you away."

"And glad we both will be to leave this hateful castle of Zillenstein."

"But it's not that you will fare better. There will be no chance of freedom now. You are to be sent into the higher mountains in the wilderness to a hunting lodge belonging to Auersperg. You will be hidden from all but a few of his most trusted followers."

"Then we're not afraid. We shall even be glad to go there, anywhere from this terrible place. We do not fear the woods, my mistress and I. I can think they're more friendly than those old stone walls above us."

"But tell her this, Suzanne, I pray you, that I shall follow her there."

"How?"

"I don't yet know, but I shall find a way. Tell her, Suzanne, that I'll never leave her so long as I'm alive."

The eyes of the grim woman softened singularly, as she gazed in the dusk at the young man. A devotion such as his, a devotion so evident, would have moved a heart of stone. Her young mistress was dearer than anyone else in the world to her, dearer than her own father, and her stern spirit relaxed when she saw that another could love her in a different way, but as well.

"I'll tell her," she said, "but I tell you that 'tis needless. She knows already that wherever she goes you will follow. Does that bring any comfort to your soul, Mr. Scott?"

"Aye, Suzanne, it fills it with thankfulness. Don't forget to tell her that she will go soon. Von Arnheim, Pappenheim and Kratzek are her friends, but they can't prevent it if they would. It may be too that they will not know when or where she goes."

"She shall hear everything you say and, remember, that she has a brave heart. She has less fear for herself than for you."

She slipped away in the darkness and John went back to his own little place over the stables where he passed a night that was all but sleepless thinking over his problem and finding no good solution. He meant to follow Julie and Suzanne in any event to the hunting lodge, but it was not sufficient merely to follow. He must appear in some capacity that would permit him to be of service. And yet Providence was working for him at that moment.

Prince Karl of Auersperg in his magnificent modernized apartments in the huge castle was also troubled by an inability to sleep. Hitherto in his fifty or more years of life he had always got what he wanted. His blood was more ancient than that of either Hohenzollern or Hapsburg. The Auerspergs had been princes of the Holy Roman Empire for a thousand years and now he was a prince of both Teutonic empires and a general of the first rank in the army of Germany. His wealth was so vast that he scarcely knew the extent of his own lands and here in Zillenstein he could maintain the power and state that appertained to a baron of the Middle Ages.

A mind that has only to wish for a thing to get it becomes closed in fifty years. It mistakes desire for right. It regards opposition as sacrilege. Other minds that differ from it are wicked because they differ. The thick armor of Prince Karl's self-complacency had been pierced as it were by a tiny needle that stung, however tiny, as if its point were laden with poison.

He, the omniscient and omnipotent, had been defied and by whom? A mere slip of a girl! A child! She was not even of his own race! But perhaps it was this very defiance that made him wish for her all the more. He loved her as he had never loved that long-dead wife, a plain princess who always thought what she was told to think.

But he would take Julie in all honor as his wife. He could not make her a princess but he could make her a countess, and he would clothe her in a golden shower. There had been hundreds of morganatic marriages. They implied no disgrace. Noblewomen themselves had been glad to make them. And yet she had refused. Nothing could move her. She had not even flinched a particle when he had threatened her otherwise with death as a spy, although the threat was merely words on his lips and had no abiding place in his heart. She was most beautiful then, when the defiant fire flashed in her dark blue eyes and the sunshine coming through a tall stained glass window made deep red tints in her wonderful golden hair. It was maddening to think of her, just a child turning into a woman, and wholly in his power defying him as if he were some humble lieutenant and not the mighty Prince Karl of Auersperg.

He rose and walked angrily back and forth. Now and then he went to a window and looked out at the dusky panorama of valley, mountain and shaggy forest. As far as he could see and farther it was all his and yet he was powerless in the matter that now concerned him more than all others. She was his prisoner, and yet she was as free as air. Her soul and her heart were her own, and he could not reach either. He knew it. That knowledge like the little poisoned needle had punctured the triple-plate of his complacency and pride and left him no relief from pain, a pain that would have become intolerable had he known that of all the bars that stood between her and him the one that nothing could move was a young peasant in his employ, who watered and fed horses, and who often led them up and down the road within his plain view.

And yet knowing what he did, knowing that she would not marry him, he had no thought to give her up. Hope will often spring anew in the face of absolute knowledge itself, and deep in his heart a belief would appear now and then that he might yet break her to his wish. He knew that von Arnheim, Pappenheim and Kratzek knelt at the same shrine and he laughed harshly to himself because he was sure that they knelt in vain. They were young, handsome, attractive, men of the world, men whom any girl might love but she did not love any of them. He knew the signals, and Julie certainly hung out none for von Arnheim, nor for Kratzek nor for Pappenheim.

He ran his fingers through his great brown forked beard, just such a beard as many a robber baron might have worn, and thought deeply of what he should do with her, before the great council of princes and generals assembled in his castle. She must not be there then. Awkward questions might be asked, but if she were well hidden no trouble could befall. Von Arnheim or Kratzek or Pappenheim might speak, but any words of his would outweigh all of theirs and that term of a spy was wonderfully convenient.

But he wished only himself to know where Julie had gone. He wanted no tattle and gossip about the castle and where there were so many servants and followers it could not be prevented unless they were kept in ignorance. It would be best to use a stranger, one who was known but little at Zillenstein, and he recalled such a man. Second thought confirmed first thought and his decision was made.

CHAPTER XII
THE HUNTING LODGE

John passed a troubled night. He could not yet see his way to follow Julie and Suzanne to the hunting lodge in the manner he wished, and the signs were multiplying that they would soon go. He had no doubt that the arrival of von Arnheim would hasten their departure. Auersperg at such a time could not tolerate the attitude of the young prince toward Julie and he would avail himself of what he considered his feudal rights to send her somewhere into the dark at the quickest possible moment.

But Providence was working for John. His courage and skill which tempted fate were winning new points in his great battle. Walther told him a little after noon that he was to take him into the presence of the august Prince Karl himself. In some manner he had fallen under the favorable eye of His Highness who was about to assign him to an important duty. It was an honor that seldom fell to one so young and ignorant and he hoped that he would conduct himself in a manner to reflect credit upon his superior and instructor, Walther.

John gave his faithful promise but he wondered what the prince could want with him personally and he did not look forward to the interview with confidence. Perhaps his identity and the nature of his errand had been discovered, and it was merely an easy method of making him walk into the lion's jaws, but he could not have refused nor did he wish to do so. His curiosity was aroused and he was willing to meet Auersperg face to face and talk with him.

Cap in hand he followed Walther, also cap in hand, into the interior of the castle. Auersperg sat in a great room overlooking the valley. His chair stood on a slightly raised portion of the floor, and he was enthroned like a sovereign. John, following Walther's example, bowed low before him.

"You may go, Walther," said Auersperg. "I wish to speak alone with this young man."

The master of the stables withdrew reluctantly, consumed by curiosity, and the young peasant in his rough brown dress stood alone before the prince. One seemed the very personification of power and pride, the other of obscurity and insignificance, and yet so strangely does fate play with the fortunes of men that the fickle goddess was inclined toward the peasant in the matter that was nearest to the hearts of both.

John, be it said once more, had not the smallest faith in the supernatural, but it often seemed to him afterward that some power greater than that of man moved the prince to do what he was about to do.

Prince Karl of Auersperg stroked his great brown beard and looked at him long and thoughtfully. John stood before him in the position of an inferior, even a menial, but his heart was far from holding any feeling of inferiority. He was awed neither by the man's rank nor his power nor his ancient blood. He knew that rank could not stop a bullet, nor turn aside a shell. He knew that inherited power could be overthrown by power acquired. There was nothing to make either sacred. He knew that old blood was usually bad blood, that in a thousand years it became a poisonous stream, for the want of fresh springs to purify it. But the head of the young peasant was lowered a little, and the last representative of ten centuries of decadence did not see the gleam of defiance, even of contempt in his eyes.

"You have not been at Zillenstein long," said the prince.

"But a week, Your Highness."

"Walther speaks well of you. The Walthers have served the Auerspergs for centuries and his judgment and loyalty are to be trusted."

John's heart, stanch republican that he was, rose in rebellion at the thought that one family should serve another for a thousand years, but of course he was silent.

"Walther tells me also," resumed the prince, "that you can handle an automobile with skill and that you understand them."

"Herr Walther is very kind to me, Your Highness."

"It was you also who rode the horse of Pappenheim. A great feat. It showed ability and courage. For these reasons I am selecting you to do a deed of trust, one of great importance to me. I am informed by Walther that you are from Lorraine and that your name is Castel."

"Yes, Your Highness, I'm Jean Castel and I was born near Metz, a subject of His Imperial Highness, the German Emperor, the Winner of Victories."

Auersperg smiled and continued to stroke his great brown beard. The young peasant pleased him. Though of humble station and ignorant of the higher world he was undoubtedly keen and intelligent. He was just the man for his task, and fortune had put this useful tool in his hand.

"Go back to the stables, Castel," he said, "and make ready for the high duty to which I am going to assign you. You are to ask no questions and to answer none. Walther will receive instructions to equip you. There is a small gate in the rear wall of the castle. Be there at nine o'clock tonight, and you will then know the work that you have to do. Now go and be silent and, if you fail to be at the gate at the appointed time, that which you like little may happen to you."

John bowed and left the illustrious presence. He was on fire with eagerness and curiosity, and there was apprehension too. Would his trust take him away from Julie at a time when he was needed most? It must not be so, and his faith was strong that it would not be so. Yet his heart was beating very hard and his impatience for the night to come was great. But he strove his utmost to preserve at least the appearance of calmness. He saw that Walther was full of curiosity and now and then asked indirect questions, but John remembering his instructions gave no answer.

Once he passed Ilse and Olga, those twin spirits of mischief and kindness, and they stopped him to speak of the great company that was coming.

"They say it's to be the mightiest array of princes and generals gathered at Zillenstein in a hundred years," said Ilse.

"So I hear," said John.

"And you may be called from the stable to serve in the castle. The man who rode the horse of Count Pappenheim may have to carry a plate and a napkin."

"One can but do his best."

"But it will be a great scene. Perhaps the Kaiser himself will be here, or the old Emperor."

"Perhaps."

"Aren't you eager to see them?" asked Ilse, piqued a little at his lack of curiosity.

"Oh yes," replied John, recalling that he must make believe, "but I've seen the Kaiser several times and once at Vienna I could almost have reached out my hand and touched the old Emperor, as he rode on his way to Schonbrunn."

He passed on and they looked after him. They liked the bearing of this young peasant who was respectful, but who certainly was never servile. But it was in John's mind that however brilliant the great council might be he would not see it. He was surely going from Zillenstein but it was for the future to say whether his absence would be short or long.

While John was at the stables young Kratzek sent for his horse, and John, after his custom, led the animal to him. He had long since ceased to fear discovery by the Austrian, and his immunity made him careless, or it may be that Kratzek's eyes were uncommonly keen that day. He stood beside John, as the young American fixed the stirrup, and some motion or gesture of the seeming peasant suddenly appeared familiar to Kratzek.

Before John had realized what he intended Kratzek suddenly seized him by both shoulders and turning him around, looked straight into his eyes.

"Scott, the American, and a spy!" he exclaimed.

John's heart missed several beats. He knew that it was useless to deny, but in a moment or two he had himself under full control.

"Yes, it's Scott, and I'm in disguise, but I'm not a spy," he said.

"The penalty anyhow is death."

"But you'll not betray me!"

"You saved my life at the great peril of your own."

John was silent. He felt that the time had come for Kratzek to repay, but he would not say so. Now his own look was straight and high, and it was Kratzek's that wavered.

"You pledge your word that you are not seeking to pry into our military secrets?" asked the Austrian at length.

"No such purpose is in my mind at all, and I leave here within twenty-four hours as ignorant of them as I was when I came."

"Then, sir, I do not know you. I never saw you before, and I believe you are the peasant you seem to be."

Kratzek gave him one look of intense curiosity, then sprang upon his horse, and rode away, never looking back.

"There goes a true man," thought John, as he returned to the stable.

Toward evening Walther gave him a heavier suit of clothes which he put on, a great overcoat like an ulster falling almost to his ankles, and an automobile cap and glasses. John could see that he longed to ask questions but he did not do so and John too was silent. A few minutes before nine o'clock Walther told him to go to the small gate in the rear wall.

"Reach it without being seen if you can," he said. "But if you are seen be sure to answer no questions. I would go with you myself, but it's forbidden. You're to be absolutely alone."

John, shrouded in the overcoat and cap and glasses, made his way in the dark to the designated gate.

As he approached the place he saw the black shadow of a heavy bulk against the dusk. No person was yet in sight and there was utter silence. The beat of his heart was so hard that it gave him actual physical pain. The shadow he knew was that of a large closed automobile, but no driver was in the seat, and he did not believe that anybody was inside. Both the silence and the loneliness became sinister.

John slipped forward boldly. It required no divination to know that he was expected to drive this machine. The gate was open and two figures hooded and cloaked came forth. But hooded and cloaked as they were John knew at once the first and slenderer one. The step disclosed the goddess. Julie and Suzanne were going somewhere and he was to take them and there was the prince himself coming through the open gate to give him his instructions.

John's first emotion was one of extraordinary wonder, qualified in a moment or two by humor. Suzanne opened the door of the machine and Julie stepped in. Then the maid followed into the darkness of the interior and closed the door. Truly that variable goddess, Fortune, had chosen to play one of her oddest tricks and for the time, at least, she had chosen him also as her favorite. But with a presence of mind bred in the terrible school of war, he stood waiting ready to receive all her gifts with a thankful heart. "These are two Frenchwomen, prisoners, whom I hold," said the prince in a whisper. "There are reasons of state why they should be taken from Zillenstein and be hidden at my hunting lodge in the mountains. Follow the road that you see there in the moonlight leading up the slope, and on the crest six leagues away you will come to the lodge. You cannot miss it because no other building is there. It lies off the road in a deep pine forest, and here is a letter to my forester Muller who lives there. You and he will hold the women at the lodge until I send for them, and let them speak with nobody, though there is little chance of such a thing on the mountain, where the winter has not yet gone. I hold you responsible for them. Do you understand?"

"Yes, Your Highness," replied John, and he meant it.

"And here is a purse of gold for you. See that you serve me well in this matter, and there is another purse at the end of it. Now go at once!"

John touched his cap, sprang into the seat and started the great automobile up the mountain road. He could not look back, but he knew instinctively that the prince had gone into the castle as silently as he had come from it. And he was alone at the wheel with Julie and Suzanne inside. In very truth chance or fortune had moved the pawns for him in a way that the most skillful player could not have equaled. For a moment, the whole world seemed to swim beneath his feet.

The night was dark and cold, and although the road up the slope showed for a long distance in the moonshine the top of the mountain was wrapped in mist. A wind began to blow and he felt raw and damp to his face. But there was nothing to check his exultation. Come wind or rain or snow they were all one to him. He was away from Zillenstein, out in the great free world and Julie was with him. Auersperg himself, unknowing, had provided the way and he was sending them not only in comfort but in luxury. John knew the big automobile. It was the prince's own and it was surely equipped in a princely way. The man who bad brought it to the gate had been forced to go away and he, John Scott, and Prince Karl of Auersperg alone knew where they were going. All the better! He laughed under his breath as he handled the wheel with hands now skilled and sent the great automobile along the smooth white road that stretched away and away up the mountain side.

At a curve a mile or more distant, he could look down almost directly upon Zillenstein. The vast castle was bathed in whitish mists floating up the valley in which it loomed gigantic and enlarged, a menacing creation that had survived far beyond its time. He shuddered at the thought that Julie and he might still be there, had not fortune been so kind, and then, pressing the accelerator, he sent the machine forward a little faster.

The road owing to the steepness of the ascent now wound a great deal, but it was smooth and safe, and the automobile, despite its size, had an organism as delicate as that of a watch. It obeyed the least pressure of his hand, and his exultation became all the greater when he fully realized that he had such a powerful mechanism at hand, subject to its lightest touch. The thought, in truth, had come to him that he might turn back into the valley, and seek escape from the mountains. But consideration showed that the idea was foolish. So large a machine by no possibility could escape from the valley. It was better to go on.

The cold increased sharply. He expected a fall in the mercury owing to the ascent, but it was greater than the height alone warranted. All the signs betokened foul weather. The castle was now wholly lost in great masses of vapor and the moon was withdrawing from the sky. The wind had an edge of ice. He knew that mountains were the breeding place of storms and he made another increase of speed in order that they might reach the hunting lodge before one broke.

He had not heard a sound from the interior of the automobile since he started. They were sitting only a few feet away, but the whistling of the wind and the crunch of the wheels on the sanded road would have drowned out all slight noises, and they did not speak, nor did he look back.

He knew that they could see only a broad back in front of them and the muffling coat and cap. He longed to say a word or two, but he deemed it wisest to wait yet a while. His full attention was concentrated upon the machine and the road and it was all the more necessary because the night was growing darker and the wind cut.

But his confidence was so high that he handled the automobile through all the dangers with a firm and sure hand. It sped on and on, climbing in a rapid series of circles up the side of the mountain. Behind him the gulf was filled with vapors and before him the clouds were growing darker on the crest, but he could yet trace the road, and it would not be long now until they reached the crest and the pine forest in which the hunting lodge stood.

He wondered what kind of man the forester Muller would prove to be. If he were suspicious, keenly alert, he might prevent their ultimate escape, but if he were merely a simple hunter John might make friends with him and use him for his purposes. Then his thoughts came quickly back to Julie. He believed that she had left the castle without resistance of any kind. She would be glad to escape from Zillenstein and Auersperg, no matter where that escape might take her.

Another half-hour and the crest was but a hundred yards or so away. How thankful he was now that he had put on extra speed despite the ascent and had driven the machine hard, because the road would soon be blotted from sight! Heavy flakes of snow had begun to fall and with the rising wind they were coming faster and faster.

He dimly made out a pine wood on his right, and, then, in the center of it the outline of a low building which he knew must be the hunting lodge. He slowed down the machine, took the last little curve, and stopped before the door of the lodge. But in that minute the snow had become a driving white storm.

He leaped out, knocked hard on the door of the lodge, and, no answer coming, threw himself heavily against it. It burst open, revealing only an interior of darkness, but he turned quickly back to the automobile, threw wide its door and beckoned with peremptory command to the two dark figures sitting within.

They stepped out, Julie first, and entered the lodge. John followed them, and there they stood, staring at one another until their eyes might grow used to the dusk and they could see their faces. It was evident that Muller was not anywhere in the building, or he would have come at the sound of the machine.

John glanced toward a window set deep in a heavy timbered wall and admitting enough light to disclose a lantern and a box of matches on a shelf. Still in his shrouding coat, cap and glasses he stepped forward, struck a match and lighted the lantern. Driven by a sudden impulse, he swept off the cap and glasses and held up the light.

He saw Julie's face turn deadly pale. Every particle of color was gone from it and her blue eyes stared at him as if he were one newly risen from the dead. Then the color flushed back in a rosy tide and such a tide of gladness as he had never seen before in human eyes came into hers.

"You! You! Is it really you?" she cried.

John was once more the knightly young crusader. No such moment had ever before come into his life. His heart was full. Triumph and joy were mingled there, and something over and beyond either. In that passing flash he had read the light in her eyes, a light that he knew was only for him, but in the instant of supreme revelation he would take no advantage. The manner as well as the spirit of the young crusader was upon him.

He knelt before her and taking one of her gloved hands in his kissed it.

"Yes, dearest Julie," he said, "by some singular fortune or chance, or rather, I should call it, the will of God, I was chosen to bring you here, and I glory because I have fulfilled the trust."

"'You! You! Is it really you?' she cried"

Suzanne, tall and dark, stood looking down at them. Her grim features which relaxed so rarely relaxed now and her eyes were soft. The young stranger from beyond the seas had proved after all that he was a man among men, and no Frenchwoman could resist a romance so strong and true in the face of all that war could do.

John felt Julie's hand trembling in his, but she did not draw it away. Her lashes were lowered a little now, but her gaze still rested upon him, soft yet confident and powerful. He had believed in her courage. He had believed that she would suffer no shock when she should see that he was the strange man who had been at the wheel, and his confidence was justified.

"And it was you who brought us up the mountain?" she said.

"The Prince of Auersperg himself chose me because I was a stranger and he did not wish anyone else in the castle to know where you were sent."

He released her hand and rose. The soft but strong gaze was still upon him, as if she were yet trying to persuade herself that it was reality.

"I felt all the time that some day we should leave the castle together," she said, "but I did not dream that it was you who sat before me as we came up the mountain."

"But it was," said John, joyfully. "I think Wharton himself would have complimented me on the way I drove the machine. I have a letter in my pocket for Muller, the prince's forester who lives here, but it seems that he is absent on other duty."

"And then," said the practical Suzanne, "it becomes us to take possession of the house at once. Look forth, sir! how the storm beats!"

Through the open door they saw the snow driven past in sheets that seemed almost solid. John handed the lantern to Suzanne and said:

"Wait here a moment."

"Where are you going, Mr. Scott?" exclaimed Julie. "You will not desert us?"

"Never!"

He was out of the door in a couple of strides, and then he sprang into the automobile. He had noticed a small garage back of the lodge and he meant to save the machine, feeling sure that they would have need of it later. In a few minutes it was safely inside with the door fastened so tightly behind him that no wind could blow it loose, and he was back at the lodge with the wind and snow driving so hard that he opened the door but little, and, slipping in, slammed it shut. Then he turned the heavy key in the lock, and stared in surprise and pleasure at the room.

It was a great apartment, the heavy log walls adorned with the horns and stuffed heads of wild animals. Several bear skins and other rugs lay upon the oaken floor. There were chairs and tables with books upon them, and, at one end, the dry wood that filled a great fireplace was crackling and flashing merrily. The practical Suzanne, noticing the heap, had set a match to it at once, and already the room, great as it was, was filled with warmth and light. Julie, having taken off her heavy furs, was sitting in a chair before the fire, the leaping flames deepening the light in her eyes and the new rose in her cheeks.

John's heart swelled with thankfulness and joy. He had not dreamed that so much could be achieved. A day before he would have said that it was impossible. As the whistling of the wind rose to a fierce roar and the snow drove by, he realized, with a shudder at the danger escaped so narrowly, that they had arrived just in time. The automobile itself would have been driven from the path by the fierce Alpine storm now raging.

The stern but gifted Suzanne had found lamps and had lighted them, and like a capable soldier she was already looking over her field of battle.

"Not so bad," she said. "His Highness, Prince Karl of Auersperg, builds a little palace and calls it his hunting lodge. But his heart would turn black within him if he knew who was one of the guests in it today."

John smiled, and meeting Julie's eyes, he smiled again. He saw a flame there to which his own soul responded, and he tingled from head to foot. The omens had not been in vain. The blessings of the righteous had availed. Again it may be said that he had no faith in the supernatural, at least here on earth, but all things must have worked for him in a world that seemed wholly against him. He believed that he read such a thought too in the glowing dark blue of her own eyes.

"You are wonderfully right, Suzanne," said John. "Probably the Prince of Auersperg had the lodge especially prepared for the coming of Mademoiselle Julie. Perhaps there is a telephone."

"Truly there is, Mr. Scott," said Suzanne. "Here it is, in the corner."

"Then," said John, "it's very likely that we'll hear very soon from Zillenstein, and since he has kept your journey secret it is sure to be Prince Karl himself who will call you up. I must be the one to answer. Now will you sit here by the fire, Miss Julie, and rest while your most capable Suzanne and I look further into our new residence. There is no possibility of any caller, save the worthy Muller, to whom

I bear a letter from the prince, in which I have no doubt I am highly recommended."

"Very well, Mr. John, I obey you," said Julie, sitting down again in a large armchair before the flames, where the ruddy light once more deepened the gold of her hair and the rose of her cheeks. "It seems that you intend to be master here."

"I'm master already. My rule has become supreme, nor am I any usurper. Do I not hold a commission from Prince Karl of Auersperg, the owner of this lodge, and did he not intrust you to my care? I mean to do my duty. And now come, Suzanne, you and I will see what this wilderness castle of ours contains."

The hunting lodge was worthy of a prince. It was built of massive logs, but the interior was improved and finished in modern style. There were no electric lights, but it contained almost every other luxury or convenience. Besides the great room in which Julie was now sitting, they found on the ground floor a writing-room well supplied, a small parlor, a gunroom amply equipped with a variety of arms and ammunition, a dining-room containing much princely silver, a butler's pantry, a kitchen and a storeroom holding food enough to last them a year. Above stairs were six bedrooms, any one of which the capable Suzanne could put in order in half an hour. All the house had running water drawn from some reservoir in the mountains.

John had seen such luxurious camps as this in the Adirondacks in his own country, and there were many others scattered about the mountains of Europe, but he was very grateful now to find such a refuge for Julie. Again he realized how fortunate they had been to arrive so early. As he looked from an upper window he saw that the storm was driving with tremendous fury. Even behind the huge logs he heard the wind roaring and thundering, and now and then, through the thick glass of the windows, he caught a glimpse of a young pine torn up by its roots and whirled past.

Where was Muller, the forester, who had charge of the lodge and who lived there, and what kind of a man was he? It was the only question that was troubling him now. If he did not come soon he could not come that night, nor perhaps the next day. The snowfall was immense, with every sign of heavy continuance, and by morning it certainly would lie many feet deep on the mountain. Traveling would be impossible. He heard the distant sound of a bell, and knowing that the telephone was calling, he ran down the stairway to the great room. Julie had risen and was looking at the instrument with dilated eyes, as if it sounded a note of alarm, as if their happy escape was threatened by a new danger. John believed that she had fallen asleep before the heat of the fire, and that the ring of the telephone had struck upon her dreaming ear like a shell.

"It's he! It's the terrible prince himself!" she exclaimed, her faculties not yet fully released from cloudy sleep.

"Very likely," said John, "but have no fear. Zillenstein is only six leagues away at ordinary times, but it's six hundred tonight, with the greatest storm that I've ever seen sweeping in between us."

He took down the receiver and put it to his ear.

"Who is there?" asked a deep voice, which he knew to be that of Prince Karl.

"Castel, Your Highness."

"You arrived without accident?"

"Wholly without accident, Your Highness. We reached the lodge a few minutes before the storm broke."

"The lady, Mademoiselle Lannes, is safe and comfortable?"

"Entirely so. Your Highness. The maid, Suzanne, is preparing her room for her."

"You found Muller there waiting for you according to instructions?"

Some prudential motive prompted John to reply:

"Yes, Your Highness, he had everything ready and was waiting. I presented your letter at once."

"You have done well, Castel. Keep the lady within the house, but the storm will do that anyhow. Do not under any circumstances call me up, but I will call you again when I think fit. Bear in mind that the reward of both you and Muller shall be large, if you serve me well in this most important matter."

"Yes, Your Highness. I thank you now."

"Keep it in mind, always."

"Yes, Your Highness."

His Highness, Prince Karl of Auersperg, replaced the telephone stand upon the table in his bedroom at Zillenstein, and John Scott hung up the receiver in the hunting lodge on the mountain.

"It was Prince Karl," he said to Julie, who still stood motionless looking at him. "He wanted to know if you were safe and comfortable and I said yes. He said he would call us up again but he won't."

He lifted a chair and shattered the telephone to fragments.

"It might afford a peculiar pleasure to talk with him," he said, "but it's best that we have no further communication while we're here. An incautious word or two might arouse suspicion and that's what we want most to avoid. When he fails to get an answer to his call he'll think that this huge snow has broken down the wire. Most likely it will do so anyhow. And now, Miss Julie, Suzanne has your room ready for you. If you wish to withdraw to it for a little while you'll find dinner waiting you when you return."

"And the day of the abandoned hotel in Chastel has come back?"

"But a better and a longer day. We're prisoners here together on the mountain, you and I, and your chaperon, servant and sometime ruler, Suzanne Picard, who I find is not as grim as she looks."

There was a spark in his eyes as he looked at her, and an answering fire leaped up in her own. He was in very truth a perfect and gentle knight, who would gladly come so far and through so many dangers for her and for her alone. He was her very own champion, and as her dark blue eyes looked into the gray deeps of his her soul thrilled with the knowledge of it. Deep red flushed her from brow to chin, and then slowly ebbed away.

"John," she said, putting her hand in his, "no woman has ever owed more gratitude to a man."

"And I am finding repayment now for what I was happy to do," he said, kissing her hand again in that far-off knightly fashion.

Again the red tide in her cheeks and then she swiftly left the room, but John threw himself in a chair before the great fire and gazed into the coals. Wide awake, he was dreaming. He knew they would be days in the lodge. The storm was so great that no one could come from Zillenstein in a week. Providence or fortune had been so kind that he began to fear enough had been done for them. Such good luck could not go on forever, and there, too, was the man Muller who might make trouble when he came.

Nevertheless his feeling was but momentary. The extraordinary lightness of heart returned. The storm roared without and at times it volleyed down the chimney, making the flames leap and dance, but the sense of security and safety was strong within him. The war passed by, forgotten for the time. History, it was true, repeated itself, and this was the abandoned hotel at Chastel over again, but they were in a far better position now. No one could come against them, unless the man Muller should prove to be a foe. And he resolved, too, gazing into the flames, that they should not steal Julie from him here, as they had taken her at Chastel.

Darkness, save for the gleam of the snow, came over the mountain, but the flakes were driving so thick and fast that they formed a white blanket before the window, as impervious as black night itself. It reminded him of a great storm he had seen once on his uncle's ranch on the high table land of Montana, but to him it came that night as a friend and not as an enemy, cutting them off from Zillenstein and all the dangers it held.

He lighted candles and lamps in the great room and all the smaller rooms clustering about it. He would have everything cheerful for Julie when she returned.

He had seen Suzanne take several heavy packages from the automobile and he had no doubt that they had come amply provided with clothing, that for Julie, belonging doubtless to a young cousin or niece of the prince who stayed sometimes at Zillenstein.

As for himself, if they remained long he must depend upon the spare raiment of the forester, and, remembering suddenly that he might effect his own improvement, he hunted for Muller's room and discovered it on the second floor. Here he found shaving materials, and rapidly cleared his face of the young beard that he despised. Muller's clothing was scattered about, and he judged from it that the forester was a man of about his own size. After some hesitation, he took off his own coat and put on a brilliant Tyrolean jacket which he surmised the owner reserved for occasions of state.

"If you come, Mr. Muller, I'll try to explain to you why I do this," said John aloud. "I know you'll forgive me when I tell you it's in honor of a lady."

Then he laughed at himself in a glass. It was a gorgeous jacket, but one could wear more brilliant clothes in Europe than in America, and his appearance was certainly improved. He returned to the great room and someone sitting in the chair before the fire rose to receive him.

It was Julie all in white, a semi-evening dress that heightened in a wonderful fashion her glorious, blond beauty. He had often thought how this slender maid would bloom into a woman and now he beheld her here in the lodge, his prisoner and not Auersperg's. A swift smile passed over her face as she saw him, and bowing low before him she said:

"I see, Mr. John, that you have not wasted your time. You come arrayed in purple and gold."

"But it's borrowed plumage, Miss Julie."

"And so is mine."

"It can't be. I'm sure it was made for you."

"The real owner wouldn't say so."

"You will forgive me if I tell you something, won't you?"

"It depends upon what it is."

The red in her checks deepened a little. The gray eyes of John were speaking in very plain language to Julie.

"I must say it, stern necessity compels, if I don't I'll be very unhappy."

"I wouldn't have you miserable."

"I want to tell you, Julie, that you are overwhelmingly beautiful tonight."

"I've always heard that Americans were very bold, it's true."

"But remember the provocation, Julie."

"Ah, sir, I have no protection and you take advantage of it."

"There's Suzanne."

"But she's in the kitchen."

"Where I hope she'll stay until she's wanted."

She was silent and the red in her cheeks deepened again. But the blue eyes and the gray yet talked together.

"I worship you, your beauty and your great soul, but your great soul most of all," said the gray.

"Any woman would be proud to have a lover who has followed her through so many and such great dangers, and who has rescued her at last. She could not keep from loving him," said the blue.

Suzanne appeared that moment in the doorway and stood there unnoticed. She looked at them grimly and then came the rare smile that gave her face that wonderful softness.

"Come, Mademoiselle Julie and Mr. John," she said. "Dinner is ready and I tell you now that I've never prepared a better one. This prince has a taste in food and wine that I did not think to find in any German."

"And all that was his is ours now," said John. "Fortune of war."

Suzanne's promise was true to the last detail. The dinner was superb and they had an Austrian white wine that never finds its way into the channels of commerce.

"To you, Julie, and our happy return to Paris," said John, looking over the edge of his glass. Suzanne was in the kitchen then and he dared to drop the "Mademoiselle."

"To you, John," she said, as she touched the wine to her lips—she too dared to drop the "Mr."

And then gray depths looked into blue depths and blue into gray, speaking a language that each understood.

"We're the chosen of fortune," said John, "The hotel at Chastel presented itself to us when we needed it most, and again when we need it most this lodge gives us all hospitality."

"Fortune has been truly kind," said Julie.

After dinner they went back to the great room where the fire still blazed and Suzanne, when she had cleared everything away, joined them. She quietly took a chair next to the wall and went to work on some sewing that she had found in the lodge. But John saw that she had installed herself as a sort of guardian of them both, and she meant to watch over them as her children. Yet however often she might appear to him in her old grim guise he would always be able to see beneath it.

Now they talked but little. John saw after a while that Julie was growing sleepy, and truly a slender girl who had been through so much in one day had a right to rest. He caught Suzanne's eye and nodded. Rising, the Frenchwoman said in the tone of command which perhaps she had often used to Julie as a child:

"It's time we were off to bed, Mademoiselle. The storm will make us both sleep all the better."

"Good night, Mr. John," said Julie.

"Good night. Miss Julie."

Once more the stern face of Suzanne softened under a smile, but she and her charge marched briskly away, and left John alone before the fire. He had decided that he would not sleep upstairs, but would occupy the gunroom from which a window looked out upon the front of the house. There he made himself a bed with blankets and pillows that he brought from above and lay down amid arms.

The gunroom was certainly well stocked. It held repeating rifles and fowling-pieces, large and small, and revolvers. One big breech-loader had the weight of an elephant rifle, and there were also swords, bayonets and weapons of ancient type. But John looked longest at the big rifle. He felt that if need be he could hold the lodge against almost anything except cannon.

"It's the first time I ever had a whole armory to myself," he said, looking around proudly at the noble array.

But he was quite sure that no one could come for days except Muller, and the mystery of the forester's absence again troubled him, although not very long. Another look at the driving snow, and, wrapping himself in his blankets, he fell asleep to the music of the storm. John awoke once far in the night, and his sense of comfort, as he lay between the blankets on the sofa that he had dragged into the gunroom, was so great that he merely luxuriated there for a little while and listened to the roar of the storm, which he could yet hear, despite the thickness of the walls. But he rose at last, and went to the window.

The thick snowy blast was still driving past, and his eyes could not penetrate it more than a dozen feet. But he rejoiced. Their castle was growing stronger and stronger all the time, as nature steadily built her fortifications higher and higher around it. Mulier himself, carrying out his duties of huntsman, might have gone to some isolated point in the mountains, and would not be able to return for days. He wished no harm to Muller, but he hoped the possibility would become a fact.

He went back to his blanket and when he awoke in the morning the great Alpine storm was still raging. But he bathed and refreshed himself and found a store of clothing better than that of the forester. It did not fit him very well, nevertheless he was neatly arrayed in civilian attire and he went to the kitchen, meaning to put himself to use and cook the breakfast. But Suzanne was already there, and she saluted him with stern and rebuking words.

"I reign here," she said. "Go back and talk to Mademoiselle Julie. Since we're alone and are likely to be so, for God knows how long, it's your duty to see that she keeps up her spirits. I'd have kept you two apart if I could, but it has been willed otherwise, and maybe it's for the best."

"What has happened shows it's for the best, Suzanne. And, as you know, you've never had any real objection to me except that I'm not a Frenchman. And am I not becoming such as fast as possible?"

"You don't look very much like one, but you act like one and often you talk like one."

"Thanks, Suzanne. That's praise coming from you."

"Now be off with you. My mistress is surely in the great room, and if you care for her as much as you pretend, you will see that she is not lonely, and don't talk nonsense, either."

John, chuckling, withdrew. As Suzanne had predicted he found Julie in the large room, and she was quite composed, when she bade him good morning.

"I see that the storm goes on," she said.

"So much the better. It is raising higher the wall between us and our enemies. Our fire has burned out in the night, leaving only coals, but there is a huge store of wood in the back part of the lodge."

He brought in an armful of billets to find her fanning the coals into a blaze.

"You didn't think, sir," said she, "did you, that I mean to be a guest here, waited upon by you and Suzanne?"

"But Suzanne and I are strong and willing! Don't lean too near that blaze, Julie! You'll set your beautiful hair on fire!"

"And so you think my hair beautiful?"

"Very beautiful."

"It's not proper for you to say so. We're not in America."

"Nor are we in France, where young girls are surrounded by triple rows of brass or steel. We're in a snowstorm on top of a high mountain in Austria. There are no conventions, and Suzanne, your guardian, is in the kitchen."

"But I can call her and she'll come."

"She'd come, I know, but you won't call her. There, our fire is blazing beautifully, and we don't have to nurse it any longer. You sit here in this chair, and I'll sit there in that chair at a respectful distance. Now you realize that we are going to be here a long time, don't you Julie?"

"Miss Julie or Mademoiselle Julie would be better and perhaps Mademoiselle Lannes would be most fitting."

"No, I've said Julie several times and as it always gives me a pleasant thrill I'm sure it's best. I intend to use it continually hereafter, except when Suzanne is present."

"You're taking a high stand, Mr. John."

"John is best also."

"Well, then—John!"

"I'm taking it for your good and my pleasure."

"I wonder if Suzanne is ready with the breakfast!"

"You needn't go to see. You know it's not, and you know, too, that Suzanne will call us when it is ready. A wonderfully capable woman, that Suzanne. She didn't look upon me with favor at first, but I believe she is really beginning to like me, to view me perhaps with approval as a sort of candidate."

"Look how the snow is coming down!"

"But that's an old story. Let's go back to Suzanne."

"Oh no. She's coming for us."

It was true. The incomparable Suzanne stood in the doorway and summoned them to breakfast.

CHAPTER XIII
THE DANGEROUS FLIGHT

It snowed all that day and all the next night. The lateness of the season seemed to add to the violence of the storm, as if it would make one supreme effort on these heights before yielding to the coming spring. Many of the pines were blown down, and the snow lay several feet deep everywhere. Now and then they heard thunderous sounds from the gorges telling them that great slides were taking place, and it was absolutely certain now that no one from the valley below could reach the lodge for days.

The sight from the windows of the house, when the driving snow thinned enough to permit a view, was magnificent. They saw far away peak on peak and ridge on ridge, clothed in white, and sometimes they beheld the valley filled with vast clouds of mists and vapors. Once John thought he caught a glimpse of Zillenstein, a menacing gray shadow far below, but the clouds in an instant floated between and he was not sure.

Yet it was a period of enchantment in the life of John Scott. Their very isolation on the mountain, with Suzanne there in the double rôle of servant and guardian, seemed to draw Julie and him more closely together. The world had practically melted away beneath their feet. The great war was gone for them. He was only twenty-two, but his experience had made him mentally much older, and she, too, had gained in knowledge and command of herself by all through which she had passed.

She showed to John a spirit and courage which he had never seen surpassed in any woman, and mingled with it all was a lightness and wit that filled the whole house with sunshine, despite the great storm that raged continually without. In the music-room was a piano, and she played upon it the beautiful French "little songs" that John loved.

There were books and magazines in plenty, and now he read to her and then she read to him. Sometimes they sat in silence and through the thick glass of the windows watched the snow driving by.

The hours were too few for John. He served her as the crusader served his chosen lady. The spirit of the old knights of chivalry that had descended upon him still held him in a spell that he did not wish to break. Often she mocked at him and laughed at him, and then he liked her all the better. No placid, submissive woman, shrinking before the dangers, would have pleased him. In her light laughter and her banter, even at his expense, he read a noble courage and a lofty soul, and in their singular isolation it was given to him to see her spirit, so strong and yet so rarely sweet in a manner that the circumstances of ordinary life could never have brought forth. And the faithful Suzanne, still in her double rôle of servant and guardian, served and guarded them both.

John at this time began to feel a more forgiving spirit toward Auersperg. It might well be that this man of middle years, so thoroughly surrounded by old, dead things that he had never seen the world as it really was, had been bewitched. A sort of moon madness had made him commit his extraordinary deed, and John could view it with increasing tolerance because he had been bewitched himself.

He made another and more extended survey of their stores and confirmed his first opinion that the lodge was furnished in full princely style. They need not lack for any of the comforts, nor for many luxuries, no matter how long they remained.

On the morning of the third day the storm ceased and they looked out upon a white, shining world of snow, lofty and impressive, peaks and ridges outlined sharply against a steel-blue sky. John had found a pair of powerful glasses in the lodge and with them he was now able to make out Zillenstein quite clearly. Clothed in snow, a castle all in white, it was nevertheless more menacing than ever.

John believed that Muller would surely come, and many and many a time he thought over the problem how to deal with him. But the new, windless day passed and there was no sign of the forester. John himself went forth, breaking paths here and there through the snow, but he discovered nothing. He began to believe that Muller had been forced to take shelter at the start of the storm and could not now return. His hope that it was so strong that his mind turned it into a fact, and Muller disappeared from his thoughts.

The garage, besides the great automobile, contained a smaller one, but John kept the limousine in mind. He intended when the time came to escape in it with the two women, if possible. There might be a road leading down the other side of the mountain, and toward Italy. If so, he would surely try to get through when the melting of the snow permitted.

Meanwhile he devoted himself with uncommon zest to household duties. He cleared new paths about the lodge, moved in much of the wood where it would be more convenient for Suzanne, cleaned and polished the guns and revolvers in the little armory, inspected the limousine and put it in perfect order, and did everything else that he could think of to make their mountain castle luxurious and defensible.

Julie often joined him in these tasks, and John did not remonstrate, knowing that work and occupation kept a mind healthy. Wrapped in her great red cloak and wearing the smallest pair of high boots that he could find in the lodge, she often shoveled snow with him, as he increased the number of runways to the small outlying buildings, or to other parts of their domain. Thus they filled up the hours and prevented the suspense which otherwise would have been acute, despite their comfortable house.

She continually revealed herself to him now. The shell that encloses a young French girl had been broken by the hammer of war and she had stepped forth, a woman with a thinking and reasoning mind of uncommon power. It seemed often to John that the soul of the great Lannes had descended upon this slender maid who was of his own blood. Like many another American, he had thought often of those marshals of Napoleon who had risen from obscurity to such heights, and of them all, the republican and steadfast Lannes had been his favorite. Her spirit was the same. He found in it a like simplicity and courage. They seldom talked of the war, but when they did she expressed unbounded faith in the final triumph of her nation and of those allied with it.

"I have read what the world was saying of France," she said one day when they stood together on the snowy slope. "We hear, we girls, although we are mostly behind the walls. They have told us that we were declining as a nation, and many of our own people believed it."

"The charge will never be made again against the French Republic," said John. "The French, by their patience and courage in the face of preliminary defeat and their dauntless resolution, have won the admiration of all the world."

"And many Americans are fighting for us. Tell me, John, why did you join our armies?"

"An accident first, as you know. There was that meeting with your brother at the Austrian border, and my appearance in the apparent rôle of a spy, and then my great sympathy with the French, who I thought and still think were attacked by a powerful and prepared enemy bent upon their destruction. Then I thought and still think that France and England represent democracy against absolutism, and then, although every one of these reasons is powerful enough alone, yet another has influenced me strongly."

"And what is that other, John?"

"It's intangible, Julie. It has been weighed and measured by nearly all the great philosophers, but I don't think any two of them have ever agreed about the result."

"You are a philosopher, sir, too, are you not? How do you define it?"

"I don't know that I've arrived at any conclusion."

"And yet, John, I thought that you were a man of decision."

"That's irony, Julie. But men of decision perhaps are puzzled by it more than anybody else."

"Then you can neither describe it nor give it a name?"

"It has names, several—but most of them are misleading," said John, thoughtfully.

"So you leave it to me to discover what this mysterious influence may be, or to remain forever in ignorance of it."

In her dark red cloak with tendrils of the deep golden hair showing at the edge of her hood, she seemed to John a very sprite of the snows, and the blue eyes said clearly to the gray:

"I know!"

And the gray answered back in the same language:

"I know!"

Nevertheless John would not let words betray him. He thought that the mountain and their isolation gave him an unfair advantage, and the young crusader upon whom the mantle of chivalry had descended had too knightly a soul to use it, at least in speech.

"And so, sir," she said, "you will not venture upon such an abstruse subject?"

"No, I think not. I don't believe you could call it an evasion, but perhaps it's fear."

"Fear of what, John?"

"I'm not sure about that, either. Perhaps elsewhere and under more suitable circumstances I may be able to put my thought into words, precise and understandable. It will take time, but that I shall do so some day I have no doubt."

She looked away, and then the two, the snow shovels in their hands, walked back gravely to the lodge. Suzanne stood in the doorway watching them. She knew that they were wholly oblivious of her presence, that they had not even seen her, yet the heart of the stern peasant woman was warm within her, although she felt that she now had two children instead of one under her care.

Neither was Suzanne given up wholly to the present. She spent many anxious hours thinking of the future. The deep snow could not last forever. Already there was a warmer breath in the air. When it began to melt it would go fast, and then Auersperg—if he were still at Zillenstein—eaten up with impatience and anger because he could hear nothing from the lodge, would act, and he would show no mercy to the young man with the brown hair and the gray eyes, who was now walking by the side of her beloved Julie.

John himself took notice the next day of the signs. Spring, which already held sway in the lowlands, was creeping up the slope of the highlands. The sun was distinctly warmer and tiny rivulets of water flowed along the edges of the runways. In a few more days retainers of Auersperg or troops would come up the mountain. The prince himself might have been compelled to return to the war, but he would certainly leave orders in capable hands. John never deluded himself for a moment upon that subject. His shoveling in the snow made him quite sure now that a road led over the mountain and southward, and he had made up his mind to take the automobile and the two women and try it, as soon as the snow melted enough to permit of such an attempt. One might get through, and he had proved for himself that fortune favors the daring.

In his explorations on the southern slope he came to a deep gulch in which the tops of scrub pines showed above the snow. Following its edge for some distance his eye at length was caught by a dark shape on the rocks. He climbed slowly and painfully down to it and saw the body of a man, clothed like a German forester. His neck and many of his bones were broken, and his body was bruised frightfully.

John had no doubt that it was the missing Muller, and it was altogether likely that in the storm he had made a misstep, and had fallen into the ravine to instant death.

"What are you going to do?" asked Julie, who saw him going out, spade on shoulder.

"I've found Muller at last," he replied soberly.

"Oh! I am sorry!" she said, shuddering as she looked at the spade.

"It's all I can do for him now."

"I'm glad you thought to do as much."

When John returned he had carefully wiped all the earth from the snow shovel. The subject of Muller was never again mentioned by either of them, and while he experienced sorrow for a man whom he had never seen and who was an official enemy, he felt that a shadow was lifted from them.

The sun grew much warmer the next day, and the snow began to melt fast. The rivulets in the runways swelled rapidly. The snow sank inch by inch, and warm winds blew on the slopes. The pines were now clear and little rivers were running down every ravine and gulch. The thunder of great masses of snow, loosened by the thaw and gathering weight as they rolled down the mountain side, came to their ears. The sky was a brilliant blue, pouring down continuous warm beams, and it was obvious that it would not be long before the automobile road was clear. Then the blue eyes turned a questioning gaze upon the gray.

"Yes, I'm preparing for us to go soon," said John.

"Which way?" asked Julie.

"Toward Italy, I think."

"Is it possible for us to get through?"

"I don't know. The hardships and the dangers undoubtedly will be great."

"But one can endure them."

"You have little to fear. Prince Karl of Auersperg offers you morganatic marriage, and he thinks that he is honoring you."

"But do you, John, think that he is honoring me?"

"Although you would probably be a mere countess and not a princess, your position nevertheless would be great in most continental eyes, far grander than if you were to marry some obscure republican."

"You haven't answered me. Do you think the Prince of Auersperg would be honoring me?"

"I'm not a judge to make decisions. I'm merely stating the facts on either side."

"But suppose I should meet this simple and obscure republican and, through some singular chance, should happen to love him, would it not be better for my pride and more promising for my happiness to marry him on terms of full equality rather than to marry Prince Karl of Auersperg, a man old enough to be my father, and yet remain all my life his inferior? As we understand it in France and as you understand it in America, republicanism means equality, does it not, sir?"

"If it doesn't mean that it means nothing."

"Then, sir, being what I am, you may be sure that I shall not stay here to await Prince Karl of Auersperg, and his unsought honors."

"You are the judge, Julie, after all, and I believed it was the decision you would make. Yet, it was only fair to lay the full facts before you."

John knew that the attempt to escape southward through the mountains would be attended by great danger, not only from the Austrians, but from the risks of the road itself, when the great automobile, slipping on melting snow and ice, might go crashing at any moment into a gorge. Yet it must be done. Another day brought home the extreme necessity of it. All the mountains thundered with the sliding snow, and the prince's men would certainly come soon.

The garage contained an ample supply of gasoline and extra tires, and John saw that the machine was in perfect order. He also stored in it clothing, food for many days, two rifles and many cartridges. It was thus at once a carriage, a home and a fortress. Then he told Julie that they must start the next morning. Enough snow was gone to disclose the road leading southward, and he believed that he could drive the limousine down the mountain.

"Are you willing to trust yourself to me, Julie?" he asked.

"Through everything," she replied.

Suzanne also was eager to go, and, in her character now as a full member of the little company, she did not hesitate to say so.

"Our comfort here may cause us to linger too long, sir," she said to John, when Julie was not present. "My mistress has been twice in the hands of the Prince of Auersperg and twice through you she has escaped him. There is certain death for you if he finds you and I know not what for my mistress if she should be taken by him once more. Hardened by his years and her resistance he would seek to break her. It has seemed to me sometimes, sir, that you were sent by God to save us."

The woman's faith, which had so completely replaced her original distrust and hostility, moved John.

"Suzanne," he said, "she shall never again be in the power of that man. I don't know what the future holds for us, but I think I can promise her escape from Auersperg."

"And others will come to help us," said Suzanne, with all the intensity of a prophetess. "You left word, you have said, which way you were going, and it will reach Monsieur Philip. It will not be so hard to trace us to Zillenstein, and he will surely follow. He flies in the air like the eagle, and we will see him some day black against the sky."

The two by the same impulse looked up. But there was nothing showing in the blue vault, save feathery white clouds. Nevertheless the faith of neither was dimmed.

"I feel the certainty of it, too," said John. "Philip and the *Arrow* will answer to our call."

"And my father," said Suzanne in the same tones of unshakable faith. "He was left a prisoner in Munich, but few prisons can hold Antoine Picard. He will surely seek us through all the mountains."

John's faith was already strong, but Suzanne's made it stronger. A high nature always tries to deserve the trust it receives. Early the following morning the automobile was ready, and Julie and Suzanne, wrapped in their cloaks, took their places inside. John stood beside it, in chauffeur's garb with cap and glasses.

"It's the last look at the lodge, Julie," he said. "When the Prince of Auersperg built it he never dreamed that it would serve as a refuge for those who were escaping from him. But it hasn't been such a bad home, has it?"

"No," she replied. "It will always have a place among my pleasant memories."

"And among mine."

He sprang into his seat and grasped the wheel. The automobile began a slow and cautious descent of the mountain's southward slope. However reluctant one is to prepare for a start there is invariably a certain elation after the start is made, and John felt the uplift now. He could not yet see his way out of Austria, but he felt that he would find it. He did not even know where their present road led, except that it disappeared in a valley, filled with mists and vapors from the melting snows.

John had preserved the pass given to him by the German officer, and thinking he might be able to make use of it again, he dropped the name of John Scott once more and returned to that of Jean Castel, asking Julie and Suzanne to remember the change, whenever they should meet anyone. But it was a long before they saw a human being.

They came at last to the bottom of a narrow valley, and the strain of driving under such dangerous circumstances had been so great that John felt compelled to take a rest of a half-hour. Julie descended from the machine and walked back and forth in the road. They saw that they were in a narrow valley down which flowed a stream, much swollen by the melting snow. But the grass and foliage were heavy here and the air was warm.

"I have resolved, Julie," said John, "to say, if we are pressed closely, that you are a lady of the household of the Prince of Auersperg, accompanied by your maid, and that, wishing to get out of the war zone, I'm deputed to carry you to the port of Trieste. I can't think of anything else that seems likely to serve us better."

"We're in your hands."

"Aye, so we are, sir," said the bold Suzanne, "but we also have hands of our own and can help."

"I know it, Suzanne, and I know that you will not fail when the time comes."

Julie returned to the machine and John put his hand on the wheel again, finding it a great relief to drive on a fairly level road. Throughout the descent of the slope he had been in fear of skidding and a fatal smash. Although much snow was left on the crests and sides of the mountains, none was visible in the valley, and the great mass of green foliage was restful to the eye.

"The first inhabitant to greet us," said John.

A man driving a flock of sheep was coming toward them. He was a sturdy fellow, with a red feather in his cap, which was cocked a bit saucily on one side of his head. It was evident that he was a shepherd, whose sheep had been driven into the lowlands by the storm. John, both from prudence and natural consideration, brought his machine down to a slow pace, and spoke pleasantly to the man, who was looking at them with much curiosity.

"We're from the family of the Prince of Auersperg," said John, "and we're making our way toward the coast. The prince wishes a lady whom he esteems very highly to reach Trieste as soon as possible. Where can we find the best inn for the night?"

"The village of Tellnitz, which you should reach about dark, has a famous inn, and there is no finer landlord than Herr Leinfelder."

John thanked him, and drove on, increasing his speed, after he had passed the sheep. He looked back once, and saw the shepherd placidly driving his flock before him. He was singing, too, and the musical notes came to them, telling them very clearly that one Austrian, at least, did not suspect them.

"Our first test has been passed successfully," said John, "and I look upon it as a good omen. But don't forget that I'm Jean Castel of Lorraine, French by descent, but a devoted German subject, in the service of the Prince of Auersperg. I intend that we shall pass the night in the inn of the good Herr Leinfelder at Tellnitz, and I believe that we will go on the next day still unsuspected. I've seen no telephone wires in the valley, and doubtless there is no connection between Zillenstein and Tellnitz."

They passed more peasants, none of whom asked them any questions, but they saw no soldiers.

Toward night they beheld the usual lofty church spire, and then the huddled houses of a small village. One rather larger than the others and with a red-tiled roof John thought must be the inn of the good Herr Leinfelder, and his surmise proved to be correct.

"It's fortunate that you are blond," said John to Julie, "as most people think the French are dark. Still, both you and Suzanne look French, and I recommend that you do not take off your wraps until you go to your room, and that you also have your dinner served there. It's best for you, Mademoiselle Julie, to be seen as little as possible, and your rôle as a great lady of the semi-royal house of Auersperg permits it. Now, may I lay the injunction upon both you and Suzanne that you permit me to do all the talking?"

"I obey," said Julie, "but I'm not so sure of Suzanne."

"I never talk unless it's needful for me to speak," said Suzanne with dignity.

Many eyes watched the great limousine as it rolled into Tellnitz, and stopped before the excellent inn of Herr Johann Ignatz Leinfelder. Herr Leinfelder himself appeared upon the gravel, his round red face beaming at the sight of guests, evidently of importance, at a time when so few guests of any kind at all came. John in his rôle of chauffeur said to him with an air of importance:

"A lady of the family of Prince Karl of Auersperg, on her way to Trieste. She wishes a room, the very best room you have, to which she can retire with her maid and seek the rest she so badly needs after her long journey over bad roads."

The good Herr Leinfelder bowed low. John's manner impressed him. It was a perfect reproduction of the style affected by the flunkies of the great.

"We have a splendid chamber for the princess and a smaller one adjoining for her maid," said the host. "It's an honor to Tellnitz and to me that a lady of the house of Auersperg should stop at my inn. The prince himself, we hear, has returned to the great war."

"Ah!" said John, but there was immense satisfaction under the subdued "ah" over the important information coming to him by mere chance. He opened the door for Julie and Suzanne to alight, and still heavily muffled they were bowed into the house by Herr Leinfelder.

"I shall be on guard tonight," whispered John to Julie, as she passed. "Did you hear him say that the Prince of Auersperg had gone back to the war?"

She nodded as she disappeared into the interior of the inn, and he knew that a weight had been lifted from her heart also. The pursuit surely could not be so fierce and lasting when the one who gave it impulse was gone.

There was a small garage behind the inn, and the great automobile almost filled it, but John, clinging to his rôle of chauffeur, which was expedient in every sense, would not trust it to any of the servants of the hotel. He inspected it carefully himself, saw that everything was in proper order, and not until then did he enter the inn in search of food and fire.

"My mistress?" he asked of August, the head waiter. "Has she been properly served? His Highness, Prince Karl of Auersperg, will not forget it if a lady of his family does not receive the deference due to her."

"Dinner has just been served to the princess," said August, deferentially, as the chauffeur's tone had been peremptory. "I return in a moment myself to see that every detail is attended to properly."

"Then look to it," said John, as he slipped a five-kronen piece into his hand, "and see also that she is not disturbed afterward. Her Highness wishes a good night's rest."

August bowed low with gratitude and hurried away to do his commission. John himself, as a man who carried gold, was treated with deference, and he had an excellent dinner in a dining-room that contained but three or four other guests. Here in accordance with his plan he talked rather freely with Herr Leinfelder, and the few servants that the war had left him.

He enlarged upon the greatness of Prince Karl of Auersperg and the ancient grandeur of his Castle of Zillenstein. He referred vaguely to the young princess whom he escorted as a cousin or a niece, and spoke complacently because he had been assigned to the important duty of taking her to Trieste. There was need of haste, too. He knew his orders, and he would start in the morning at the very first breath of dawn. He was also empowered, if necessary, to fight for her safety. The rifles and pistols in the automobile were sufficient proof of it, and he had been trained to shoot by the Prince's head forester, Muller.

Herr Johann Ignatz Leinfelder was much impressed. This young chauffeur who spoke with such assurance was a fine, upstanding fellow, obviously strong and brave, the very kind of a man whom a prince like Auersperg would employ on a duty of such great importance. Hence, Herr Leinfelder bowed lower than ever, when he spoke to John.

After dinner, the waiter, August, came with word that the princess was much refreshed and bade her chauffeur come to her apartments for orders. He found her standing by a window with the watchful Suzanne hovering near, but he did not speak until the waiter withdrew and closed the door.

The paleness begat by the long weariness of the ride was gone from her face, the beautiful color flowing back in a full tide, and she stood up straight and strong. The room was lighted by two tall candles, and the glow in John's eyes was met by an answering glow in hers.

"You think it wise to spend the night here?" she asked.

"It seems to me that we should risk it. In the darkness the roads will be dangerous from the melting snows. Nor should we exhaust ourselves in the first stage of our flight. It's scarcely possible that any word from Zillenstein can reach Tellnitz tonight and tomorrow we'll be far away. What say you, Suzanne?"

"I agree, sir, with you, who are our master here," replied Suzanne with uncommon deference. "A start at dawn, and we can leave pursuit behind for the present at least."

Julie smiled a little at this proof that young Scott's conquest of her stern maid was complete.

"I'll bid Herr Leinfelder have breakfast for us at the earliest possible moment," he said, "and now, I think it would be better for you two to sleep, because tomorrow we may need all our strength. You know as well as I the dangers that lie before us."

Outside the door he was the haughty chauffeur again, the subservient servant of Auersperg, and the arrogant patron of the innkeeper and waiters. He secured a good room for himself, in which he slept until he was called by his order at the first light of dawn, and he was assured by the manner of Herr Leinfelder that no word of the fugitives had come in the night.

"Breakfast is ready for the princess," said the innkeeper, bowing.

John knocked at her door, and she came forth at once, followed by Suzanne, both fully dressed for the journey.

"No alarm has yet come to Tellnitz," whispered John, as she passed. "Remember that they think you a princess of the house of Auersperg, and that we must start in a half-hour."

He ate his own breakfast at another table, and within the appointed time the great limousine was at the door. Herr Leinfelder and his staff had no reason to change their belief that the lady of such manifest youth and beauty was a princess, as their chauffeur gave gratuities in truly royal style, and then whirled them away in a manner that was obviously ducal.

The morning was fresh and beautiful, silver as yet, since only an edge of the sun was showing over the hills, but it was fragrant with the odor of foliage and of wild flowers, blossoming in the nooks and crannies under the slopes. John felt a great surge of the spirits and he sent the machine forward at a rate that made the air rush in a swift current behind them.

"The first stage of our flight has been passed in safety," he said to Julie.

"It's an omen that we'll be as fortunate with the second."

"And with the third."

"And with all the others."

She flashed him a brilliant smile, and John felt that he could drive over any obstacle. He sent the machine forward faster than ever, and the road stretched before them, long and white.

CHAPTER XIV
THE HAPPY ESCAPE

They said very little now. John drove on through a great happy silence. All the omens were good, and he believed that they would escape. Surely, fortune was with them when they had been able to come so far without challenge. The sun swam over the earth and threw golden beams into the valley. On their right a swift stream chattered over the stones and further away on their left rose the steep slopes, heavy with forest. They passed farmers and shepherds who had little time to take notice, as they saw the great machine but a moment, and then it was gone.

John had his mind set on escape by the way of the Adriatic. He had heard rumors that Italy might enter the war on the side of the Allies, but he knew that it had not yet taken any action and he had high hopes of finding a path to safety in that direction. Meanwhile, and whatever came of it, he must press on.

Toward noon he slackened speed, and they ate a little from the supplies they carried in the automobile. Just as they finished Suzanne held up her hand: "I think I hear another machine coming," she said.

"You are right," said John, after he had listened intently for a full minute. "It's the humming sound of tires, but it's only one automobile. Of that I'm sure, and I think it's a light one. We'll drive on at moderate speed, attending strictly to our own business."

But he loosened the revolver in his belt, and while he appeared to look straight ahead he had eye and ear also for the approaching machine, which obviously was coming at a great pace.

"It's a small automobile with only one person in it," said Julie.

"Then we have nothing to fear," said John. "But the figure of the man at the wheel looks familiar."

"Ah!" said John, drawing a deep breath. In that region a familiar face could scarcely be the face of a friend. He stiffened a little, and cast another look at the revolver in his belt to see that it was convenient to his hand. Then, to indicate that he was not running away and to prevent suspicion, he slackened the speed of the machine. As he did so the humming behind them rapidly grew louder and a light runabout drew up by their side. John uttered a cry of amazement as he saw the man at the wheel.

It was Weber, the Alsatian, in civilian clothing, his black beard trimmed nicely to a point, his eyes flashing a smile of welcome, as he took off his cap and bowed low to John and Mademoiselle Julie Lannes, but lower to Julie. John brought his machine down to a slow pace, and there was room for Weber's by their side in the road.

"You never dreamed of being overtaken by me here," said the Alsatian, smiling again, and showing his white teeth.

"No," replied John. "It never occurred to me that it was you behind us."

"After all, I am, I think, your good angel. In your flight with Mademoiselle Lannes you need advice and guidance, and I can give both."

"You do appear at the most opportune times. It has become a habit for which I am grateful."

"It's not chance that I'm here. It's pursuit and design. You know my duties as a spy, an ugly name, perhaps, but one that calls for daring and patriotism. Hearing of the council held at Zillenstein by Prince Karl of Auersperg I went there to learn what I could of it. The information that I was able to secure is in the hands of a confederate now on his way to Paris, and I remained to probe into the mystery of Mademoiselle Lannes' disappearance."

"Then you learned of the hunting lodge on the mountain?"

"Very quickly. I discovered, too, that Mademoiselle Lannes and her maid had been taken away by a young chauffeur, coming from somewhere in Lorraine, who had been only a short time at the castle. Knowing you for what you are, Mr. Scott, and understanding your devotion, I leaped at once to the conclusion that it was you. I slipped away as soon as the snow melted sufficiently, and was the first from the outside world to reach the lodge. The absence of the limousine, the tire tracks leading toward Tellnitz and other evidence at the lodge showed without doubt that my conclusions were right."

"And you followed immediately?"

"Without delay. I reached Tellnitz, where you stopped, obtained this light machine and came on at speed. It will be my pleasure to help as much as I can you and the sister of the great Philip Lannes, the first aviator of France."

"You left France after we did, Monsieur Weber," said Julie. "Did you hear anything of Philip?"

"That he had recovered fully of his wound, Mademoiselle, and that he and the *Arrow* were once more in the service of his country. He knows of your abduction by Prince Karl of Auersperg. A friend, an aviator, Delaunois, furnished him with many facts, and I cannot doubt that he will come over Austria in the *Arrow* to seek your rescue."

The eyes of Julie, John and Suzanne, as with one impulse, turned upward. It seemed to John, for a moment or two, that his vivid imagination could fairly create the slender and graceful shape of Philip's aeroplane, outlined against the sky. But the heavens were flawless, a pure, unbroken blue, without speck or stain, and he suppressed a little sigh of disappointment.

"Do you know the country at all?" he asked of Weber.

"Somewhat. It was a part of my work before the war to pass through all the regions of Germany and Austria, and learn as much of them as I could. At the end of this valley is a small village called Obenstein, where perhaps it would be wise for us to spend the next night. After that we must devise some method of getting out of Austria — and I do not seek to conceal from you that it will be a most difficult task. Perhaps it would be better to change your plan and enter Switzerland, a neutral country. It, of course, would end your service as a soldier, but that, I take it, would be no great hardship to you now."

The color came into John's face, but he was bound to admit that Weber was right. His interest in the war had become far less than his interest in Julie Lannes.

"Perhaps we can tell better after we spend the night at Obenstein," he said.

"Nothing can be hurt by reserving our verdict until tomorrow," said Weber. "Obenstein is very secluded. I believe that it has neither telephone nor telegraph, and we'll surely be able to leave it tomorrow before any pursuit can reach us."

"Do you think the plan a good one?" said John to Julie.

"I know of no better," she replied in English. "I trust to you and Mr. Weber."

"Then it's agreed," said John to Weber.

"It's agreed."

The Alsatian now led the way in his light machine, and the limousine followed at an interval of fifty or sixty yards. One hour, then two and three passed, and nothing came in the way of their easy and rapid progress. It all seemed too smooth and fortunate to John. It was incredible that they could travel thus great distances through Austria, the land of the enemy. He knew that chance had a way of finding a balance, and violent and fierce events might be before them.

But as he drove on he scanned the heavens now and then with a questing eye. It had not occurred to him until Weber spoke that all of them might escape through the air. Lannes would trail them, not on the earth, but through mists and clouds. He would come, too, with friends almost as daring and skillful as himself, perhaps with Caumartin and the two, Castelneau and Méry, who had responded to the thrilling signal near Salzburg, when he took his first flight. His blood leaped and danced, and once more his eyes roved over the blue in search of the *Arrow*.

They came to Obenstein a little before dusk. It was a tiny village, almost hidden in a recess of the mountain, with a shaggy pine forest rising above it and casting its shadow over the houses. But there was a small, neat inn, and a garage for the machines, and the guests were received with the same hospitality that had been shown at Tellnitz. John again spread the rumor that it was a princess of the house of Auersperg who came, and he added Weber to the list of those who were attending her in her flight to a safer region. Julie withdrew as before to her room with her maid, but giving John, before she went, the brilliant smile of faith and confidence that would have sent him, sword in hand, against dragons.

He and Weber sat awhile in the little smoking-room talking in low tones of their journey. Most of the time they were alone, a waiter merely passing through now and then, and they had no fear of being overheard.

"Weber," he said, "I've learned from the innkeeper that a mountain road leads from here toward Switzerland and I feel sure already that your suggestion about our escaping into that country is good. You, of course, when you reach the border will do as you choose, as you will want to continue the dangerous work upon which you're engaged. But you may be sure that if we do get through, Mademoiselle Lannes and I will never forget the help that you have given us."

"All that I do I do gladly," said Weber. "You may not have spoken to each other but it is easy for me to tell how matters stand between Mademoiselle Lannes and you."

John was silent but his color deepened.

"You must not mind my saying these things," said Weber, speaking easily. "I'm older than you and the times are unusual. When you reach Paris you and Mademoiselle Lannes will be married."

John was still silent.

"And you will take her to America for the present, or at least Until the war is over. Ah, well! You're a happy man! Youth and the springtime! Beauty and love! Kings can procure no more and seldom as much! I think I'll walk in the air a little and have a smoke."

"And I," said John, "will go to sleep. I've a tiny room on the ground floor, but it's big enough to hold me. Good night."

"Good night, Mr. Scott."

There was only a single window in John's little room, but before undressing he opened it and stood there to breathe the cool night air for a while. It looked upon the forest that ran up the slope of the mountain, and the odor of the pines was very pleasant. Looking idly at the trunks and the foliage he saw a shadow pass into the depths of the forest and something, a pulse in his temple, perhaps, struck a warning note.

A shiver ran down his back and his hair lifted, as if touched with electric sparks. Acting at once under impulse he touched the pistol inside the pocket of his jacket to see that it was all right, and slipped out of the room.

He had marked the point at which the shadow disappeared in the forest and he followed it on light foot. He had been awakened as if a stroke of lightning had blazed suddenly before his eyes, and now his brain was seething with fierce thoughts, called up by a long chain of incidents, all at once made complete.

His hand slipped again to the revolver and he drew it forth, holding it ready for instant use. Then he went forward swiftly again on noiseless steps, and once more he caught a glimpse of the flitting shadow straight ahead. He increased his speed and the shadow resolved itself into the figure of a man, a figure that seemed familiar to him.

Two or three times the man stopped and looked back, but John had shrunk behind a tree and no pursuit was visible. Then he resumed his rapid flight up the steep slope, and young Scott persistently followed, never once losing sight of the active figure.

The way led to the crest of the mountain which hung about two thousand feet above the village and it was a climb requiring some time and endurance, but though John's pulse beat fast it was with excitement and not with exhaustion. At the summit he saw the figure emerge upon an open space upon which stood a slender round tower of considerable height.

John stopped at the edge of the pines and saw the figure disappear within the tower, upon the summit of which something presently began to flash and crackle. He caught his breath and the blood leaped fiercely through his veins. He knew that the tower was a wireless signal station and that it was talking to another somewhere. It sent, too, as he well knew, through the velvety blue of the night the message that Mademoiselle Julie Lannes, Suzanne, her maid, and John Scott, the American, were in the village of Obenstein where they could be taken.

He cursed himself for a fool, thrice a fool! Why had he not understood long before? Why had he not seen that so many coincidences could not be the result of chance? Only design and skill could have brought them about! Who had disabled the automobile in that flight with Carstairs and Wharton from the Germans? Who had sought to delay Lannes until he could be caught by the enemy? Who was the mysterious man in the aeroplane who had wounded Philip, who had led John from the château under the very rifles of the waiting marksmen, and who had been responsible for Julie's capture at Chastel? That letter, purporting to be from Philip, and directing her to come to Chastel, was surely a forgery!

These and all the other details crashed upon him with cumulative force, and he was so mad with fury that he thought his heart would burst with the surging blood. Why had the man worked with such energy and such cruel persistence against him? But his wonder quickly passed, because the reason did not matter now. Instead he put his finger on the trigger of the automatic and waited.

The wireless flashed and crackled for five minutes, then five minutes of silence and the figure of Weber reappeared at the base of the tower. He lingered there for a little space looking warily about him, before he began the descent of the mountain, and John quietly withdrew further into the pines. Weber presently crossed the open space, entering the forest, and John, noiseless, retreated before him.

Thus they proceeded down the mountain until the wireless tower was left several hundred yards behind and they were buried deep in the pine forest. Then John stepped suddenly into the road not twenty yards before the Alsatian and leveling his automatic said sharply:

"Hands up, Weber!"

Weber started violently and slowly raised his hands. But he said with composure:

"Why this sudden violence, Mr. Scott?"

"Because you have been upon the wireless tower signaling to our enemies. I've just understood everything, Weber. You're a German and not a French spy, and you've played the traitor to Julie and Philip Lannes and me all along."

There was enough moonlight for John to see that Weber's face was distorted by an evil smile.

"You've been a trifle slow in discovering just what I am," he said, calmly. "I've wondered that a young man of your perception didn't find me out earlier."

John flushed. The Alsatian's effrontery, in truth, had been amazing and in that perhaps lay his success—so far.

"It's true," he said, "I should have suspected you sooner, but it did not occur to me that human nature could be so vile. To undertake such risks and to use so much trickery and guile there must be a powerful motive, and in your case I can't guess it. Now, Weber, why did you do it?"

"Let me drop my hands, Mr. Scott, and I'll answer you," said Weber. "It's difficult to argue a case in such a strained and awkward position."

"Put them down, then, but remember that I'm watching you, and that I'm willing to shoot. Now, go ahead. Why have you been such a persistent enemy of Mademoiselle Lannes, her brother and myself? Why have you been such a triple traitor?"

"Don't call me a traitor, because a traitor I am not. On the contrary I am loyal with a loyalty of which you, John Scott, an American, know nothing. I've called myself an Alsatian, but really I am not. I am an Austrian. I was born on the Zillenstein estate of Prince Karl of Auersperg. My family has served his for a thousand years. Great as I hold Hapsburg and Hohenzollern, Auersperg means even more to me. The Auerspergs are the very essence and spirit of that aristocracy and rule of the very highborn, in which I believe and to which your country and later the French have stood in the exact opposite. Every time that my pulse beats within me it beats with the wish that you and all that you stand for should fail."

John did not feel the slightest doubt of Weber's sincerity. The increasing moonlight, falling in a silver flood across his face, showed too clearly his earnestness. Yet that earnestness was not good to look upon. It was sinister, tinged strongly with the beliefs of an old and wicked past. He too, like his master, was of the Middle Ages.

"And so in all these deeds you were serving Prince Karl of Auersperg?" said John.

"To the death. It was a false escape that I planned for you at the château. You were to have been shot down, but by an unlucky chance you escaped in the water."

"I've surmised that already."

"I'm an aviator, not so great as your friend Lannes, but no mean one nevertheless. It was I who pursued him, when you were with him in the *Arrow* near Paris, and wounded him."

"I've surmised that, too."

"And when Prince Karl coveted Mademoiselle Julie Lannes — and I do not blame him — I was of the most help to him in that matter so near to his heart. Do you understand that it was a great honor he offered Mademoiselle Lannes, to make her his morganatic wife? He need not have offered her so much."

The great pulse in John's throat beat heavily and his hand pressed the automatic, but he compressed his lips and said nothing.

"I see that my words anger you," continued Weber, "but from my point of view I am right. I serve my overlord!"

"What message were you sending by the wireless from the tower?"

"Doubtless you have guessed it. I was sending word to the detachment now on the road from Zillenstein to come here for Mademoiselle Lannes, her maid and you. They're ahorse, and they should arrive in three hours and you can't possibly escape. Before Prince Karl was compelled to leave for the theater of war he put this most important affair in my charge. He has not yet yielded all hope of Mademoiselle Lannes."

"It may be true that we can't escape, but what of yourself, Weber? We're alone in the forest and I hold the whip hand. The score that I owe you is large. You may have wrecked the life of Mademoiselle Julie and perhaps you will destroy my own, but you said it would be three hours before the detachment arrived, and I need only a few seconds."

"But I don't think you'll fire, Mr. Scott."

"Why, Weber?"

"Because I fire first!"

Absorbed in the talk John had unconsciously lowered the automatic, and, as agile as a panther, Weber suddenly leaped to one side, snatched a revolver from his own pocket and pulled the trigger. But the bullet flew wild. A huge shadow hovered over him and a weight crashed upon his head, smiting him down as if he had been struck by a giant shell. He sank in the path and lay motionless, dead ere he fell.

John stared, stricken with horror. The great shadow bent down a moment over the fallen man, then straightened itself up again, and two eyes in which the vengeful fire had not yet died gazed at John. Then as his dazed mind cleared he saw and knew. It was Antoine Picard, the gigantic and faithful servitor of the Lannes family.

"Antoine! Antoine!" cried John. "How did you come here? I thought you were in Munich!"

"It seems, your honor, that I'm here at the right moment. His bullet would certainly have found your heart had not my club descended upon his head at the very instant that his finger touched the trigger. He'll never stir again."

"But Antoine, it's you, yourself! It doesn't seem real that you should be here at such a time!"

"It's none other than Antoine Picard, your honor, and he never struck a truer or more timely blow. They were to hold me a prisoner in Munich, but I escaped. I did not return to France. I could never desert Mademoiselle Julie, and I followed. My size drew their attention, but in one way or another I kept down suspicion or escaped them. I traced Mademoiselle Julie and my daughter to the great castle and then to the lodge on the mountain. I saw the traitor who lies so justly dead here talking with German troops, and I knew that there was need for me to hasten. In the night I stole the horse of a Uhlan and galloped to Obenstein.

"I approached the inn just in time to see the traitor come forth, and knowing that he was bent upon some devil's work I followed him to the signal tower. I did not see you until he started back and then I bided my time. I was in the bush not ten feet from him while you talked."

"Lucky for your mistress and lucky for us all that you were, Picard!"

"We must leave Obenstein, your honor, at once!"

"Of course, Picard. We must take flight in the machine."

"As it would be hard to explain my presence, your honor, suppose I wait down the road for you. I've already turned the horse loose in the forest. First I'll move this from the path lest someone see it and give the alarm too soon."

He lifted the body of Weber and hid it among the bushes. Then they separated, John returning quickly to the inn. He saw a light in Julie's window and inferring that she had not yet retired he went hastily to her room and knocked on the door.

"Who's there?" came the brave voice of his beloved.

"It's John!" he replied, guardedly. "Open at once, Julie! We're in great danger and must act quickly!"

He heard the bolt shoot back, the door was opened, and Julie stood before him, pale but erect and courageous. Behind her, as usual, hovered the protecting shadow of Suzanne. John stepped inside and closed the door.

"Julie," he said, in a whisper, sharp with anxiety, "we must leave Obenstein in fifteen minutes! Weber is a traitor in the service of Prince Karl of Auersperg! He followed us to get you back to him! He has been signaling from a wireless station on the mountain! A detachment of hussars will be here in three hours!"

Her pallor deepened, but the courage that he loved still glowed in her eyes.

"But Weber?" she said. "He will stop our flight?"

"He will never harm us more, Julie. He is dead."

"You—"

"No, Julie, I did not kill him. It was a stronger arm than mine that struck the blow. Suzanne, your father is waiting for us in the forest. He has followed us all the way from Munich to Zillenstein, to the lodge, and here to Obenstein. It was he who sent Weber to the doom that he deserved."

"Ah!" said Suzanne, and John saw her stern eyes shining. She was the worthy daughter of her father.

"Put on your cloaks and hoods at once," said John, "and I'll have the automobile out in a few minutes! It doesn't matter what they think at the inn. We disregard it and fly."

Suzanne, quick and capable, began to prepare her mistress and John went down to the innkeeper. He was so swift and emphatic that the worthy Austrian was dazed, and, after all a princess of the house of Auersperg had a right to her whims. It was not for him to question the minds of the great, and the heavy gold piece that John dropped into his hands was potent to allay undue curiosity.

The automobile properly equipped was before the main door of the inn within ten minutes. John helped into it the hooded and cloaked figure of the great lady, and her maid, also hooded and cloaked, followed. Then he sprang into his own seat, turned the wheel, and the huge machine shot down the road. But at the first curve it slackened speed, then stopped for an instant beside a dark figure, and when it went on again four instead of three rode.

Picard sat beside his daughter and in those two faithful hearts was no doubt of their escape.

"Antoine," said Julie, "I know that we owe our lives to you."

She offered him a small gloved hand. It rested in his giant grasp a moment, then he raised it to his lips and kissed it.

"I'd have followed you across the world, my lady," he said.

"I know it, Antoine."

John, watching intently, sent the machine forward at fair speed. The road again stretched before him lone and white in the moonlight, which fell in a heavy silver shower. He did not know where they were going, but there was the road, and the hussars could not ride hard enough to overtake them. Now and then he stole a glance at Julie, and the same indomitable courage was always shining in her eyes. She was not weary and she was as wide awake as he. By and by both Antoine and Suzanne slept, sitting upright, but Julie, wrapped almost to the eyes in cloak and hood, was still quiet, watching everything with wide fearless eyes. John brought the machine down to a slow pace and guided it for the moment with one hand.

"Julie," he said softly, "I don't know where we're going, but I know that we'll escape, and knowing it I now have something to ask you."

"What is it, John?"

"When we reach Paris, you'll marry me, Julie?"

"Yes, John, I'll marry you."

The other hand came from the wheel and as he leaned back, they kissed in the moonlight. The great machine ran on, unguided but true.

They kissed again in the moonlight, and for a splendid moment or two her arms were about his neck.

"Julie," whispered John, "will your mother consent?"

"Yes, when I tell her to do so."

"And Philip?"

"Yes, without telling."

The automobile, still unguided, ran on straight and true as if it were alive, and knew that it carried the precious freight of two young and faithful hearts, and that nothing else in all the world was so tender and true as young love.

Far in the night, when the road had climbed up the hills, John saw a light flashing and winking in the valley, and from a more distant point another light winked and flashed in reply. He read the fiery signals and he knew that the alarm was abroad. The hussars had come to Obenstein, only to find that the birds had flown, and doubtless, too, to find among the bushes the dead body of Weber, Prince Karl's most trusted and unscrupulous agent. Julie had gone to sleep at last and Antoine and Suzanne slumbered on.

He alone watched and worked, and for a few moments he felt a chill of dread. The hussars would spread the alarm and the whole country would now be seeking them. He saw a road turning from the main one, and leading deeper into the mountains. Instinctively he followed it, like an animal seeking hiding in the wilderness, and now the machine rose fast on the slopes, dense forest lining the way on either side. Far below in the valley the lights and the wireless signals talked incessantly to one another and the hounds were hot on the chase.

It was about halfway between midnight and morning when John stopped the machine among dense pines on the very crest of a mountain, where the road, without any reason, seemed to end. Antoine awoke with a start and, springing out, began to curse himself under his breath for having gone to sleep.

"Take no blame, Antoine," said John. "You could have done nothing then, and it was much better for you to have slept. You now have back all your strength and we may need it."

Julie awoke with a start and after a moment or two of bewilderment understood. Then she gave John that old brilliant, flashing look, softened now by the memory of a kiss when no hand was at the wheel.

"Julie," said John, trusting as ever in her courage, "we seem to have come to the end of things. Our enemies are in the valley following us, and it's not hard to trace the path of our automobile. I don't know how many will come, but Antoine and I can make a stand with the rifles."

"All hope is not yet lost!" said Suzanne, in a voice as deep as that of a man. "Remember that when the earth cannot hide us the air may open to receive us. Remember, too, Mademoiselle Julie, that your brother seeks you, and when the time comes we are to look aloft."

Driven again by that extraordinary impulse, John and Julie gazed up. But they saw only the dancing stars in the blue velvet of the sky.

"He may come! He may come in time!" said Suzanne, speaking like an inspired prophet of old, and her manner carried conviction. John, clinging to the last desperate hope, recalled how Lannes and he had summoned Castelneau and Méry from the sky to save them, and though it was a wild hope he resolved to send up the same signal.

It was a quick task to gather dry wood and build a little heap, Julie and Suzanne helping with energy and enthusiasm. There were plenty of matches in the car, and presently John lighted the heap, which crackled and sent up leaping tongues of flame.

"It may serve also as a signal to those who follow us," he said, "but we must take the chance. Cavalry can't reach us except by the road that we came and with our rifles we can hold it a long time."

The mention of the word "rifle," put a thought in the head of Antoine Picard, in whose veins the blood of Vikings flowed, and who that night was a veritable Viking of the land. Leaving John and the two women to feed the signal fire, he secured one of the powerful breech-loading rifles from the automobile, and quietly stole down the path.

Antoine, although he held a modern weapon in his hand, had shed centuries of civilization. As still as death as he trod lightly in the dark road, he was, nevertheless, consumed with the wild Berserk rage against those who followed him. He knew that hussars would soon appear on the slope, but he intended that a lion should be in their path and he stroked lovingly the barrel of the powerful breech-loader. Behind him the flames were shooting higher and higher, pouring red streaks against the velvet blue of the sky. But all of Picard's attention was concentrated now on what lay before him.

He heard soon the distant beat of hoofs and he drew a little to the side of the road, down which he could see a long distance, as it stretched straight before him, narrow and steep. He made out clearly a half dozen figures, hussars struggling forward on tired horses, and he chuckled a little to himself. It was a splendid weapon that he held in his hand, and he was a great marksman. Armed as he was, he felt that he had little to fear on that lone mountain road from six or seven horsemen.

He pushed the rifle forward a little and waited in the shadow of the pines. The hoofbeats rang louder, and the shadows became the distinct figures of horses and men. Picard uttered a deep "Ah!" because he recognized the one who led them, a powerful, erect man, the Prussian Rudolf von Boehlen, now in the very center of the moonlight.

When they were yet two hundred yards away, Picard stepped into the middle of the road and called to them in a loud voice to halt. He saw von Boehlen throw up his head, say something to his troop, and then try to urge his horse to a faster gait.

Picard sighed. He knew that von Boehlen was a brave man and he respected brave men. A disagreeable task lay before him, one that must be done, but he would give him another chance. He called again and louder than before for them to halt, but von Boehlen came on steadily. Then Picard promptly raised his rifle and shot him through the heart.

When von Boehlen fell dead in the road his hussars halted and while they were hesitating Picard shot the horses of two under them, while a third received a bullet in the shoulder. Then all of them fled on horse or on foot into the valley while Picard went calmly back to the fire which was now sending its signal across the whole heavens. He told John in a whisper of what had befallen, and soon he returned to his place in the road to watch.

John and Julie by and by left Suzanne to feed the fire and they stood hand in hand gazing now at the heavens and now at the dark pine forests. The velvet blue of the sky faded into the dark hour and then the dawn came, edged with silver, turning to pink and then to gold, like a robe of many colors, drawn slowly out of the infinite. Suzanne suddenly uttered a great cry.

"Look up! Look up, my children!" she cried.

Coming out of the west which was yet in dusk was a black dot and then three others—behind it in Indian file.

"We're saved," cried Suzanne. "It's Monsieur Philip and his friends'"

"How do you know? You can't see yet," said John, almost afraid to hope.

"I don't need to see it! I feel it, and I know!" replied Suzanne. "Look, how they come!"

John trembled and the hand of Julie in his own trembled too, but it was not fear, it was the feeling that a miracle, a miracle to save them, was coming to pass.

The four black dots moved on out of the west and John knew that they were aeroplanes coming swiftly and directly toward their mountain. The dawn reaching the zenith spread also to the west and the flying machines were outlined clearly in the luminous golden haze. Then John, too, uttered a great cry.

He knew the slender sinuous shape that led. As far as eye could reach he would recognize the *Arrow*. The miracle was done. They had called to Philip in their desperate need and he had come.

"Philip and the *Arrow*!" he exclaimed. "We're saved!"

"I knew that he would come!" Julie said, as she stared wide-eyed into the blue and gold of the heavens.

Now the aeroplanes flew at almost incredible speed, the *Arrow* always at their head, poised for a few moments directly over their heads, and then came down in a dazzling series of spirals, landing almost at their feet.

"Philip, my brother!" exclaimed Julie, as the slender compact figure that they knew so well stepped gracefully from the *Arrow*.

He took off his heavy glasses and gazed at them as they stood, forgetting that they were still hand in hand. Then he smiled and lifting his cap in his old dramatic way he said:

"It seems that for several reasons I didn't come too soon."

"No," replied John, calmly, and holding firmly the little hand in his, "you have arrived just in time to give your consent to my marriage with your sister."

"And what does Mademoiselle Julie Lannes say?"

The rising sun clothed Julie in a shower of gold. Never before had the wonderful golden hair seemed more wonderful. Never before had she seemed to the youthful eyes of her lover more nearly divine.

"Julie Lannes says," she replied bravely, "that if John Scott wishes her to be his wife and her mother and brother consent she will gladly marry him."

"Now the aeroplanes flew at almost incredible speed, the *Arrow* always at their head"

"Then we must hurry away, or it will be a wedding; without either a bride or a bridegroom. Are not those Austrian hussars at the bottom of the slope, Picard?"

"Yes, monsieur."

"Then it's up and away with us. Here are Caumartin, Méry and Castelneau, old friends of yours, John, but it was Delaunois who brought me the last news of you. Caumartin has the *Omnibus*, and in it the bridal pair must travel. I can't take you with me in the *Arrow* now, John, as it admits of only a single passenger. But do you, Picard, take the rifles and come with me. We'll cover the rear of our flight. Now, hasten! Hasten!"

John and Julie in an instant were side by side in the *Omnibus*, Picard, forgetting all fear of aeroplanes, was with Philip, and the four machines rose, circling above the mountain, Caumartin's big plane leading. John and Julie sat very close together and her hand was again in his.

"Fear not, dearest," he said. "When all seemed lost Philip came for us."

"But you came for me first and you risked your life many times. To give myself to you seems but a small reward for all that you've done."

"It's a reward that kings and princes in their power cannot win."

Then they fell silent, their emotion too deep for speech. Philip had spoken in jest, but it was almost like a wedding trip. The hussars below had reached the abandoned automobile, and fired vain shots at the disappearing aeroplanes, but John and Julie heeded them not. War and brute passions were left behind, and they were sailing through the calm blue ether.

Caumartin, the stalwart, was wholly absorbed in steering his great machine and they sat behind him, very close together, still hand in hand, watching the great panorama of the heavens, unrolled before them. It was the most beautiful sky that they had ever seen, dyed that day into intensely vivid colors by the master hand. Far away were great pink terraces of color, changing to blue or gold or silver, while below them revolved the earth, clad in deepest green, save where far peaks were crested with snow.

Both John and Julie breathed an infinite peace. The war sank farther and farther away, as they sailed on through peaceful heavens, surcharged with infinite color. Both felt, with the certainty of truth, that their troubles and dangers were over, and they now left the journey and its needs to Philip and his able comrades.

"After we're married, Julie, you'll go to America with me for awhile," said John, "but we'll come back to France. We shall divide our time between two homes, your country and mine, now the countries of both."

The hand within his own returned his pressure. Caumartin turned his machine toward the north, avoiding neutral Switzerland, and sailing at great speed they passed beyond the German lines and over the fair land of France that all of them loved so well.

Caumartin kept his place in front. Suzanne was in the machine just behind and Philip and Picard in the *Arrow* always hovered in the rear. That night they descended within the French lines, and John heard the next day that Prince Karl of Auersperg had been killed in battle. It was singular, perhaps, but John felt a touch of pity for him. He had wanted something very greatly and, powerful prince though he was, his power had not been great enough to win it for him.

They were married in Notre Dame by the Archbishop of Paris. The influence of John's uncle, the senator and great mining millionaire, was sufficient to procure John's release from the army. In truth, General Vaugirard, although he was fat and sixty, had a strong vein of sentiment, and he was one of the most distinguished guests in Notre Dame, where he puffed mightily and kept himself with great difficulty from whistling his approval. He and Senator Pomeroy stood together and he nodded emphatically when the senator told him, with a certain pride in his whisper, that while John, his sole heir, was not a prince, he could buy and sell many who were.

General Vaugirard was not the only distinguished officer at the marriage. There was a lull in the operations and all of John's friends came to Paris to see him wed the beautiful Julie Lannes. A little man, with the brow of a Napoleon, the famous general, Bougainville, whose rise had been so astonishing, stood beside General Vaugirard.

Daniel Colton, now a colonel, his arm in a sling, was not far away. Carstairs was there, a bandage about his head, and Wharton was with him, his shoulder yet sore from the path that a bullet had made through it. It was decreed that while these friends of John's should receive many wounds, all of them were to survive the great war.

They were to spend three days at the little house beyond the Seine before sailing, and as the twilight came on they sat together and looked out over the City of Light, melting into the dusk after a golden day. The subdued hum of Paris came to them in a note of infinite sweetness and peace.

John was stirred to the depths, but his emotion, like that of most deep natures, was quiet. He felt Julie's hand tremble a little in his own, as the voice of Paris grew fainter but sweeter. The twilight faded into the night and the buildings grew misty.

"We have passed through many dangers, Julie," said John, "but for me at least the reward is greater than them all. When did you begin to love me?"

"You were my gallant knight from the first, but, if it had not been so, how could I have kept from loving the fearless crusader who dared all and who risked his life every day in the country of the enemy to save me?"

"I'd have been a poor and worthless creature if I hadn't done so, Julie."

"Few men have done so, though, even for love."

Stirred by an emotion deeper than ever, and wholly pure, he put his arms around her, and their lips met in a long kiss of young love.

The first dusk thinned away, the sky turned to a vault of burnished silver, and, the infinite stars coming out, danced their approval.